I0710290

Wolf Bound

Wolf Bound

BERRING COLLEGE BOOK 1

KAYLA BROOKS

Copyright © 2024 by Kayla Brooks

All rights reserved.

No part of this book may be reproduced in any form or by any electronic or mechanical means, including information storage and retrieval systems, without written permission from the author, except for the use of brief quotations in a book review.

Cover design by getcovers.com

Editing by oneloveediting.com

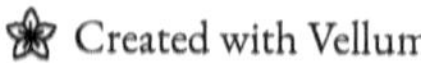 Created with Vellum

For Mom, who made up bedtime stories about princesses who talk to animals, and Dad, who introduced me to J. R. R. Tolkien and C. S. Lewis, and Leland, who got me through my first D&D campaign.

A Note About Content

Dear Reader,

This is a steamy female/male romance novel. It has elements that will not be appropriate for all readers, so please proceed with caution. I try to give a comprehensive list of content warnings so everyone can make an informed decision about whether to read this book or not, but it is possible that I overlooked or forgotten something. If you find an element that should have a content warning, please let me know so I can fix it. My email address is kayla@kaylabrooksauthor.com and I will *always* want to hear your feedback, especially if it involves making the reader's (your) experience better.

You can find the full list at https://kaylabrooksauthor.com/content-warnings

I completely understand if any of these elements prevent you from reading this book. Please take care of yourself.

Sincerely,
Kayla

Chapter One

GLORIA

I stifle a groan as the wheel of my suitcase catches a crack in the pavement and the whole son of a bitch careens out of my control. I look around to see just how many people saw, and sure enough, it takes less than five seconds for me to spot a group of girls at three o'clock, turning away from me with sneaky grins on their faces that tell me not only did they see, but they also judged and laughed. So much for everyone only worrying about themselves.

My high school guidance counselor's voice echoes in my mind. "Gloria, you need to stop worrying so much about what other people think of you. No one is ever paying attention to other people because they're too wrapped up in worrying about themselves." I suspect Mrs. Harrison didn't have to move into the dorms by herself, carrying everything she owned in the world's most embarrassing set of pink floral luggage.

"I am a strong, confident woman," I tell myself under my breath. "I am going to kick ass, and make friends, and live a beautiful life far away from all of the backwater hicks I grew up with."

Okay, maybe the "backwater hick" thing is a little harsh. But I need this fresh start. I need this new life, and I really need to not do anything embarrassing like have my hand-me-down pink flower suitcase give up on me and spill all of my darkest secrets on the asphalt for all the other freshmen to see.

I'm drenched in sweat, probably raspberry red, and fully broadcasting my wolf musk in the worst possible way by the time I get across the parking lot and reach the dorm entrance.

I double-check the name above the stone arch entryway. James MacLennon Hall. Yes. That's definitely the name on all of my housing information.

The doors open onto chaos as one tide of people fights their way toward the elevators on the right to get moved in while another tide surges toward me and the exits for their next round of moving. Then, there are the poor schmucks—myself included—scattered just left of the entrance who haven't even managed to check in and get our keys yet.

I hop on my tiptoes to check the hanging signs for the name on my move-in packet.

Lacey. Lacey, the RA, who gives off those too-pretty-to-be-believed vampire vibes with her straight white-blonde hair and even straighter nose. It almost hurts to look at her perfect Danish supermodel body and her piercing ice-blue eyes. She looks flawless in a school tank top, maroon, with the words Berring Bulldogs printed in gold right under her generous cleavage. Because of course she also has amazing boobs. To me, everything about her is screaming, "I'm a vampire." Not that I would actually ask her outright, of course. I'm a backwater hick, but even I'm not that backwater. I'm burning with curiosity, though. And humiliation. If she is a vampire, she could probably smell me before I even got in the building.

Just do it, Gloria, I try to reassure myself. *This is the first step in your big adventure. Don't you think it's time to take it?*

The wind is knocked out of my pep talk sails when someone unceremoniously bumps into me, throwing me against the table where Lacey is looking perfect and calm and beautiful. Except for the wrinkle of her nose as the full force of my overripe scent hits her.

"Um, hi, sorry, I . . ." I stammer, getting more flustered with every word. Why can't lightning ever strike you down when you need it to? The first vampire I meet and I'm a sweaty, stinky, stammering mess of a werewolf, while the vampire in question is the epitome of poise and confidence that I always imagined based on what I've seen on TV. It just figures.

"Last name?" she asks, putting on an "if I have to put up with one more freaked-out freshman, I'm going to lose my shit" smile.

I realize that I have yet to look up from the name of our school on her tank top as I whip my head up and say, "I . . . Severson. Gloria Severson."

"Welcome to Berring College." She hands me a manila envelope with a not-too-fake-seeming smile. "Your keys and any information you could possibly need are in here. We'll have a floor meeting tonight at eight where we can answer any other questions you might have." Then, she dismisses me without a word by moving her eyes onto the person behind me.

I stumble away from her table to the right and join the tide of people heading toward the elevators. My feet feel like they're made of lead, and no matter how many pep talks I give myself, the snakes in my belly keep twisting around and threatening to make me puke.

I'm finally here, and all I can think is that I've made a huge mistake.

* * *

The room is tiny. And dingy. And also glorious and everything I've ever dreamed of. There's an alcove just to the right of the door with a sink and tiny vanity. As you walk into the room past the wall that divides the sink from the rest of the room, there are two closets to the left that take up the entire left wall of the room. The first skinny bed is tucked up next to the partition wall on the right, with the end of the bed facing the closets. A second bed at the end of the room faces the same way, with two large desks on the wall between them. As I look closer, I can see that the desks also have small nightstands between them and each bed. Directly across from the door, on the back wall, is a window with a pretty view of lots of green trees and some other brick building peeking through. I take a moment after wheeling my suitcase inside to close the door and shut out the world so I can actually take a breath. The bustle of move-in day continues outside, but my door muffles it.

I flop back on one bed with a grateful sigh. Both maroon-clad beds are uncovered and waiting to be claimed, so I guess my roommate isn't here yet. I'm thankful to have a moment to myself, but I almost wish someone had already claimed one of the beds so I wouldn't have that decision ahead of me.

I suppose I can just ask my future roommate if she wants to switch whenever she gets here. I set my things on the bed at the back wall, farthest from the door, then second-guess that decision and move everything to the other bed before panicking and moving everything back to the far bed again.

I need to get out of my head.

I need to get out of this room.

I dig through the giant atrocity of a suitcase to find a towel. Yet another embarrassingly old hand-me-down that I didn't quite—but kind of actually did—steal from the pack when I left. But it's not like anyone was going to take me to the mall on move-in day and make sure I had a matching set of towels to go with my comforter.

With my towel in one hand and keys in the other, I make a quick dash to the shared bathrooms that are conveniently just around the corner from my room. Of all the potential humiliations I might face today, my body odor is one of the few I can actually do anything about.

I scrub down as well as I can without soap or a washcloth in the tiny shower stall. The summer heat, mixed with the anxiety of starting college and moving away from home, has kicked my sweat and scent production into overdrive. As I scrape what feels like an inch-deep layer of sweat off my scalp, I remind myself of everything I need to accomplish in order to be successful here.

Get into college: check. Fix up one of the broken-down, never-used pack cars so I can get to college: check. Meet a vampire and become more worldly: maybe? Did Lacey give off actual vamp vibes, or am I just being closed-minded? Maybe it isn't exactly racist to assume the first pale, beautiful person I meet is a vampire, but I probably shouldn't make assumptions. If I go around assuming things, someone's going to figure me out. Someone's going to find out that I'm the worst kind of know-nothing country hick from one of the last of the unaffiliated packs. Though, I suppose our unaffiliated status has more to do with the fact that the Council isn't interested in us than anything else. If the pack leader decides to take an interest, I'm sure he could turn my world on its head. What-ever else might happen while I'm in school, the possibility of being found out is what keeps me up at night. Like, waking up drenched in cold sweat at one in the morning from nightmares type of keep me up at night. No, thank you. I would much rather avoid that.

* * *

I struggle to dry off enough in the cramped shower stall, but I'm also not willing to risk navigating the busy dorm halls in only a towel just for the possibility of drying off more comfortably in my room.

Maybe later. If I feel like my self-esteem is getting too high and I need another potential disaster to bring me back down to Earth.

After everyone is moved in and it's only the other freshmen in the dorm. For now, I slide my still-somewhat-stinky clothes back onto my still-somewhat-sticky body and head back to my room to start unpacking.

I guess the bright side of coming to college with almost nothing is that unpacking will be a breeze.

There we go. Bright side: found.

My room is occupied when I get back. By the type of delicate, perfect blonde waif that I always wished I could be. My moment of jealousy at her silky, golden waves almost overrides my nervousness at meeting someone new.

"You must be Bethany. I set my things on that bed, but if you want it, it's no problem at all to move to the other bed. Let me know if you want me to move." The words barely come out coherent, piling on top of each other like I'm just speaking one desperately long sentence.

"Oh." The pretty girl, who I assume is the roommate Bethany who I literally know by name and not a damn thing else, turns in a slow circle, taking in the room and looking like she's not sure what to do with it. "No, I don't think you have to move anything. Unless you want to, that is. Are you Gloria?"

I reach forward to take her hand, just like I would if I were sealing a pack agreement. She stares at me for a moment, a rabbit who's just seen a fox, and then she blinks and snaps back to reality. She gives me a brief handshake.

"Um, yeah." I take my hand back and surreptitiously wipe it on my pants, wondering if there's something about me that's scaring her off. "It's nice to meet you?"

"Oh!" Her face lights up like this is the first time she's spoken to a real, live person in real, live life. "Yes! It's nice to meet you!"

I can't tell if she's really laying it on thick, just pretending to be clueless, or truly doesn't know what to do when someone offers to shake her hand.

I deflate a little bit. "Yes, I'm Gloria, your totally safe, not-at-all-crazy roommate?"

She gives a slow, wide-eyed nod. "Yeah, I'm Bethany, but, um . . . call me Bee? Okay, I guess I'll take this bed, then." She points a finger over to the empty bed. "I'm afraid I still have a lot of things to move up. What about you?"

"Oh, I . . . don't have a whole lot of stuff," I say in my most diplomatic voice. Here's the moment of truth. Will my roommate buy it, or will I end up outing myself as the loser I am and have my roommate spend the rest of the year ridiculing me?

She doesn't leap at the chance to dig into my past, so I let out a relieved breath.

"I guess I'll go back down so I can move some more things," she says, still looking a little lost.

She may not be overly curious about me, for which I am very grateful, but I am itching with curiosity to figure out what her deal is. "Do you need some help carrying things?" I offer hesitantly.

She lights up. "Oh my gosh! That would be so amazing!"

I'm tired. And don't feel like my shower actually got me clean. And would love to sit back and relax right now. But I was raised to make myself useful, not to sit back and watch someone struggle, so I guess I'd better help her. It might have been nice to have her hesitate a moment before accepting my offer, though. Just saying. I make sure I've got my essentials with me—phone, keys, ID—then gesture for her to lead the way.

Where she leads is a moving van with a very hot, very annoyed-looking dude standing next to it. A very, very hot dude, for sure, but also the type of bored, annoyed, bro-dude wolf shifter that I've already had enough experience with in my life. Dark blond hair, bulging muscles, vacant golden-brown eyes, expects the world to serve him and not the other way around. Oh yes. I know this type.

"Ma'am," he practically growls, "if you needed the full moving service, you should have paid for the full moving service. I'm supposed to be back at the depot with this van already."

Bee gives her lost look again. "I'm sorry. I didn't realize. I promise, I'll try to be quick."

Something about the way her eyes are filling with tears, or maybe the fact that his voice sounds like the high school bully from every movie ever, puts my hackles up.

"Oh, I'm sorry." I poke him in the chest, hard enough to make my finger hurt, but I refuse to let him see that weakness. "I had no idea that us expecting you to do your job would be such an inconvenience to you. You're going to help us move all of this up to our room—without complaining—and it's going to take as long as it needs to take, and then and only then will you go back to your depot and be done with this job. Now, start grabbing some boxes."

Bee shoots me a grateful smile.

He makes a face like he's about to argue with me, but I counter it with a wave of my index finger and a raised eyebrow. I've never been more grateful for my ability to channel my mother. Say what you will about her, but she knows how to keep people in line. He rolls his eyes and, with an exaggerated salute in my direction, opens the van and starts grabbing boxes. Do I take a moment to stand back and enjoy the way his jeans mold to his ass while he bends over? Yes. Because I've earned it after dealing with his bullshit, and this is something he can do for me after being an asshole. Bee catches me looking and gives me a reproachful look. I look back at what might actually be the best ass I've seen in my life and shrug. Maybe we just don't have the same taste in guys.

In the end, it only takes a few trips with the three of us working together, and if part of me notices that Bee only ever seems to carry one or two small items at a time, well, it's not like she has my natural wolf strength to help her out. It makes the most sense that I carry the heavier stuff. The moving goes fast enough, but the summer heat means I'm definitely going to need another shower. Preferably twenty minutes ago, but I'll settle for right now. Except there's still a giant male shifter in my room when I turn to look for my shower things.

What the fuck? Why is the moving guy still in my space?

JIMMY

I have been known—on occasion—to make some fairly questionable decisions. Arguably, that's why I'm here, pretending to be a put-upon moving guy with better things to do than help Bee move into her dorm. Pretending I don't know Bee at all, for that matter. I guess that was really her decision, so I don't have to claim all of the choices that led up to this moment.

The questionable decision I am most definitely, not a chance in hell going to make today is to go panting after the first attractive female I come across. That would defeat the purpose of this whole exercise. But, damn, when this girl got in my face about helping Bee move in? Something inside me sat up and took note. Two pretty big notes, actually. Two pretty big notes that I'm currently trying not to stare directly at. Now, I'm just trying to make sure she doesn't notice any other parts of me showing my appreciation in a very inappropriate and inconvenient way. I force myself to look up at her face instead, but I'm still in trouble. She's got dark hair that curls wildly around her face, working hard to escape the hair tie she has pulling it back. Her ink-dark eyes and rose-pink lips look used to smiling, or at least smirking, and that just feels like a challenge for me to make her smile and smirk for me.

The sensible part of me knows I need to follow my father's instructions. Lay low. Get the lay of the land. Feel free to sniff as much tail as I can, but don't get attached. Not that he said that part explicitly, but it was definitely implied. The less sensible part of me is already one hundred percent on board with the idea that I've met the only girl whose tail I ever want to sniff again.

But that is a terrible, nonsense idea. That's mystical fated mates bullshit, and I know that stuff isn't real. I don't even know her name, but all I can think about is how much I already want to make her mine.

And it's not because her boobs have the type of size and jiggle that could smother a man in his sleep so he would die happy.

Well, at least it's not all because of that. She also has a very grabbable-looking ass. I can imagine those curves denting under my fingers while I hold her still so I can bury myself deep inside of her. Not to mention, I'm desperate to tangle my fingers in that mane of brown curls. Oh, and also the fact that she stood up to me to defend Bee. I'll feel a lot better about leaving my sister alone if I know someone else has her back.

I'm already in deep shit, and the semester hasn't even really started.

I help Bee get everything moved up, then stand in their overly stuffed dorm room, scrambling for any excuse to stick around, any conversation starter that might get this girl even half as interested in me as I am in her. Hell, I'll settle for an excuse to get her name at this point.

"So." I search the space around me for inspiration. "You're both freshmen here?"

Bee waits for her roommate's back to turn and then makes a shooing motion at me. I get it. I promised to keep an eye on her and not get in her way. I can't help it that my wolf instincts aren't letting me leave the room right now, though.

"Weren't you complaining that you had places to be?" the sexy, commanding, enigmatic, off-limits roommate asks.

Inspiration strikes. "Well, now I'm already late getting back. And I lugged all those boxes for you. The polite thing for you to do would be to offer me a drink or something."

Bee glares. Bee's roommate raises both eyebrows like I just peed in the corner or something. We all stand frozen in the awkward moment I created until Sexy Roommate stomps across the room, unzips a gigantic, ugly, flower-printed suitcase, pulls out a mug covered in what appear to be hand-printed flowers and rainbows, fills it with tap water from the tiny vanity near the door, and hands it to me with a scowl.

"Thank you for helping. Now . . . bottoms up, and get the hell out!"

I shouldn't be grinning. I made her mad. I gave her a bad first impression. I'm continuing to impose on her. And yet, here I am, holding a ridiculous mug of funky-tasting tap water, and I cannot wipe the smile off my face.

"If you need any help again, maybe you can call me."

The girls give me matching, wary looks but don't say anything.

"Or maybe we'll have classes together. What's your major? We could start a study group?"

"What?" Bee bursts out. "What do you mean about having classes together?"

I press back against a pile of boxes in case she decides to come after me. Being human, she's never been trained as a fighter, but I know from experience that she can deliver a swift kick to the balls if provoked enough. I may have overplayed my hand.

Lowering the mug defensively in front of my groin, I say, "What? You just assume because I drive the moving van that I can't be a student too? All I said was we might have some classes together."

Sexy Roommate—god, I have to learn her real name before I slip up and call her that to her face—slips between Beth and me and grabs the mug, her fingers almost brushing against my fly. Hope springs to life in my pants, and I have to work to tamp it down. "I guess we'll deal with that scenario if we actually encounter it. For now, you should probably get going so no one thinks we've stolen a moving van."

Admitting defeat, I shuffle out of the dorm and down the stairs. I don't even notice the bustle around me as I see my way out of the dorm. I'm practically surrounded by good-looking girls, most of them wearing shorts and tank tops to survive the August swelter, and all I can think of is the one I completely failed to impress upstairs in Bee's dorm room.

Me: Come on, B. We're doing this for me as much as you. Give me a name, at least. Better yet, set up a meet.

There's no response for long enough that I'm pretty sure she's never going to answer. I'm formulating plan B when my phone buzzes.

Bee: You cannot stick so close to me. Chase after someone else.

Me: Please please please. I am literally begging you right now. And if you help me out, I promise to back off.

Bee: I'll let you know when we go out someplace. That is all I'm willing to do so don't ask for anything else. Besides, what would your father say about it?

I know exactly what he would say about it. "Blah blah, life experience. Blah blah, who your real friends are. Blah blah, family duties." But he's not the one who met Sexy Roommate today and now can't seem to think of anything else, so I'm not that interested in what he would say.

Me: Name?

Bee: Nope. If you're going to do this, you have to put the work in. I am not enabling this humongous mistake only to watch you crash and burn and be miserable in the aftermath.

Me: Bee's Lickable Roommate. RILF. Roommate I'd Like to Fuck.

She sends a GIF of someone flipping the bird at me.

Me: When did you get to be so jaded?

Bee: Pot? Kettle? You were as jaded as me just a few hours ago. What happened?

I'm not going to admit it to Bee, but I'm pretty sure I fell in love a few hours ago. And, yes, I realize how ridiculous and improbable and not to mention idiotic that is. But I can't stop thinking about this girl. I can't stop remembering her scent and imagining the feel of her hips under my body and wondering what her major is. What else could I be feeling? Maybe all those bullshit fated mates stories I've been told have some kind of truth to them. Or maybe this is just lust at first sight, not love, and I'll lose interest as soon as I learn her name or see her naked.

Considering the thought that I might possibly see her naked gets me harder than I have any right to be, I'm not going to hold my breath for these feelings to go away.

GLORIA

Some of my hope for Bee has been restored. Once we got all of her stuff moved up and got rid of the weirdly clingy moving guy, she got to work unpacking everything with gusto. I don't think I could have helped her even if I had wanted to, considering that I had no idea what half the stuff she was pulling out of her boxes and bags was.

Thank goodness, because I've already carried enough of her stuff for her.

The only thing that seemed to slow her down was her smartphone, which kept going off, causing her to pause from her unpacking whirlwind to punch a response back. After the first few times of this, she told her phone to "Fuck off" before throwing it to the other side of her bed.

Even without having everything unpacked, her things fill up all of the shelf, dresser, and closet space available, while mine neatly fits in my closet or the little bedside table. We sit on our respective beds and stare awkwardly at each other. My mind races for conversation starters. How do people normally do this? I don't want to ask anything rude and then have to face a year as roommates with someone who hates me. The only comfort is that Bee looks about as lost as I do.

Her dinging phone interrupts the awkward silence, and she huffs out an annoyed sigh as she checks her message.

"Something you need to deal with?" I ask.

She gives an exaggerated eye roll. "No. Nothing that won't deal with itself. Hopefully." She looks up at me with more truth in her eyes than I've seen before. "Do you have any siblings?"

"Ugh! Too many siblings! And all of them are happy to live the shifter dream. And by dream, of course I mean wasting your life working on a farm forever while being used to push out wolf litters at the same rate as the sheep. Not to mention always being poor and never doing anything for yourself—" I clap my hands over my mouth in horror at the stream of too much truth that just poured out of my mouth.

"Wow . . . are you sure you don't want to tell me how you really feel? I take it you have other ideas? Have you chosen a major yet?" she asks with a shy but amused look on her face.

I sigh in relief while being filled simultaneously with jealousy that she was able to think of a safe topic of conversation. "Undeclared right now," I admit. "I know my parents really want me to do . . . well, let's just say they have very particular ideas about what kind of degrees are useful." A girl like Bee, who has a truckload of belongings, probably wouldn't understand the agriculture vs pre-vet war that has been waging in my family for the past year, ever since I insisted that I wanted to go to college. And my family still doesn't understand what I'm actually hoping to get out of college.

A name for myself. A place in the world that isn't the farm I grew up on. And the easiest way for someone like me to have a chance at that is to find a rich husband to give me a step up in the world.

"What about you?"

Bee gives a dreamy sigh. "There are so many things I want to do. I just can't choose yet."

Must be nice, I think. "No reason to choose yet," I say. "Isn't freshman year when we're supposed to go out and find ourselves?"

"I guess it is." She gives a definitive nod of her head, then says, "Yeah, that's exactly what I'm here to do, now that you put it that way." She smiles at me. "I feel like I've never really known who I am or where I belong. But here, no one knows who they are or where they belong, so I guess that means I'll fit in more than I ever have before, don't you think?"

In spite of my jealousy, I find myself charmed by her utter earnestness. We may be from different worlds and have different experiences, but I feel like we might actually get along just fine. I decide to take a risk. "I heard all of the Greek houses put on, like, a huge block party during move-in weekend. Kind of a pre-rush thing? Would you . . ."

"Yes!" Bee's eyes light up. "I've never done anything like that, and I want every new experience I can get while I'm in school."

Alright, taking the risk paid off. Some of my nerves ease up. "I love that idea. Try every new experience while I'm here. Starting with my first frat party."

Bee screams. "Oh my god, look at the time! We're late! We're going to be late for the orientation meeting!"

I check the time, and sure enough, our orientation is starting right now. We race across the pavement between the freshmen dorms, only to find the meeting hall completely full of freshmen.

Shit.

Chapter Two

GLORIA

"**A**nd we encourage everyone to visit the clinic before you have a health emergency." Lacey is lecturing the room full of freshmen when we squeeze through the doors. She cuts off to give a cold look that slices right through me. "As I was saying, I realize that many of you have never visited a doctor before. The Campus Health Clinic can help you out with all sorts of issues you might not have thought about. Headaches. Toe fungus. Oh! You! Late girls in the back! I was just saying the Health Clinic might be able to help anyone with any body odor issues you might be having. Just wanted to make sure you heard that part. The clinic can really help, so don't feel embarrassed, and go see them as soon as you can. You wouldn't want to force your roommate through that now that you're living in close quarters."

"Sorry!" a short, fit guy with deeply tanned skin, perfectly sculpted, shiny black hair, and the most mischievous white smile I have ever seen shouts next to me. "I swear, I've been working on the body odor issue, but I just haven't found the right cocktail of antiperspirant and body spray to keep it under control." He shrugs with a *what can you do?* kind of smile. "You, on the other hand, smell amazing. What is that? Strawberry? No, guava! Maybe we could meet up later and you could show me what makes you smell that good?"

I can't help letting out a chuckle, along with most of the people around us.

Lacey's eyes narrow in a death glare at him. "Tempting, but pass. Anyway, please make use of the free clinic. It's for everyone. Don't make your bad hygiene my problem."

The short guy isn't deterred at all. He salutes with a cheeky grin at Lacey. "Roger that."

I give him a small nod of my head to say "thank you" before turning back to the front of the room.

Each RA has some preplanned spiel to go through. One says to make sure we stop by the bookstore before classes start to make sure we get our textbooks before they run out.

Another RA has a fun pep talk about meeting new friends through various campus organizations, which will have a fair on the quad tomorrow. I probably should go and get a feel for what's out there, but I'm feeling too nervous right now to really think about it.

There's a human RA who talks about proper condom use, which has shifters—and possibly also some vampires—all around the room rolling their eyes. A condom that actually prevents shifters from getting pregnant has yet to be invented. It might reduce the chances, but it will never really keep you safe. And everyone knows that vampires have their own shit going on in that department. I guess that's the thing about going to a mixed school like this. They need to address the needs of everyone, not just the shifters or the vampires.

Bee follows me as I ease through the crowd to get closer to the guy from earlier who saved us from the icy terror that is Lacey the RA so I can thank him.

"Are you sure you want to stand so close?" he whispers to us with a playful grin. "I've heard that my hygiene may be an issue for some people."

"I'll hold my breath if it gets to be too much."

He holds his hand out to shake. "I'm Jeff. So, just out of curiosity, do you have some long and sordid history with her, or am I imagining things?"

"What, you mean you can't tell that she and Gloria are long-lost twins separated from birth?" Bee says with a grin.

I give Bee a shocked look before realizing that she is joking and introduce us both. "I'm Gloria, and this is my roommate, Bethany."

"But you have to call me Bee. After all that, I insist." Bee smiles at him.

Right then, Lacey raises her voice above the RA who's telling us about all of the different libraries on campus. "Excuse me! I'm sorry if you're having so much trouble understanding this simple presentation that you need to rub all your brain cells together, but maybe you could wait just a few more minutes?"

Jeff's smile widens. "I'll wait as long as you want me to, rubbing whatever I can together," he calls out to her with an accompanying wink, then turns to Bee and me and whispers a fervent "God, I think I'm in love."

"Do you think he's"—Bee points to her temple—"you know . . . okay?"

I can hear Lacey's teeth grinding from across the room, but at least her glare is directed at him instead of me now.

It really is just a few more minutes before the RAs release us. All of the information could have been shared along with the move-in packet, of course, and I would have happily avoided being embarrassed by my RA in front of a crowd.

Jeff turns back to Bee and me as the crowd of freshmen

mills around us and starts trickling out. "So, was that just in my head, or does she have something against you?"

I shrug. "It's possible she really is offended by my smell."

"Hey, don't worry about it. Coming from a house with four sisters, I can honestly say you do not smell." Jeff chuckles as he throws his arm over my shoulder. "And man, can my sisters stink up a place!"

I take a surreptitious sniff at the collar of my shirt. "*Would* you tell me if I was stinking things up?"

Jeff removes his arm from my shoulder and turns to me with a solemn expression on his face and only the tiniest twinkle in his eyes as he holds up his pinky finger. "Gloria, I will pinky promise with you right now, if you get too smelly, I will book you an appointment at the student health clinic myself."

"And I'll buy you some of Lacey's strawberry guava antiperspirant!" Bee giggles and adds her own pinky so we can shake our tangled fingers together.

"So what are you ladies doing after this?"

Bee and I share a look.

"Well," I say, "I've heard there are a lot of parties at the frat houses tonight. I want to go, but I also know I have nothing to wear for a party."

Bee cuts in. "Don't worry about that. You can borrow something from me. You'll look great!"

Jeff claps his hands in excitement. "It's decided, then! Meet me back here at nine, and we'll go party hunting together. Sadly, I'll have to miss the makeover, but I have faith in your abilities.

* * *

Bee gets to work as soon as we get back to our room, pulling out skirts, tops, and dresses like a tornado passing through.

"Now, I realize we're not the same size, but let's see if there's anything here that we can work with." She hands me a red dress made of soft, stretchy fabric. "Try this first."

The red dress doesn't even make it over my bulky shoulders before I'm trapped, flailing my hands above my head like an idiot. Bee helps peel it off me and sets it aside with a frown.

"Okay. I thought that one might be stretchy enough to work, but obviously, I was wrong."

We then go through several skirts that either won't close properly or don't even make it past my thighs.

I flop down on my bed, wearing my underwear and nothing else. "Let's face it. This is not going to work. I appreciate you trying, though."

Bee crosses her arms and stands over me with a scowl. For a tiny human, she's actually pretty intimidating right now.

"I'm not giving up yet, so you aren't allowed to either. It looks like the only thing we can share is my shoes. Thank goodness for small miracles, huh!"

Then she turns to the drawer with my clothes in it and starts rifling through it.

"What are you doing?"

She tosses one of my flannel shirts to me with a "Tie that, don't button it. Do you have a black bra? Yes, that's perfect!" while I stare at the shirt in confusion. "I think we need to play to your strengths. You have beautiful hair, great legs, and perfect freakin' boobs." Bee sighs as she looks down at her own chest. "I think if we add some jewelry and some high heels . . ." She trails off as she casually takes a pair of scissors, approaches my closet, and picks up a pair of my jeans.

"Wait! What the fuck are you doing?"

"Don't worry. You'll thank me for this later," she tells me with a wink.

Chapter Three

GLORIA

My nerves are back with all of their buddies from a few hours ago as we walk toward Greek Row.

I can admit that the outfit Bee put me in—a red flannel shirt tied around my boobs like a swimsuit top and faded cutoff jeans that I can feel my ass cheeks hanging out of, pulled together by a pair of Bee's strappy sandals and some dangly earrings—is an improvement over my regular dusty farm clothes, but I don't really know what people normally wear to parties like this. First impressions matter, and I am painfully aware that I would turn myself away at the door if I was the one in charge.

And then there's Bee, looking elegant and effortless in the red dress that I couldn't even put on, which of course looks flowy in all the right places and clingy in all the other right places when she's wearing it. She looks like a sexy siren, while I look . . . well, I at least look sexy. I just look like a sexy farm girl. Okay, I guess my jealousy has also returned in full force. I love that she, in all her innocent sweetness, offered to let me borrow something to wear. I hate that we've now confirmed that I'm about three sizes bigger than her if you only count my skeleton before adding all of the meat onto my bones. Farmwork has not made me into a delicate lady. My wolf shifter genes haven't helped either. Even when I was only living with other wolves, I learned that "swarthy" is the best word to describe my body type. And Bee is both dainty and delicate.

What was I thinking? Every single plan I've made in the past year revolves around me being able to pass myself off as just like all the other freshman girls.

I roll my shoulders back and check my posture. I may be completely out of ammunition in my arsenal, but I'm going to march into battle and do my best anyway. Maybe it's a fake-it-'til-you-make-it situation. Maybe the goddesses will take pity on me? I have to keep hope alive somehow.

"Are you ready?" Bee's earlier confidence has wilted some.

I grab onto her hand. "Let's go. The worst that can happen is they turn us away."

* * *

We meet up with Jeff and are immediately rewarded with a brilliant smile as he gets down on his knees and worships at our feet. "All hail the goddess of makeovers! I am ready to worship at the short shorts altar!"

Both Bee and I look extremely embarrassed as we each grab hold of one of his arms to haul him to his feet.

"Oh please, we are nothing compared to a vampire like Lacey. Stop being dumb," I say as Jeff brushes some grass off his jeans.

"Hey now! I will hear none of that. All asses are to be revered in my religion!"

Bee gives him a small smack on the shoulder as I hide a

smile. Who knew having a handsome man grovel at your feet, even in jest, makes a person feel pretty good.

Jeff holds out an arm to each of us and leads us down the quad to a house that is blasting music. As we go inside, I am relieved to find I don't stick out quite as badly as I feared. I can smell that there are other wolves around me. Not a majority, and not a pack by a long shot, but I'm not the only sturdy-boned girl giving off extra sweat and scent in this place.

Bee gets enveloped into a gaggle of ultra-feminine girls mere moments after we walk through the door, but no one looks askance at me. No one tries to turn me away or asks if I'm sure I'm in the right place. Jeff says he'll grab us something to drink, and a minute later, someone places a red plastic cup filled with light brown liquid in my hands.

"I thought we might see each other again," an already too-familiar voice says in my ear.

I turn to face him. "Ah, Thirsty Moving Guy. What are you doing here?"

"I told you, I'm a student. And the name is Jimmy, not 'Thirsty Moving Guy.' Though now that you mention it, I am starting to feel a little thirsty.'" He gives me a sexy grin as he raises his own red cup for a toast. "Enjoy!"

I sniff at the beer skeptically—just regular, cheap lager, as far as I can tell—and take a cautious sip. "If I get roofied, I'm blaming you, and I will make you pay. Painfully."

He holds up his hands. "I would expect nothing less. But I promise it's just regular beer that I got from the keg over there." He points to the corner of the room where a shirtless guy is doing a keg stand. "So if I get roofied, I'll have to tell everyone to look for my last client's sexy roommate as suspect number one." He takes another sip from his matching red plastic cup.

"Excuse me? Did you just call me sexy roommate? You obviously need to have your eyes checked or maybe your whole head," I say as I try to avoid making eye contact with him, thankful to have a cup to hide my face in.

"Maybe if you have time later, you can give me a look over. So, since I've proven my worth as a bringer of beer, can I get your name now? Or would you prefer I just keep calling you Sexy Roommate until my head exam?"

I look sidelong at him and sip my drink. I tried to ignore it before, when he was drinking from my embarrassing rainbow mug and complaining about helping Bee move, but he actually is a good-looking guy. Okay, maybe more than just good-looking. I'm a grown-ass woman and can admit it, at least to myself. He's probably the sexiest guy I've ever actually talked to. And he has a wolfy-masculine musk that has me all kinds of turned on right now. And it's not like I'm going to meet my rich, well-bred future husband tonight anyway. If I did, it's not like I'd be impressing him in my made-over farm clothes.

"If I give you my name, you might get ideas that this could be more than it is."

"What is this?" He looks serious as he asks, "I thought we were talking about an eye exam." He says it in an innocent voice while sneaking the quickest look at the top of my plaid shirt. I can't help feeling like maybe I'm the butt of a joke and I just haven't figured it out yet.

"'This' is a you get one night to take me somewhere where we can enjoy ourselves, then we go our separate ways and live our separate lives and never see each other again kind of an eye exam."

His eyebrows shoot up. He stares at me with his mouth hanging open long enough that I'm about to slink away in shame from the whole proposition. "Okay." He grabs my hand before I can finish turning away. "I can take you someplace. Let's go."

I throw back the rest of my cup of beer, wishing for something stronger but glad that it's nothing that will make me sick. I had a bad experience with red wine as a kid, and I've never been the same since. I let him pull me away from the party and out the back door of the house, pausing just long enough to set my now empty cup on a table as I walk past.

"Do you have a car?" he asks once we get enough from the noise to talk.

"No. Were you expecting me to drive us somewhere?"

He laughs. "No, I thought I should check in case we needed to take it into account. I'd rather run anyway. If that's alright with you?"

It goes against every one of my plans. It's probably the worst idea in the world. It sounds delicious, and the wolf in me is already sitting up and begging to be let loose.

"Okay," I say, trying to sound coy or reluctant or cool. Anything other than what I feel, which is suddenly desperate beyond belief. "I could go for a run. Oh, wait! I should probably tell my roommate that I'm leaving. I don't want her to worry."

He starts to take off his shoes as he says, "It's fine, I'll text her."

"Wait. How do you have her number?"

He pauses from undoing his belt and looks back at me.

"I helped her move, remember? I had her number to help her schedule everything."

Realizing that Bee and I haven't exchanged numbers yet, I'm about to ask him if he could share her number with me, but before the words are fully out of my mouth, he's stripping off his shirt and ever so slowly sliding the zipper of his jeans down. He quirks an eyebrow at me in challenge as he starts to push down his jeans. "Well? Were you planning on running like that?"

"Turn. Around," I grind out through clenched teeth. "I am not stripping for you."

"Oh, come on. Are you seriously the one wolf in the world who has some kind of hang-up about being naked?"

Of course I'm not. I'm as comfortable in fur as I am bare skin, and clothes don't go well with fur. Therefore, clothes are only for when I'm in my human body and not always even then. That doesn't mean I want to put on a show for this guy I just met.

"Look," I say in my calmest voice. "I've already told you my expectations here. You get one night. You said you want to run. Fine, let's run. Turn around so I can shift in private, or I can happily go back to the party and find someone who's actually worth my time."

He holds up his hands in defeat and turns his back to me. "Fine. I won't look. But you have to realize that now my curiosity is piqued to a whole new level it never would have reached if we'd just seen each other naked and gotten it over with."

I don't need to say anything. We both know he's right, and we both know there's no way in hell I'll ever admit it. I whip off my clothes and shift in a few seconds flat, then give a quiet "woof" as a signal that I'm ready. For all my insecurities in my human form, I preen a little in wolf form, knowing how striking my almost midnight-black coat is.

He turns around, still partially clothed and fully human, to look at me. Asshole. I have a moment of panic, wondering if this was all just a prank and he's going to steal my clothes and disappear, but he stands there with a grin spreading across his face instead. With my heightened wolf senses, I can smell his arousal, practically hear the quickening thrum of his heartbeat. If I still had a human mouth, I'd tell him to get on with it, but I have no choice now but to wait for him to make the next move.

Giving me a very meaningful stare, he finishes taking off

his boxers ever so slowly, sliding the material down his legs until it hits the ground.

"You'll let me know if I'm making you uncomfortable with my nudity, right?" he teases me.

For once, I'm not going to complain. The fact is, while I didn't want to put on a show for him, I have no problems at all with watching him put on a show for me. My wolfish mouth actually salivates as I watch him bend over to rearrange our clothes in a neat pile and send a quick message to Bee on his phone, keeping his eyes on me as he does so. Now I can see his arousal in plain view, and I'm having trouble remembering why I told him to turn away from me, why I insisted that we could only have one night.

When his cock—darker than the rest of his skin and with visible veins pulsing just beneath the surface—starts to stand even more erect, I can't stop myself from panting in anticipation. And the asshole notices too. "See something that interests you?" he asks with that infuriating grin still plastered across his face.

I snap my jaws in response, just a little reminder of who currently has the sharpest teeth.

He just laughs and shifts to meet me in wolf form.

And his wolf form is, well, impressive. There's nothing else to say about it. Broad and tall, with thick grey-and-silver hair, he truly is a prime specimen as far as wolves go. Too bad my big college plans don't involve falling into the trap of a relationship with the first townie I come across. If I was going to go for a townie, this guy would be it.

I take the appropriate amount of time to sniff and be sniffed before dashing off in the direction that seems most likely to lead away from town and lights and loud noises. Right now, I just need to get away more than anything else. And if my getaway happens to be with a sexy silver wolf I just met, so be it.

It feels amazing to really stretch my legs after a day of walking upright and slow. Living on a farm, I don't know if I've gone a day in my life without unleashing my wolf and letting her ramble. I'm not sure how I'm going to deal with those needs at college when people expect me to do human social activities. When I expect myself to do human social activities. My new friend seems to be enjoying himself just as much.

I start at an easy lope, but when I sense him gaining on me, instinct kicks in, and I run from him in earnest. He falls back, but I get the sense he still has energy to burn. I stretch myself, pushing my running speed to my limit, trying to escape his pursuit until we leave the lights of civilization behind us, and I flop down in an exhausted, panting heap in a field overlooking the city lights.

Chapter Four

JIMMY

I'm not sure what to do now. She's still in that beautiful, black-furred wolf form, and since she hasn't shifted back to human, it's not like I can ask what she wants now. And getting frisky as wolves has some major inherent risks. Like the fact that I don't exactly have any wolf condoms with me, and my wolf cannot be trusted to pull out at the appropriate time. I'm pretty sure my wolf wants nothing more than to mate her and move on to the next phase of life: cubs and pack and more cubs until we're too old for any of that. Fuck, but we would make some beautiful wolf babies.

My father will actually kill me, like, run straight to campus without stopping and straight up murder me on the lawn, if I get someone pregnant before the semester is over.

My human mind is way too sensible for this. Get to know her better, sure. Maybe even have sex, as long as we have protection, fine. My wolf takes control of my faculties, though, bringing me to lie down right beside her and give her a playful nip at her ear.

She shakes her head, then nips me back. Oh, now it's on. I up the ante by crouching over her and nuzzling my entire snout into the thick fur around her neck.

Danger! Danger! my human mind is screaming at me.

She smells like home is the oh-so-helpful thought my wolf provides. If I don't get this situation under control and fast, I'm going to be fathering a litter of wolf pups before classes start.

I'm saved by the obviously better-functioning brain of Sexy Roommate. She tosses me off her and shifts in one smooth ripple. She lets me take her in in all her glory for a moment before I follow her lead and shift, lying a few feet away, letting the stars bathe my skin and the prickling grass bring me back to my senses.

"Thanks for that," I gasp once some blood has returned to my brain. "I really didn't mean to . . ."

"It's nothing," she says quickly, and I'm a little relieved that she seems to be breathing just as heavily as me. "Sometimes, nature tries to take over. We managed to get back under control this time around."

"Right. Yeah. Under control." I know that I'm babbling nonsense, but at this point, I need to do anything to fill the space. "Now that we're . . . back under control . . . do you think we might try kissing?"

She turns her head to give me a narrow-eyed look. "I don't think that's a good idea. Actually, considering what almost just happened, I think that's an extremely bad idea."

I puff out a breath. Just because I know she's right doesn't mean I have to like it. "Okay. No kissing. And no fucking probably goes without saying. What about any kind of touching?"

"Only if it's to save a life," she says drily.

"If I tell you I have a condition where I will literally die if you don't touch my dick?"

She cracks out a loud, harsh chuckle. "Show me the shifter medical journal on it, and it's a deal. Sadly, I'm afraid I've never heard of any kind of disease like that. Do you have any other 'proof' you could show me?"

"What about you?" I change the subject. "I bet you've got a few places that feel tender enough to kill if you don't get some . . . relief . . ."

She scowls. "How can you be suggesting that when you just established that losing control with each other would be a very bad thing?"

My grin matches her scowl. "The thing is," I slowly admit, "I really am having an issue at the moment, which is preventing me from thinking clearly, and the more I try to remember why I can't put one of those amazing tits in my mouth here and now, the more it actually seems like a pretty fucking good idea."

"Or why I can't see how it would feel to have you pressing my back against a tree," she says, her eyes focused on my pecs.

"Hmm, I could do that . . . It would mean I'd have to hold those fucking sexy hips that have been driving me crazy and squeeze until I can see my handprints." I can almost see it in my mind. I get even more turned on as I watch her gaze drift to my hands like she is imagining it.

"Well, it's a terrible idea whether you remember the reasons or not," she counters, the smell of her arousal filling the air around us.

Just as I step toward her to make everything we just said happen, she shifts and streaks back toward town and campus and rules and civilization.

God, I hate civilization.

I shift and follow her, desperately trying to imagine ways to convince her to give me a chance.

* * *

Her clothes are still where she left them, and she's nowhere in sight when I get back. She must have gone straight back to her dorm. Maybe I should have tried harder to follow her, to catch her and make her see things my way, but I know that her way is more sensible right now.

So maybe she won't be tricked into a quickie in a field outside of town. That doesn't mean I can't keep pursuing her. After all, I know where she lives. I still don't know her name or her phone number or her major, which might make things more complicated, but I'm not ready to give up hope yet.

I shift and get dressed, run a hand through my hair in hopes of jostling any stray blades of grass out before going in to face people again. I stop and gather up her clothes, taking note of the cut-up shorts, and I can't help but grin. This handiwork has Bee written all over it. I take a moment to bury my face in her clothes, the scent of Sexy Roommate still driving me insane as I go back to the party to search out Bee. I have no idea why the girls chose a frat party—of all the miserable, godforsaken social events they could have sought out—for their first night on campus, but I did tell Bee to let me know where they went. And good thing, too, because I can't in good conscience tell my father that I'm keeping an eye out if I don't at least duck back in and make sure she isn't letting the vampires or frat boys or anyone else feast on her.

The too-loud but fairly orderly party from earlier has completely devolved into chaos. Bee is nowhere to be found in the common rooms of the house, and the side yard seems to have given birth to some kind of fight club. I say a little prayer as I sneak up the stairs that I'm not about to see something that I can't unsee. I say an even more fervent prayer that nothing's been done to Bee that can't be undone. The first door I come to is closed, with the unmistakable sounds of people enjoying themselves behind it. Everyone making noise in there, at least, sounds like a very willing participant. If one of them is

Bee, I'll just have to hope she's remembered to take some reasonable precautions. And hope that she finishes up and comes out before I reach the point of having to break down doors to find her.

I've never had to be this protective of anyone before. In the past, there was always a pack around me for support, a real adult to call the shots. This situation is kind of messing with my head right now. Should I start opening doors to try and find her? Should I assume that, since she's legally an adult every bit as much as I am, I should leave her to whatever debauchery she's found? I settle with moving further down the hall, listening at each door in case I do hear a distressed voice calling out.

The second door is mostly quiet, except for the rhythmic thumping of a headboard against the wall. Please, please let me find Bee before I have to open that door to check for her.

The third door has me dashing through without a second thought when I hear a scream of pain. Oh shit, is that a mistake. Two naked men—one with . . . is that a riding crop? In his hands—glare at me from the bed.

"Do you mind?" the guy who was apparently just getting whipped shouts at me.

"Sorry! Shit, so sorry!" I shout back, getting out and shutting the door as fast as I can.

I guess that's proof that I can't trust my senses as far as which doors have people who might need help as opposed to people just having fun. I take a slow, fortifying breath, allowing myself a moment to be thankful it wasn't Beth I just barged in on.

The next door is quiet, but I've learned my lesson not to barge in. I knock loud enough that anyone inside will hear it over the noise of the party and quiet enough so hopefully anyone inside doesn't assume there's a police raid or anything.

Bee opens the door and blinks up at me in confusion. And

she's fully clothed and seems to be alone, thank every deity in creation.

"I couldn't find you and was starting to get a little worried," I admit. This night has been too long for me to play any games about this. "You okay?"

"Yeah, Grey, I'm fine," she says in a small voice that makes me want to go find someone to punch.

"Are you sure? You kind of don't look fine right now."

"I am. I really am. It's just, Gloria really wanted to come tonight, and I didn't want to hold her back, you know? But everything was kind of . . . a bit too much when it all came down to it."

I hold out an arm in invitation, and she slips under it for a hug without any protest. "Does it help at all to know that it's been a bit too much for me too?"

Bee blinks up at me. "Really? For you? I mean . . . I saw your message about you leaving with Gloria, and I assumed . . ."

"Nope." I shake my head. "You assumed wrong. We shifted, then we went for a run, then she came to her senses and ran away from me, and then I came up here and saw more than I bargained for."

Beth snickers at that. "If you saw what was happening a couple doors down from this one, then I think I understand what you're talking about."

Both of us dissolve in a bout of immature giggles.

"Wait, so where did Gloria go? Is she okay? I should get back to see if she got back okay."

"She stayed in her wolf form, so I'm sure she's fine." I unwillingly bring the bundle of clothing forward and pass it to Bee. "Here, get these back to her for me. Wouldn't want her to go without those shorts. Your work, I assume?" I give Bee a small reproachful smile, even though I am so fucking grateful for what she did with a pair of scissors. Imagining what it would feel like to take off those shorts is what is going to get me through the night.

Bee smiles as she takes the pile of clothing from me. "Yeah, that was all me. She didn't look like she felt comfortable wearing any of her clothes, and all my stuff is made for stick people like me, so I solved the issue."

"Well done, Bee."

She smacks my arm but is still smiling sleepily.

"Come on." I squeeze her to my side and start walking us toward the exit. "We've had a big night. Let's get you home."

She stays blessedly quiet the entire way back to her door, and I spend the entire time letting the name she revealed—Gloria—play through my mind. Not Sexy Roommate. She has a name. Gloria.

GLORIA

Did I leave my clothes behind at a frat party because I wasn't sure I could control my hormones?

Yes, I did.

Did I almost forget every single reason I had for coming to college in the first place in favor of a one-night stand?

Yes, I did.

Am I going to allow these facts to derail me from all of my goals and plans?

Absolutely not.

I brace myself and do my best to hold my head high as I walk into the dorm, naked as the day I was born, and ask the tall, freckled, curly-haired, red-headed girl working the front desk if she can let me into my room.

The fates are in my favor or something because she's a wolf too.

She gives me an understanding smile, then grabs her master key. "I've started wearing my important stuff on a chain around my neck," she says, lifting said chain from under her shirt to show me. "I think I lost my wallet three times during my first semester here from shifting and leaving it in random places. Stuff your parents don't prepare you for, right?"

She's not wrong. My parents spent plenty of time arguing the pros and cons of studying animal husbandry vs not going to college at all, but I'm pretty sure neither of them went through a phase where they shifted, came inches away from destroying their lives, and then had to run home without going back to the clothes they left behind. And if they did, god, I don't want to know about it.

"I'm Shelly, by the way," she says, offering her hand at the door after she opens my room for me. "I work the front desk most nights. It keeps me out of trouble." She looks up sheepishly through her eyelashes. "My parents said I had too much fun at college my first year here, and now they say I have to have a job and keep my grades up if I want them to continue supporting me here. But anyway"—she shrugs it off—"if you're interested, we've got a nice wolf community here on campus. Lots of us away from our packs for the first time. It can be good to have someone to lean on sometimes."

I'm about to jump at her offer, then remember what I'm here for and hesitate. "I . . . I'll think about checking it out sometime" is what I settle on. Nice and noncommittal so she won't get her hopes up, but not an outright lie or downright rude. I'm kind of proud of myself for coming up with a reasonably diplomatic answer on the fly like that.

She smiles like she knows I'm bullshitting, but she doesn't care enough to call me on it. "No pressure or anything. Just know we're here if you do need us. For anything."

I nod, silently vowing to not need anything from the werewolves here on campus. It's not that I don't want to be a part of the community; it's just that I can't see how it would fit in with my plans right now, or my life in general. I refuse to be that washout wolf who can't handle civilization as well as I'd hoped.

After using the spare key from the front desk, I get comfy in my pajamas and snuggle down into my freshly made dorm bed with my journal and my well-loved set of colorful pens and markers.

Nothing says "put together and powerful woman" like a colorful yet coordinated journal. At least, I hope that's the truth because otherwise, I have literally nothing going for me right now.

Nope. Negative thinking like that has no place in my fresh college life. I turn to a blank page and take the time to set it up to perfection. The more I organize my journal, the less my life seems like a mess. I take a full page to spew out all of the negative thoughts in my head, then turn it over so I can write positives without feeling like they're being poisoned by the negatives.

Positive: My roommate is turning out to be great. A kindness I haven't really come across in my life yet. Maybe a little bit ditsy, but that's not a reason to judge or dislike someone.

Positive: I went to my first college party and didn't get turned away at the door or laughed out of the party for looking like or being a country bumpkin.

Positive: I met one cute boy and one too-hot-to-touch boy.

I draw two neat lines straight through the "too hot to touch boy." I am not here to let myself be roped in by some asshole townie. Definitely not on my first day here, and absolutely not by taking risks with birth control. I shove Thirsty Moving Guy—Jimmy? Nope. I don't even need to remember his name—ferociously to the back of my mind. That makes space for other thoughts. Like the fact that I really can't show up to another party looking like I did tonight. If I keep letting Bee cut up my clothes, I am not going to have anything left to wear.

I turn to another fresh page and start a to-do list.

1. Clothes shopping
2. Meet dorm neighbors
3. Hall meeting at noon

I'm already exhausted simply from looking at my three-item list. Then it occurs to me that Bee is still not back, and I still don't have her phone number. All I can think to do is add one more item to my list.

4. Exchange phone numbers with Bee

* * *

"Buck up, buttercup," I growl at myself from the back of my throat. Four items are not exactly something to be afraid of.

But at least the dorm meeting should be fun. I'm looking forward to meeting everyone I just saw briefly in the hallways during move-in. I'm looking forward to being around new people, and people who aren't wolves, and people who maybe have some exciting new view of the world that I've never encountered. I'm excited for the chance to expand my world-view and meet my future—hopefully well-known and wealthy—husband. Hopefully sooner rather than later.

And if I have to work to shut down any kind of attraction I'm feeling toward a random wolf I met today . . . well, I guess it's not the first time someone felt inappropriate feelings toward a smokin' hot, big-dicked guy who should stay completely off-limits. One might even say that I'm in good company.

* * *

The world looks a lot brighter the next morning when I wake up. Bee is curled up, sleeping soundly in her bed. I swear her hair has gotten even more perfectly wavy while she's been lying there sleeping, and I have to tamp down another wave of jealousy.

She blinks awake and immediately locks eyes with me. Busted. I've been staring at her and have no excuse that will come off as a positive.

"I wasn't snoring too loud, was I?" she asks in a sleepy, innocent voice that brings my jealousy rushing back to me. Why does she have the ability to be all sleepy and cute in the morning while I'm pretty sure I look and sound like some kind of sub-bridge-dwelling troll.

"No, not at all. I mean, not that I noticed. I'm sure if either of us was snoring, it was me." Which is the absolute truth. Wolves are known for their loud noises and strong scents, and not all of them are pleasant.

She rubs her face and then sits up, revealing pastel pajamas that are every bit as cute and innocent-seeming as her bed head and her quiet, sleepy snuffles. "Well, good, then. I'm glad I didn't keep you awake last night. What happened, by the way? One minute, you were by my side; the next, you'd disappeared into the crowd. And Jimmy couldn't find you either. We started to get worried, but then he said that he would have been able to smell if you were under any kind of extra stress."

"Jimmy?" I cough to cover my embarrassment, trying to look as innocent as a wolf could possibly look while staring at anything other than her roommate.

Bee cocks her head to the side and gives me a skeptical look. "Yeah . . . Jimmy who was chasing after you? He helped me move yesterday, and then he was at the party last night? I take it you never got his name."

"I . . . umm . . ." I'd kind of hoped to keep thinking of him as Thirsty Moving Guy. "Right. Jimmy. I remember. But I think you've got it confused anyway," I hurry to correct her. "He wasn't chasing after me. Or, I guess he technically was, but it was just because I happened to be convenient in that moment. I guarantee he's forgotten about me and moved on already." I feel a twinge in my belly at that thought but silence it with reminders of what happens to wolves who get pregnant their first semester of college. They definitely don't finish degrees and go on to do important things with their lives.

"If you say so." Bee continues to look skeptical. "He gave me the clothes you left behind and asked that I get them back to you." Her face turns guilty. "Have I messed things up for you?"

"What? No. Not at all. I mean . . . it's fine, right? It's not like I have anything important in my pockets, except for my dorm room key, and it's not like he doesn't already know where I live, so trying to stay hidden if he does want to find me is kind of silly."

Why am I so hot right now? And why am I babbling? I am not a babbler. In fact, I don't think I can ever remember babbling like this in my life. "Speaking of clothing, I was going to go shopping today. Do you want to come with me?" Thank you, sweet change of subject inspiration.

Clapping her hands and squealing, Bee bounces right off her bed. "Yes, please! The stress of moving has me in dire need of girl time and retail therapy. Let's go early before the crowds hit."

* * *

Bee turns out to be the best shopping partner a girl—particularly a girl with a stunted fashion sense—could ever hope for. The credit card my parents gave me with the instruction to save it for emergencies gets a good workout, but I think they'll understand when I explain the emergency of arriving at school and realizing I could never fit in dressed like a farm girl.

Okay, there's no way they'll understand, but they love me and will forgive me. And I can breathe easier knowing that I have strappy sandals now instead of mud- and dust-covered boots and fluttery blouses instead of flannel button-ups. For the first time in my life, I'm going to actually feel like I'm dressed up like a real girl. Next step, find someone tall, influential, and wealthy guy to snare and live the rest of my life never having to step in sheep shit again. Yes, maybe I am being shallow, but a girl needs dreams, and this is the only one that's stuck around my whole life.

"You seem to have a lot on your mind," Bee tells me on the drive back to the dorm. "You were so chatty while we were shopping, but you haven't said a word since we left the mall. Want to tell me about it?"

There I go being awkward and bad at socializing again. Maybe new clothes will magically change that.

"I guess I was just thinking about the semester ahead of us. Trying to imagine what it's going to be like." I sigh. "And realizing that even with new clothes, my hair and makeup situation is still a disaster."

Laughing, Bee waves a carefree hand through the air. "What I'm hearing is that our girls' day gets to continue with a bit of a makeover. Am I right?"

"Would you . . . I mean . . . is there anything you can do to help me?"

"Oh, remember, I am the makeover expert. I'll make you over so good that you won't even recognize yourself in the mirror afterward. If that's what you want?"

"Yes," I breathe. "That sounds like exactly what I want." To be anyone other than my messy, social disaster of a wolf girl self? Yes, please sign me up.

Chapter Five

JIMMY

My parents—well, my father at least; I'm not sure how Mom feels about it—didn't want Bee leaving home at all. When she made it clear that she was going to college whether they supported her or not, they tried to buy a house off campus that they could station guards at twenty-four seven. Bee was never going to agree to that. After all the arguments and negotiations between the three of them, the compromise they came up with has Bee with one roommate—she insisted that she would be too lonely in a room by herself—in an all-female dorm while I get to share a suite with three other guys in the dorm next door. I suspect there were some strings pulled to make sure Bee had a wolf roommate, but that's not really my business, so I'm not asking any questions.

I, being the far less vulnerable child, have been thrown in with three random dudes and am the only wolf. Good thing I'm not bothered by that sort of thing. It also helps that, so far, all three guys seem to be pretty cool. It could have been a lot worse, considering that both Devon and Marcus are vampires, and I have no experience dealing with bloodsuckers at all. The last guy, Jeff, is a human, and I can already tell he is going to be the ringleader of all future shenanigans.

Well, except for the ones I hope to have with a certain midnight-black she-wolf.

Jeff and Devon are settled in for what appears to be a video gaming marathon when I get up the next morning. Actually, it's a lot closer to noon, but who cares? Classes haven't even started yet.

"Dude, grab a controller and get in here!" Jeff shouts at me as soon as I step into our living room area. His eyes never leave the screen.

As the only human in the suite, you might expect him to be overwhelmed or something by his stronger, more predatory roommates, but he's actually done the best job of bringing us together and making things feel homey around here. I've only known the guy for a day, but he already feels like an old friend.

Devon, the freckled vampire sitting next to him, seems nice enough. Quiet, but he's surprised me a few times by cracking jokes that I wasn't expecting. Then there's Marcus, another vampire, who I've seen for all of five minutes so far when we all claimed our bedrooms yesterday. He doesn't seem like a bad guy—from what I could tell in five minutes—but he does give this impression that he's trying to live up to some kind of Optimum Vampire Ideal or something. Cloud-white skin. Midnight-black hair. Kind of weird.

"Um." I'm still trying to get rid of the haze from last night's adventures. "Can I get coffee first?"

"Do you mind making one for me too?" Devon asks, also without breaking eye contact with the screen.

I come around behind them to see what they're playing and burst out laughing when I see that their avatars are cute cartoon bunnies fighting against each other.

"Fuck, fuck, fuck!" Jeff shouts as Devon's pink-tutued bunny gets the upper hand and starts beating the shit out of him.

And, wow. That blood—not to mention the way the pink bunny rips the other bunny's head off—is not cartoonish at all.

"Holy shit. That was not what I was expecting," I admit, still chuckling a little.

Devon jumps up and does a victory dance that could probably put a professional pole dancer to shame.

Jeff sinks down on the couch, letting out a groan that sounds a lot like "fuuuuuuck."

"What game is that?" I ask from the kitchen as I grab the coffee beans from an upper cabinet.

"It is one of my own creations, thank you very much!" Jeff seems to have recovered emotionally as he beams with pride over his game.

"No way! Seriously? That is awesome, dude. Are you a computer science major or something?" Devon asks as he reexamines the screen with new interest.

"That's the idea. *Rainbow Sparkle Bunny Battle* is the first game I've gotten to work this well. But I am hoping to create something for my younger sisters as well," Jeff says as he grabs a notebook from the coffee table to jot something down.

"Wait . . . did you say *Rainbow Sparkle Bunny Battle*? Is that seriously the name?" I ask from the kitchen.

"Fucking perfect," Devon states as he selects a new character from the screen. A rainbow llama in white, '70s platform shoes. Amused but also intrigued, I start a pot of coffee so I can jump into their afternoon of gaming.

Three hours later, we've moved on from coffee to beer, and my bunny avatar is by far the most stylish with its rainbow bows and a rainbow disco jumpsuit. I'm in last place as far as game stats are concerned, but at least I look pretty fucking fly.

And Marcus has joined us, though more in the form of him shaking his head in a judgmental way.

"Were you all planning to eat any food with all this beer?" Marcus asks us.

We all respond with, "Do we actually have any food here?" and "Maybe we should order pizza?" He sighs and proceeds to march into the kitchen to cook up a pretty impressive meal for us, considering our kitchen area consists of a minifridge, microwave, sink, and kettle. He brings it in for us and turns the coffee table into a mini buffet, leaving some paper plates at the end.

"Hey, Marcus, how are you such an amazing cook? I thought vampires didn't, you know . . . eat this stuff," Jeff asks while grabbing a paper plate and loading it up with a generous amount of Marcus's creations.

"Why would we? It tastes like shit for us, not to mention the stomachache it'll give you," Deven says as he sniffs at Jeff's heaping plate.

"If you can't eat any of this stuff, why do you know how to cook it?" I ask as I go to grab a plate for myself.

"Do farmers not know how to feed their cows?" Marcus says as he watches Jeff stuff his face.

The room goes a little quiet, and we all look at Marcus. Then Jeff breaks the silence by busting out laughing. "Good point! Maybe I should learn how to cook too. I wouldn't want my future girlfriend to get hungry either!"

Devon claps Jeff on the back and grins, "Exactly! You get it!"

I chuckle as I take a bite of the food Marcus made. I have officially renounced any bad thoughts I originally had toward the guy. I will happily let him cook for me anytime he wants. We go back to kicking each other's ass in *Rainbow Sparkle Bunny Battle*.

"Ouch! Jimmy, what is going on with you?" Jeff crows after beating my poor, rainbowy disco bunny yet again. "At some point, it must start hurting you when your avatar feels pain, right?"

"I don't know," I groan. "I swear I'm usually better at stuff like this. I just can't seem to get my brain in gear for some reason."

Jeff and Devon share an unreadable look before Jeff turns his full attention on me and says in a mock-serious voice, "Is it girl troubles? Do we need to have a little talk about what happens when—"

"Fuck off!" I half-heartedly hit him with a cushion. "Don't worry. Someone had 'the talk' with me a long time ago."

"But you aren't denying the girl troubles part of it," Devon interjects gleefully. "Dude, it is way too early in the year for stuff like that. How have you even met any girls to have troubles with?"

"What are you talking about? I've already met two girls. You're the one falling behind, man," Jeff says as he pops another bite of food into his mouth.

"What the hell? Seriously?" Devon is now looking at Jeff with new respect.

"Yeah, and they were both freaking hot, not to mention cute. That doesn't mean I'm here getting my ass kicked like a Sparkle Bunny bitch, though, so what's your excuse, Jimmy?" Jeff and Devon are both looking at me now.

I flop back in defeat. "I don't know," I say honestly. "It's not like I was looking for it or anything."

Marcus, sitting quietly in one of the armchairs the room came furnished with, gives a little chuckle and shakes his head.

"What? I wasn't!"

"It's just such a cliché, right? Saying that you're not looking for anything seems like a surefire way to find something. At least, that's what I've heard."

"In that case," Jeff announces, "I am definitely not looking for a million dollars." He gives us all a goofy wink, and I smack him with the cushion again.

"That's not what I'm talking about," Marcus grumbles. "I'm talking more like . . . Murphy's Law or something like that. If you go off to college and tell everyone that you're going to buckle down and avoid distractions and get good grades, on move-in day, you meet a big old distraction who proceeds to derail your entire semester. Anyone who's ever watched a rom-com knows that. At least, I thought everyone knew that. So. Did you meet a distraction who's about to derail your semester?"

I huff but can't lie to them.

"Yes, I met a distraction who's going to derail my semester."

"And her name is?"

"Gloria." I probably look like a complete idiot going all dreamy-eyed over her, but I can't help it. This is what she does to me.

My roommates burst out laughing at me.

Jeff wheezes, trying to catch his breath from laughing at me so hard. "Hold on. This Gloria. Your Gloria. Is she the same Gloria I went to a party with last night?"

"Yes," I sigh, then sharpen my attention on him. "And don't you dare get any ideas about getting with her yourself."

Everyone starts laughing again.

"Okay, okay, okay!" Jeff shouts to get their attention after he's had a nice long laugh at my expense. "What kind of roommates would we be if we didn't at least try to help Jimmy with his girl trouble?"

Devon tilts his head side to side like he's checking a pros and cons list. Marcus sighs and looks at the ceiling like he's searching for divine intervention, but all three of them eventually agree to help me get Gloria to notice me. The rest, they insist, is up to me.

Chapter Six

GLORIA

I hardly recognize myself by the time I sit down for the hall meeting. And I feel like I don't quite fit in my own skin either.

Are my nipples showing through my low-cut top? I look down to try checking without anyone else noticing and am confronted by my chasm of cleavage.

Bee pokes me in the ribs. "You look fantastic. Now, stop squirming like someone put cockroaches in your underpants."

"I doubt cockroaches would fit in these pants. How the hell did you convince me to get these? I thought the jean shorts were short! You swear you couldn't see my butt hanging out when we were walking here, right?"

"Your ass is perfection, especially in your new, properly constructed jean shorts. Relax. You look like someone's dream."

Easy for her to say. She actually does look like a dream, all delicate and ethereal. Her corseted dress has her perky breasts saying a friendly hello to the world before the fabric falls gently past her hips to rest at the middle of her thigh. I swear, my new, delicate clothes are mostly serving to show off how swarthy I actually am. I pluck at the V-neck of my beautiful, new floral blouse, trying to convince it to cover just a little more of my boobs. It doesn't work.

At least I'm freshly showered, so I don't have to worry about my sweaty wolf smell. I still can't help listening for someone to shout, "Wowzer! Look at how burly this girl's shoulders are!" Bee insisted that the fluttery scraps of fabric over my shoulders would help me look lighter and narrower and more spritely, but I'm not convinced. Oh, and the super-adorable strappy sandals that seemed perfect when I first tried them on? Now, they seem to be making my feet look cartoonishly large and clumsy.

"I can't help it," I hiss back at her. "This was the worst idea I've ever had. I look ridiculous. I feel uncomfortable. I'm returning everything tomorrow and just accepting my reality as an awkward, graceless giant."

"No, you're not," Beth laughs at me. "You look great! Once you get used to dressing like the total babe you are, this won't bother you."

My protest is cut short by Shelly taking a seat beside me. "She's right, you know. It took me two months before I really settled in, but don't worry. You'll get comfortable, and before long, you won't even remember why you felt so self-conscious."

"I hope you're right," I grumble. Gods and goddesses, I hope she's right.

I introduce Shelly and Beth, who already seem like good friends as they lean their heads together in front of me to discuss . . . more girly shit, I guess . . . well, I lose track of their conversation because I'm back to uncomfortably squirming in my seat until Lacey shows up and starts the meeting.

* * *

I have to give it to Lacey. I was nervous about meeting my first vampire, and she really lived up to my unrealistic expectations. Who knew something so bitchy could come in such a stunning package? Probably something I should remember for later. Maybe I should give her the benefit of the doubt? Maybe she was dumped by a smoking hot wolf shifter and is now scarred for life and resents all wolves? Maybe a wolf like Thirsty Moving Guy?

Jimmy.

What the fuck! I can't believe I can't even go a day without thinking about him again. He would totally be the kind of guy to make a beautiful woman like Lacey swear off our kind. I could almost sympathize with her. I've been a mess of insecurities that have been on overdrive since I stepped foot on campus.

It takes me a second to focus back on what Lacey is saying, something about how freshmen are encouraged to reach out to their species' organizations on campus to help with adjusting to college life. I wonder if she ever reached out to the vampire organization when she first got here, and what a vampire organization might help with that's different from a shifter organization, and whether Bee is going to join a human-specific organization.

My head is spinning with more questions by the end of the meeting than the beginning.

"Oh, and don't forget to check out the info booth the campus clinic has set up in the lobby!" Lacey shouts as the meeting breaks up and people start wandering their separate ways.

I raise an eyebrow at Shelly. "What do you think? Is the clinic set up for shifters?"

She gives a derisive snort. "I've never been. Don't worry, no one is going to expect you to show up for a physical."

I let out a relieved chuckle. "Good. I've never been to a doctor in my life. I'm not planning to start going now."

Shelly nods in agreement.

Wolves heal fast. Way faster than humans, and a healthy wolf can generally come back from an injury faster even than a vampire. And if things are really bad, we've got healers. I like to think I'm pretty open-minded, but the thought of a human —or worse, a vampire—doctor poking around at me gives me the full-on heebie-jeebies. No, thank you.

Bee doesn't seem surprised by our anti-clinic conversation. I guess she's probably more worldly than me. Maybe she's heard wolves bad-mouth doctors before.

"I think I will go take a look," she says.

"Are you feeling okay?" I ask, trying to keep a concerned look off my face.

"Yeah! I feel fine! Just curious. I'll catch up with you later?"

"Sounds good," I say.

Shelly links her arm through mine and starts leading me out the door. "Well, since we don't have to go talk to any creepy doctors right now, I'm going to take this opportunity to introduce you to some friends."

I should have seen this one coming.

"Look, I really appreciate you trying to help me out and everything, but it's really not necessary."

She rolls her eyes. "I promise I'm not going to make you sign any pack oaths or anything. I just think it's important for us wolves to know we have a support system. Besides, the main pack lives just outside of the city. It might be useful to have some connections just in case you need something from the higher-ups, you know?"

Right. That's fine. But how do I tell her that I'm already trying my hardest to wash my wolf scent off so I can fit in here and I'm worried about that support system holding me back? Right now, my support system is back on the farm where they belong, and anyone with a closer connection to the pack leader can fuck right off before they try to trap me into following pack rules.

So, I don't tell her any of it, simple as that. I let her guide me to another meeting room where a small group of wolves is gathered, but I've already decided to not get too involved. I need less wolf involvement in my life, not more.

Chapter Seven

If I were a smart man, I would probably just accept that Gloria wants nothing to do with me and let her live her life without interfering. I never, ever, ever in my life claimed to be smart. In fact, I'm so dumb that I had to get help to track down Gloria's schedule so I could change all of my classes to match hers. My only real intelligence comes from knowing my weaknesses and being willing to outsource to cover them.

If I had some way to delegate going to all of these very intimidating math and science classes for me, I would. Unfortunately, Monday morning sees me stumbling into a math class that I had to waive the prerequisites for to sign up.

And there she is, right at the front of the room. She looks different, somehow. Trendier, maybe, than the last time I saw her. But that's okay with me. It's her sweet scent wafting through the lecture hall that has my dick already wanting to stand at attention.

I slide into the empty seat beside her with a grin. "Well, of all the gin joints . . ." I start to say but trail off at the look of horror in her eyes.

"What the hell are you doing here?" she asks in a terse whisper.

"I'm . . . taking a math class?" This is going south a lot faster than I expected.

The sweetness of her scent sours a little with fury as she glares at me. "You can't be here. I can't have you here, messing up my plans. Go. Someplace. Else."

I let my very real hurt feelings show on my face, then amp it up a bit for the sake of drama. "I have as much right as anyone else to take this math class. Math is available to any and all who are looking for the opportunity to . . . add or subtract!" I tell her through my biggest puppy dog eyes. "Maybe we could get coffee after this and compare notes?"

"No. I told you, you're messing up my plans," she says with a scowl.

"What plans are going to be messed up by getting coffee? I mean, in my experience, coffee is the solver of most problems in my life. What bad could coffee possibly do?"

"Coffee is going to keep me from meeting people who have higher standards. People who are actually important. Unlike you. If I spend time with you, that will be time wasted that I could be spending doing something useful. Like comparing notes with . . ." Her eyes search the room for a second. "That guy over there, who obviously spent more time thinking about what he should wear today than you did."

I give my own scowl to the guy she indicates, who shall henceforth be known to me as "Pretentious Khakis Guy"— PKG for short—then look down at my own comfortable sweatpants and T-shirt in comparison.

"Just because someone doesn't have the body to pull off this look for their first day of class does not make them worth your time," I say.

"And showing up looking like the probably homeless townie you are does?"

"I think you mean extremely fit, probably homeless townie, and I'll have you know—" I start, but she cuts me off.

"You're right. It seems unlikely that you're homeless, considering you apparently really are a college student. It was unfair of me to call you a homeless townie when you're probably actually a townie who actually lives with his mother."

She turns back to the front of the room, and I can't even answer. Partly because I can't think of a good comeback and partly because the professor comes in and starts in on a math lecture that goes completely over my head. Who starts lecturing from the very first day? Isn't the first day supposed to be for going over the syllabus or something? I spend the entire class frantically trying to write down everything the professor says, hoping I'll be able to find a good tutor to explain everything to me later. By the time I look up from my notes at the end of class, Gloria is gone, and my head is spinning.

* * *

Class number two. Maybe our first class together didn't go so great, but I've got good feelings for class number two. I didn't even have to sign any special waivers to sign up for this class. Just regular old biology. I took that back in high school, right?

She's not only already in the front row by the time I get there, but she's already flirting with some other guy in khakis by the time I get there. Okay, so there are two PKGs. Maybe there's a club, a "Pretentious Khakis Guys Club," at this school. I vow to never learn any of their real names.

I plunk my ass down in the empty seat next to Gloria's, at the very goddamned front of the lecture hall, and turn to her with a grin. "Fancy seeing you here."

She spares a single moment to scowl at me before going

back to her flirting with PKG. And that's all it takes for me to be hard as a rock in my—thankfully—not-khaki pants under the desk. I'm pretty sure the stiffness of khakis would kill me if my erection brushed against them.

I try to think of every unsexy thought I've ever encountered—spiders, old people holding hands, poopy baby diapers—anything to make my erection go away. Gloria is literally doing nothing. Why am I so hard just from sitting next to her?

I eventually give up and accept that I'll be hard until the end of class. All I can hope is I won't have a reason to stand up until she leaves.

Gloria does an admirable job of note-taking whenever the professor is talking, but every time he slows down to check his notes, she's giving sly glances and suggestive finger taps toward the guy to her right.

That's right.

Suggestive finger taps.

I never knew such a thing existed, but now I'm hyperaware of every single time her skin touches the laminate of her desktop. In case I didn't realize it before, I know it now, down all the way to my core. I want this girl. I need this girl. I cannot let this girl get away to follow some pea-brained, khaki-wearing frat boy.

I double down on taking notes to prevent myself from jumping up and breaking the face of every PKG in the lecture hall. When I woke up this morning, all my wolf wanted was to fuck. Unfortunately, we've gone way beyond that now. He wants to claim what's his, mark his territory, and exert his dominance over everyone who has ever worn khaki pants.

I'm sweating with the exertion of keeping my shit together by the time the lecture is over.

At the end of class, I hold a notebook strategically in front of myself and jog to catch up with Gloria.

"What are you doing?" She doesn't bother turning around to see me following her.

"What do you mean?" I ask, all innocence.

She spins to face me. "I mean, what the hell are you doing in my classes? What the hell are you doing following me right now? I don't even really believe that you're a student, which means you're probably a stalker. I don't know why you're stalking me, but please, just stop."

"I'm not a stalker, I swear. And I really am a student, though, yeah, I guess switching my schedule to be in your classes could come off as creepy."

"You think?" Her eyes are giant and give a sarcastic roll.

"Okay, but, really, I'm harmless. I just wanted a reason to see you. Let me get you a coffee to make up for it? And maybe we could talk while we drink our coffee? We can even stay out in the open. There's no danger of me jumping your bones if we're in a crowded public space, right?"

She narrows her eyes and tilts her head back and forth, like she's staring deep into my soul and judging every crime I've ever committed.

"Fine. Coffee. But we stay human and clothed and platonic. You can tell me what classes you were going to take before becoming a stalker and changing your schedule. And I will tell you which ones you should switch back to. I also reserve the right to walk away at any point and not have you follow after me. Deal?"

"Deal," I say with a grin. "But you should know that we also have freshman history together this afternoon, so even if I don't follow you, you're going to see me again."

She rolls her eyes again and starts walking toward the student union building. I allow myself an eyeful of her perfect backside before rushing to catch up again.

* * *

GLORIA

What kind of a name is Jimmy, anyway? I stare at him over my coffee. And yes, I did choose the most expensive coffee on the menu just to see if he would pay for it, and he did, which means I'm now stuck drinking an overly sugared mess of a frozen drink when I should have just ordered something plain that won't give me a stomachache.

"How does yours taste?" Jimmy asks with a grin that makes me wonder if he's figured out how disgusting my drink actually is.

I take a slurp and make a big show out of swallowing it and then licking my lips with an orgasmic noise that probably has the entire student union building turning to stare at me.

His eyes darken, and his smile disappears. He slides his tongue across his lower lip and gulps, staring at my lips like a starving man would stare at a roasting pig.

"That's . . . completely not fair," he stammers at me.

"What's not fair?"

"You, making sexy noises in public like that right after I promised not to jump you. It's not fair at all and should be . . . I don't know . . . generally off-limits or something."

Now, it's my turn to grin. "It was your idea to track me down and to get coffee together. Don't complain about the fact that you didn't think through the consequences."

Jimmy lets out a strangled little moan. "How was I supposed to know what the consequences would be? A girl has never made noises like that for me in public before. How was I supposed to guess that you would?"

I have to admit, toying with him like this is making me feel pretty fucking good. Powerful, even. Sure, he can figure out my schedule and follow me to my classes, but I can make him twist in his seat, and it's obvious he won't do anything about it.

"Are you saying . . ." I lean forward so I can whisper in his ear, and he leans forward eagerly to meet me. "That I'm your first?"

Jimmy slumps back in his chair with a dramatic groan, barely hiding a grin.

I sit back, satisfied, and slide my cup toward him on the table. "Want a go at it?" I challenge him without breaking eye contact. I really can't help myself. I have never felt so confident teasing someone before.

He stares at the drink before looking back at my lips, then my eyes. "Hell yes I do," he says as he grabs the drink and takes a fast drag on the straw. Before I can say anything else, his face twists into the best expression I have ever seen, cute even. It makes me laugh out loud as he sets my cup as far away from us on the table as possible.

"Okay, maybe I deserved that. Man, that is sweet. Don't get me wrong. I am a dessert guy, but that drink is . . . special. My stomach is gonna pay for that later." He proceeds to take a big gulp of his black coffee. I feel a little bad for offering it to him. I also like sweet things, but whatever I ordered from this coffee place has a whole different level of sugar toxicity than I've encountered before.

"So, anyway. Have you always gone by Jimmy, or are you trying to run away from your old identity or something?"

"Oh. That's really what you want to ask me? Seems a little unfair if you consider that I still don't know your name. Or maybe your name really is Sexy Roommate?"

I lift an eyebrow at him. "We're back to this, are we? Why would you need to know my name? It's not like we're friends."

"We are classmates, though. You might need to borrow a cup of sugar from me or something."

"A cup of . . . sugar?" I look at him with a baffled smile.

"Yeah. They use sugar in biology, right?" He smirks at me

again. "What? Did you think I signed up for your classes with no knowledge of the topics?"

"No. I mean . . . maybe?"

He laughs as he takes another sip of his coffee. "I am surprised, though, that the first thing you bring up is my name."

"Were you expecting me to ask something else?"

"I don't know." He shrugs, rubs his palms against his thighs, readjusts his seat a few times. "I guess I wasn't sure what to expect. I only thought as far ahead as convincing you to go out for coffee with me."

"Well, you don't seem like a Jimmy to me, and it's been bothering me ever since I learned your name. So . . . what's your real name?"

He throws a crumpled napkin at my face. "If I did come to school with some kind of secret identity, do you really think I would tell you about it on the third day we've known each other? Also, the only person here who's hidden their name is you, not me."

"Oh, fine. Fair enough." I throw the napkin back at him. "Do you have an actual major, or are you just vaguely stalking me and then going from there?"

"Mostly that second one, I guess, when you put it that way," he admits. He slumps forward, showing utter defeat for a moment. "What's with all the math and science classes?" he whines.

I shrug. Maybe a part of me feels smug that I haven't made this easy on him, but he looks like such a sad little boy right now. Fuck, why does he have to be so cute? I decide to take pity on him and explain part of my plan. No one gets to know the full plan, otherwise it won't happen. Call it superstition or just a healthy grasp of the reality of the world. I don't want to tell everyone my whole grand plan and then have to tell everyone later about how my grand plan failed.

"My mom wants me to focus on agriculture so I have something useful to take back with me when I go home. My dad wants me to do pre-vet so I have something more useful but also with a lot more debt to take back when I go home. Both majors include a lot of math and science classes."

"But what about what you want?"

He asks like it's so easy, and my chest clenches a little just at the thought of these things being easy.

"What about what I want? How would it make any difference?"

"But . . ." He thinks for a long time. "Wouldn't it? I mean, wouldn't it at least make some difference?"

I give my most casual shrug. "No matter what happens with college, I have to go home at some point and deal with stuff there, don't I?"

"I guess." He scratches his neck, giving the worst kind of impression that he's a dog scratching at his fleas. "What happens if you don't go home?"

I roll my eyes at him. "I can't run away and join the circus, no matter how much I might have dreamed of it as a kid."

"No, I mean—wait, did you really want to join the circus as—no. Don't distract me. I meant, don't a lot of people move away from home for college and then just . . . stay moved away from home? Why are you already planning on going home when it doesn't sound like it's really what you want to do?"

I have to blink away some inexplicable, traitorous wetness in my eyes. He's the first person I can ever remember talking as if I might actually have my own ideas about what to do with my life. With everyone else, it's all about the obligations. Kids in our family grow up to take over the farm. They find mates from nearby packs and make as many litters of new kids to continue the cycle as they can. "It's . . . it's pack . . . you know?"

I can tell by his sad smile that he does know. I also notice he doesn't volunteer any information about his own pack or his family's expectations for him. Maybe he's unaffiliated or, worse, orphaned. Or exiled. If that's the case, hearing me whine about my own family problems must be torture. I decide it's time to change the subject again.

"Are you living in the dorms this year?"

Jimmy perks up and gives me a lascivious grin. "Trying to figure out where we can go to get some privacy?" He even wiggles his eyebrows, in case I didn't catch the hint before.

"Ugh." I throw the dirty napkin at him again. "I should have known I couldn't ask you a simple question without you making it into something dirty."

"Actually, I'll have you know that I keep my dorm room very clean. We've got time right now. You could come back with me and check it out."

I stand up, grab my drink from the table, throw it in the trash, and walk away in response to that. Good thing he doesn't have access to my thoughts because going back to his room and sniffing out exactly how clean he keeps his sheets is actually exactly what I want to do right now.

"What about a name, at least?" He stands up and leans forward, looking hopeful.

"You know what? I'm fine with Sexy Roommate," I say as I walk out of the coffee shop.

JIMMY

I let her go. While it is driving my wolf crazy to watch her leave, I have to admit there are worse things. Also, there's only so much a guy's pride can take before he needs to fall back and regroup. So I fall back to my dorm room and regroup by jacking off in the semi-privacy of the shower I share with three other suitemates. If they were all wolves like me, I would assume they were used to this sort of thing and let loose. But they're not, and I'd rather not give them that particular first impression of me, so I do it as quietly as I can, biting my lip and only letting out a muffled grunt of release when I come. And, sadly, the imagined images of Gloria—naked and spreading her legs for me, licking her full lips before ducking her head and sucking my cock between them—don't let up after I've orgasmed. Something about her has me all kinds of twisted up.

I'm glad, when I come out of the bathroom, that I remembered about all of my non-werewolf roommates because Jeff is sitting on the couch and playing video games with another human when I step through the shared living area with my towel around my waist. My experience with humans mostly extends to Bee, and my experience with vampires is nonexistent, but what I've heard makes me believe no one is quite as comfortable with nudity as us werewolves.

"Hey, sorry, I was just . . ."

"No worries, man." Jeff waves off my apology without breaking his eyes from the screen or pausing his game. "This is Gabe. We met in math class."

Well, at least someone had a productive math class, I think with a little twist of jealousy in my stomach. "Cool, nice to meet you." I head back to get dressed and gird my loins for round three of classes with Gloria—I mean with Sexy Roommate.

* * *

History class is yet another round of torture. I'm not sure which classes in high school were my best classes, but I am sure that history wouldn't be at the top of the list.

Full disclosure: I barely scraped by in most of my classes in high school. I try not to think of myself as dumb, but . . . well, I figured out pretty early on that I wasn't going to be the next great mind of my generation. Good thing I don't need to be. As long as I can survive getting a college degree—any college degree—I can take my place protecting my pack. If I flunk out, I'm definitely going to have some issues, but I bet they still take me back as one of their own. Which is good because just one history class has my head spinning. And there were no seats even remotely close to Gloria, so it kind of feels like a waste. I drag myself back to my dorm room afterward and flop down on my bed, trying to regroup.

Okay, the day wasn't an entire wash. I think I've started chipping away at that hard exterior to get at the real Gloria. No, she isn't exactly putty in my hands right now, but she let me buy her a drink, and she sat at the same table as me for a whole . . . few minutes and let me get to know her. That's progress compared to her running away without her clothes, right?

* * *

GLORIA

I belly-flop onto my bed with a groan.

"Rough day of classes?" Bee asks from her desk.

My body refuses to move, so I just turn my head toward her. "Classes are fine. My fun new stalker, on the other hand . . ."

"Your what?"

"Okay, so remember your moving guy, Jimmy, who showed up at that party, and I kind of ran off with him, thinking it would just be a one-night thing. Two wolves blowing off steam by going for a run, you know?" Maybe she actually has no clue what I'm talking about, but she looks like she's following alright.

Her eyes narrow suspiciously. "Yeah, I remember him."

"Well, I guess he's more interested in me than I realized because he is magically in every single one of my classes. He even admitted that he changed his schedule to share classes with me."

"He what?"

"I know, right? How crazy is that? No sane person would do that, right?"

"You're right. No sane person would," she says, pushing away from her desk to turn to me fully.

"I mean, I may not be totally blameless here. I may have kinda invited him for more than just a run. And, yes, it was as wolves, which can get a bit intense. But, seriously, he agreed that it wouldn't go further than that night, and we didn't even do anything!" I realize I'm rambling at this point, and my face is flaming with embarrassment. I just don't want Bee thinking I'm some horny wolf shifter out to sleep with every other wolf on campus.

Bee is up and pacing the room, muttering something about a painful death and a dull fork.

"Um, Bee?" I roll over onto my back so I can see her better. "Is there something I'm missing here?"

She grabs two handfuls of her hair and pulls, letting out a groan like a rusty tractor in the process of breaking. "Okay. Yeah. I probably have to tell you since this problem isn't going away." She paces the room for a while, and I don't try to interrupt. She's obviously working through something. "The truth is, I actually know Jimmy. We went to school together before this, and I knew that he would be here at Berring, but I had no idea that I would be seeing him all the time. He promised me he would stay out of my way here. But, apparently, now he's chasing after my roommate. I can't believe he would do this after he promised to give me some space!"

With my fatigue all but forgotten, I sit up and lean toward her. "Let me get this straight. Your moving truck guy from two days ago is actually someone you've known for a long time, and he was just . . . what? Making up the bit about being a mover to mess with you or something?"

Now it's Bee's turn to belly-flop onto her bed. She honestly looks a lot like a child throwing a tantrum. "Kind of. It was actually . . ." The rest of her sentence is muffled because she turned her face down into her pillow.

"What was actually what?" I'm starting to feel a little hurt, realizing that I've been left out of the loop.

She turns back to me with a sigh. "It was actually my idea to pretend we didn't know each other. Our parents are old friends, so his parents forced him to come help me move in, but I was the one who told him to just help me move and then act like we didn't know each other. I figured there wouldn't even be a reason for our paths to cross after that first day, but I guess he's got other ideas."

Bee buries her face in her pillow and screams.

I take a moment to process what I've just heard. So Bee and Jimmy know each other. He is not just some townie moving guy. And Bee wanted to hide it because . . . I turn to face her fully. "Why didn't you want people to know you guys know each other?"

She stiffens a bit before sitting up on her bed, legs crossed at her ankles.

"I just wanted some space for once. I've never made any friends or had any freedom. I just wanted to try things on my own. That's all. It's not that Jimmy is a bad guy. It's just . . ." She stops talking as she looks at the pillow in her arms.

"I get it," I tell her. Bee's just like me. A person needing a chance to live without being constantly directed and watched. We are more alike than I realized. It makes it easier to forgive her for not telling me about Jimmy. It also makes me look at Jimmy in a different light. I'm not sure whether that light is positive or not, though.

"Okay." I snap my fingers with renewed energy and excitement. "What we both need is a distraction and a break from a certain blond shifter. I say we call Jeff and see if he has any ideas."

"Ideas?"

"Ideas for something to get our minds off the mess that is our first day of college! Parties! Social stuff!"

She opens her mouth to answer, but her phone buzzes, and she rolls her eyes at the notification that pops up. "Well, speak of the devil. You know what? I am all in if Jeff has a party for us to go to tonight." She's already tapping a message into her phone. "Tell me when and where, and I'll be there."

I smile as I pull out my own phone to text Jeff.

JIMMY

Me: Have you talked to Sexy Roommate today?

Bee: God you're pathetic.

Me: Yes or no question. Have you talked to her?

This time, she makes me wait before she answers.

Bee: Are you trying to ask me if she told me about her fun new stalker?

Me: I'm not a stalker!

Bee: You just happened to sign up for all the same classes as her by accident? Come on! You promised to give me space, remember, Grey?

Me: I know Bee, I remember and the last thing I want to do is mess up your life. I know what this chance to go to Berring means to you.

Bee: Do you? Like, really? Because the last thing I want is for people to realize that I brought a shifter bodyguard to school with me.

I hope I can turn her mood around.

Bee: Gloria is the first friend I have ever made outside of the pack, and I really like her! I don't want to share her with you so go sniff some other shifter tail and leave her alone.

Feeling a little guilty and a little hurt, I take a breath before messaging back.

Me: I'm sorry Bee, I'll give you space. You know I love you right? I only want you to be happy.

Bee: You'd better work hard in your classes. If you flunk out now you'll never get to see how popular I become.

At least it sounds like she's not permanently mad at me.

Bee: As my first decree as Popularity Princess I declare that you get your hand out of your pants and go hang out with your new roommates. You could stand to make some friends too.

Me: Hey! I do not have my hand in my pants!

Bee: Have you forgotten that I grew up with you? I know how wolves are, and I know how you are. I've lost count of how many times I've caught you with your hand in your pants. Now go get a life.

Fine. I send her a thumbs-up emoji in response.

My roommates are all sprawled on couches in our living room when I come out. Something sporty is playing on the TV, but no one seems to be paying much attention.

Instead, Jeff is holding court. "Alright, who has ideas for where to take some ladies in need of entertainment tonight?"

Marcus cocks his head to the side. "Are you taking two girls on a date at once? Because I feel like I should warn you, that's never going to work like in the movies."

"No, asshole, it's not a date. I'm just trying to think of a friendly way to get to know them better. Don't get me wrong. They are both beautiful, but I like them too much to fuck around with them like that. All of us could go out together. Make some friends? Drink some drinks? Maybe even find a hookup? It'll be fun!"

Devon shakes his head. "You do realize it's literally the first day of college, right? Who's going to be partying already?"

Jeff gives him a flat look. "Honestly, Devon, I'm disappointed in your lack of imagination and your negative energy. Jimmy, what about you? You want to come out tonight?"

What I want is to go hang out with Bee and Gloria in their dorm. What I want is to live up to my parents' expectations and stay close enough to Bee to keep her safe. But since I can't really do any of that right now . . .

"Sure." I shrug. "I've been told I need to try and make new friends. I can't say I know about any parties tonight, though."

"Don't worry about that. I'm sure, between the four of us, we know somebody who's partying tonight." He turns back to Devon and Marcus. "Vampires are creatures of the night, right? Shouldn't there be some vamps up, doing nighttime activities?"

Devon gives him a look. "First, that's kind of offensive. Second, did you not just hear me say that thing about it being the first day of school?"

Jeff waves him off with a grin.

Marcus, looking way too formal as always in slacks and a sports jacket, sits a little straighter in his chair. "Actually, I do know of something. It's probably going to be boring and cringy and not at all what you're looking for, but there is this vampire fraternity that will be hosting an event tonight."

"Um," I interject before this can go any further. "Unless the ladies in question are both vampires, that doesn't seem like the greatest idea to me."

Devon turns his attention toward me with a scowl. "What the fuck is that supposed to mean?"

"Oh, come on! I'm not trying to be offensive or anything, but you can't seriously be comfortable with the idea of two non-vampire girls going to a vampire party without any kind of protection!"

"They wouldn't be without protection," Jeff counters before Devon or Marcus can say anything in defense of their kind. "They would have us as protection."

Judging by the looks I'm getting from all three roommates, I probably shouldn't point out that Jeff is human and therefore brings nothing to the table as far as protecting anyone from vampires, and even though I like Devon and Marcus well enough, I don't really have a reason to trust that neither of them will suddenly be overcome by bloodlust and become as dangerous as any other vamp out there.

"Fine," I say in defeat. "We can go to this vampire thing, but the group sticks close together. I can't protect people who go off on their own."

Marcus seems to understand where I'm coming from, at

least. "How about I tell you the code to get in, but then I let you go in on your own. If you're uncomfortable with the idea of vampires, you won't want another one hanging out with you at the party."

Okay, he understands me, but now I'm feeling kind of guilty about him understanding me. I don't want to be the bigoted guy who doesn't trust his own roommates, but I guess maybe I am that guy. "Look, it's not that I don't think I can trust you—"

He cuts me off. "Don't worry about it. If I have to go to this thing, I'd honestly rather not show up with anyone who might draw extra attention."

Chapter Eight

JIMMY

I know I've made a mistake when Jeff leads me to Gloria and Bee standing in front of the fountain on the quad, both looking dressed up and ready to party. Both of their excited faces shut down when they see me. Just what a guy wants.

"What are you doing here?" Bee gets straight to the point.

Jeff's excitement doesn't fade. "Right! I'd almost forgotten you all already know each other. How cool does this party sound? I was looking it up, and this is actually one of the oldest fraternities formed in this country. Like, it predates the Civil War and the Tri-Race Pact. These vampires made this fraternity before humans even knew vampires existed."

"You're not making me feel any better about this," I tell him. Turning to Bee and Gloria, I say, "Look, I really didn't realize you were the girls Jeff was meeting here tonight. I'm just here as protection because I happen to think it's stupid to trust an entire fraternity of bloodsuckers to not just eat their guests. We could still leave. We don't have to go to this party at all."

The girls turn and start walking toward Greek Row without a word or glance back at me. Jeff gives me his "I'm not angry, just disappointed" face and follows them.

Really? Am I the one who's wrong just for trying to be sensible?

With an annoyed sigh, I jog to catch up with the group. "You all need to stay close to me in there, okay? No splitting off and doing your own thing. I'm serious."

Bee rolls her eyes at me. "It's just a frat party. They aren't going to try feeding on any of the guests."

"First of all—" I begin ticking off points on my fingers. "—it's not just a frat party. It's a vampiric fraternity party. Second of all, anyone who isn't a member or a rush is considered fair game for these guys. Third—"

"Then why did you come if you're so worried?" Gloria interrupts.

"Good question," I mutter to myself. Of course, her wolf ears know exactly what I said, and Bee is too smart to not pick up the gist.

"Come on, I have enough experience with him to know there is no getting rid of him now. Let's just get going." Bee grabs us both by the elbow and leads slash drags us across the street without further hesitation.

My guess is she's trying to look brave for her roommate. It looks good on her, I can't lie. She's come a long way from the scared kid I grew up with.

Our destination is a gothic mansion that takes up an entire block and gives every sign that anyone warm-blooded should enter expecting to become prey.

The guy at the door looks us up and down with a smirk. "What brings four outsiders to our door tonight?" he asks. If

Marcus hadn't prepped me beforehand, I'd just assume he's being an asshole.

"We come as four curious, with open minds and open hearts. We come to see and not to judge." Jeff says the pass phrase perfectly.

Oh, I'm judging alright. I'm judging the fuck out of this little play we have to put on at the entrance.

The doorman is dead serious, though. "Then four outsiders be welcome and have our protection." He steps aside and solemnly waves us inside.

I do my best to keep from laughing. Protection. Right.

And that's the end of the solemnity. The interior rattles with bass, which coalesces into music as we move further inside. The interior decorating continues the theme of gothic mansion that I noticed outside. Real subtle, the way they seem to lean into every single vampire stereotype. The party itself is a mishmash between ancient bacchanal and modern rave.

Sure, I know about bacchanals. That might have been the most interesting thing I learned about in my high school history classes.

While part of me can't help but appreciate the sheer amount of sex oozing from the very walls in here, my wolf is on high alert. It's too loud, too crowded, and the people I care about, who I promised to protect tonight—whether they want it or not—are going to be difficult to guard with the press of writhing bodies all around us. I'm already looking for the exit, but I can see at a glance that Bee and Gloria are entranced. I press down the heightened emotions that come along with heightened wolf awareness and grab each of my girls by the arm so we can't be separated.

"What's next?" I shout between rolling vibrations of bass, wanting to tuck tail and get the hell out of here.

Not safe, get the girls safe, my wolf keeps screaming at me. I ignore that impulse and do my best to smile at Bee and Gloria.

"Shots!" Gloria shouts, pointing across a sea of dancing bodies to a corner where someone has set up a fully stocked bar.

I suppress a groan and work to maneuver both girls in that direction.

"I'm going to check if Devon or Marcus made it!" Jeff shouts and peels off before I can grab him.

Didn't I tell all of them they needed to stay with me? What is wrong with people, and why am I apparently the only smart person today?

I let him go so I can stay with the girls. I am going to lose my shit if any harm comes to either of them. I guess Jeff will have to look after himself.

"What can I get for you ladies?" A handsome, dark-skinned vampire is smiling at Bee and Gloria and—I swear this isn't in my head—licking his lips.

"Shots!" they both shout at the same time, then collapse onto each other in a fit of giggles.

"And how about you?" he asks me with the same smile.

"Nothing for me," I tell him with a warning glare.

"Sure thing, man."

He fills two shot glasses and sets them in front of the girls. Does this guy ever stop smiling?

Bee and Gloria throw back the shots with a cheer of "To distractions!" whatever the hell that means, and our smiley vampire is ready with two more shots by the time they set their empty shot glasses down. Fuck, this is already getting out of hand.

I let them swallow the second round of shots, then give them a decisive tug away from the bar.

"I made it back!" Jeff catches me in a manly and already at least somewhat drunken hug as I lead the girls toward the dance floor.

"Good. Okay. I really mean it this time. We need to stick

together." I pat him on the back, then pull him along in the girls' wake. "What about Marcus and Devon?" I spare one quick glance around the party to see if I can spot our other roommates.

Jeff grins widely at me. "Oh, they're here. They, ummm . . . seemed a little preoccupied in a dark corner over there." He points to a niche in the wall that was probably intended to hold statues but currently holds Marcus and Devon as they make out, completely oblivious to the rest of the world. "So, I decided to come back over here and try my luck at the bar!"

"Wow," I say, trying to cover my surprise. "I did not clock that one at all. Did you?"

Jeff shakes his head, grinning, and changes direction, going back to the bar, then returning after a couple of minutes with two full shot glasses in each hand. "Time to cut loose!" He shouts to be heard over the bass reverberating through the room, and it's somehow a lot easier to just grab a glass from his hand than to argue that one of us should stay sober.

Bee surprises me by raising her glass in a toast. "To new friends," she says with a significant look at me, then tips the shot back like it's nothing.

Jeff and Gloria follow suit, and then it's just me standing there, still debating whether the watchdog side of my personality can safely take the night off.

"To new friends," I say and gulp the shot down.

I notice Gloria looking back and forth between me and Jeff with a speculative expression.

"What?" I have to lean in so my lips are almost against her ear to be heard and am gratified by the little shiver I sense passing down her neck as I speak.

"It's nothing, really. It's dumb." She bites her lip with the most adorable troubled expression on her face. I raise an eyebrow at her and wait for her to go on. "Okay, but you can't make fun of me. It's just that, I guess I kind of still thought you were lying about being a student here. But apparently, you have roommates, which implies you have a room you live in?"

My grin splits my whole face. I can't help myself. "You're thinking of coming back to my place, aren't you?" Cocky? Yes, but I don't seem to have much control over what I say to her. It's like being around Gloria turns half my brain cells off. Or maybe it's more like half my brain cells devote themselves to being turned on by her instead of doing their normal jobs. Whatever it is, this woman turns me into the village idiot, and I don't even care. "I've got my own bedroom. Mostly clean sheets on the bed. Condoms in—"

"Stop. Talking." She shuts me off, but I don't think it's because she actually hates the idea. "Just because I'm convinced you're actually a student doesn't change whether I'm willing to hook up with you, so stop trying."

"Fine." I hold my hands up in mock defeat. "I know when I'm beaten. I won't try to hook up with you anymore." I will try to spend every possible minute with her because that's what my wolf wants, but I don't say that part out loud.

Bee surprises me yet again by pressing another shot glass into Gloria's hand while Jeff hands a second drink to me.

Did I just get so wrapped up in flirting that I let my guard down? Well, shit. My claims of being a great protector are kind of falling apart, aren't they? But the more I look around, the less this seems like the dangerous nest of bloodsucking predators I was expecting.

This time, we all raise our glasses and drink together. I wonder how drunk Gloria will have to be before she starts seeing me differently. Not that I would take advantage of her being drunk, but there is a part of me that is curious to see what kind of drunk she is.

But in this moment, the second shot is bringing me a nice feeling of warmth and the slightest sense of fuzziness to everything. Whatever was in those shots, I want more of it.

"Let's dance!" Gloria shouts, derailing my plans to dive straight into another round of shots.

She doesn't have to ask me twice, though. I grab her by the elbow and maneuver us toward an open section of floor. Bee and Jeff are right on our tails, so instead of the sexy dancing I was hoping for with just the two of us, our whole group dances together in a painfully nonsexual way. And even though it is not what I was hoping for, I can't seem to remember the last time I had this much fun.

Chapter Nine

GLORIA

This party is amazing. The drinks are amazing. The music is amazing.

So, why is it that all I want to do is drag a certain overconfident werewolf into a dark corner and ride him like my life depends on it?

I smile at the group dancing with me. "I'll be back in a minute," I shout, pointing at the hallway that I'm pretty sure will lead to at least one bathroom.

"Wait. Where are you going? No one should go off alone." Jimmy looks stricken.

"It's just the bathroom. No one is going to eat me while I pee."

I can see him searching for reasons to keep me with the group, but he knows as well as I do that I can look out for myself. Bee might need his protection, but if someone tries to mess with me, I can shift and rip their throat out without blinking.

"I'll be fine," I assure him, patting his shoulder. "And if I need you, I'll Call." I try to emphasize the word so he understands I'm talking about wolf calls, not cell phones. It's not exactly forbidden to talk about these things in front of outsiders, but everyone likes to keep their secrets if possible. No one else needs to know that I could theoretically howl every wolf on campus to my aid if I needed to.

Jimmy's eyes lose some of their tension, so I guess my hint got through to him. "If you need anything at all," he says.

"I promise." Then I start making my way through the sea of dancing partiers to get away.

I actually don't need to pee, or get some air, or whatever euphemism I should have used. I just need to get away from Jimmy so I can focus on the actual goal of this party.

Reconnaissance.

I am on a mission to find the guy I'm going to date in college. Is it possible that I've taken the liberty of looking up details on all the major fraternities at this school and done research on all the members I think might be promising? It's possible, but I will go to my grave before I admit any such thing.

Anyway, there are likely to be several pre-med or poly-sci majors at this party, all looking to follow in their fathers' venerable footsteps and all desperately in need of the woman who will eventually take the role of wife for them. And I just happen to be all dressed up and ready to fall into someone's willing arms. Imagine that.

Target acquired! Nigel Walmsley III, son of some diplomat whose job description is something overcomplicated, is leaning on the wall by a pool table, deeply contemplating the contents of his glass. Okay, his name is . . . not particularly sexy, if I'm being honest, and he seems to have inherited the sickly vampiric traits rather than the sensual ones. But it's not like I'm on the hunt for a soul mate here. Not willing to discount someone on looks and pretentious name alone, I sidle over to him.

"Hey, sorry to bother you, but could you tell me where the bathroom is?" I ask in the most friendly, relaxed voice in my repertoire.

His eyes narrow at me in suspicion. Uh-oh. Not the response I was going for. He pulls his sallow, sweaty self to his full height and glares down at me. "Ha. Ha. Who sent you over here?"

"Who . . ." I look around the room, wondering what key information I'm missing. "Sent? I was looking for the bathroom, and I saw you standing here . . . alone . . ."

I trail off under the burden of his glare.

"Very funny. Unfortunately, you're not the first pretty girl someone has sent over to me to fuck with me. Tell them they're going to have to come up with something new if they want to keep messing with me." Then he stalks off without looking back.

Okay, I guess that marks Nigel off my list. "What the hell?" I ask myself under my breath.

"I guess no one warned you about Nigel ahead of time," a rich baritone says beside me.

Be still my beating lady parts, but this guy has a voice. I turn to look at him and find that he has a face and a body to match.

"Sorry, what was that?" I try to cover how flustered he's made me just by standing so close, but I'm sure it's obvious by the flush creeping up my neck and into my cheeks.

"I said, I guess no one warned you about Nigel. He gets prickly when he thinks people are making fun of him."

"But all I did was ask where the bathroom is. Does asking for directions really set him off?"

Mr. Sexy chuckles at my bafflement. "Nigel always thinks people are making fun of him. And I really do mean always."

I huff out a breath. "Well, I guess I wasn't interested in getting to know him after all, then."

"His loss is my gain." Mr. Sexy puts out a hand to shake. "Vincent Davenport. Nice to meet you."

I shake his hand. "I'm Gloria. It's nice to—wait . . . Davenport, like Davenport Pharmaceuticals Davenport?"

He wasn't on my list. I remember hearing about a Davenport heir but hadn't realized he went to Berring. Obviously an oversight on my part, but he's definitely got my attention now.

"You've heard of it?" He blinks, as if he's genuinely surprised that someone would recognize the name of one of the largest drug suppliers in the country.

"Heard of it? Oh my gosh, I've—" I catch myself just in time. I am not going to tell this god among men that his family provides the sheep dewormer that my family buys in bulk. "I mean, yeah, I suppose I've seen the name around. And I've thought about going into medicine, so I guess it goes with the territory."

He definitely doesn't need to know that the medicine I've thought about going into is veterinary medicine. That's a second date—third date?—conversation.

"Wow. I never expected to meet a fan out here in the real world," he says with a genuineness that warms me inside and out. Nigel who? I am all aboard this Vincent train right now.

"Well, I don't know if 'fan' is the most accurate term." I wave my hand airily. "I mean, it's not like I'm going to ask you to sign my shirt or anything."

His eyes darken as he looks at the shirt in question. "That's alright, actually. I wouldn't want to ruin something that is doing such great things for you."

"Oh? Is there something you do want to do with it?"

Before I have a chance to die of shock at my audacity, and before he has a chance to answer, someone comes up alongside him and smacks his back in a brotherly show of affection.

"You have got to check out Nigel's latest. He is on a whole new level this time," the stranger crows.

Vincent shares a conspiratorial look with me. "Oh, yeah?"

"Like, the brothers are taking bets on what the aftermath will be like this time."

My eyes are probably giant fish eyes right now, to go perfectly with my gaping fish mouth. "Aftermath?" I ask in a tiny voice. Surely, there can't be any aftermath simply from me going up to a guy and saying hello? If so, I'm going to have to rethink my strategy yet again.

"For sure, aftermath," the stranger says, sounding delighted to be the one to share the news. "Last time someone messed with him, all of the history TAs lost their positions. It was hilarious."

Maybe it's hilarious to him, but my stomach is twisting in knots.

"Can't you see you're upsetting her?" Vincent comes to my rescue. He looks me sternly in the eye. "No one is going to lose their job because you asked the guy for directions to the bathroom. And if Nigel can't handle a pretty girl talking to him, that's Nigel's problem, not yours."

I take a deep, calming breath, then catch on to what he just said. "So, I'm the pretty girl in this situation, right?"

"That you are," he confirms, resting a hand casually on my hip. "I can understand why Nigel thought you were trying to mess with him, honestly. You are way out of his league."

My blush is back, and I'm sure every vampire in the house can feel the blood pulsing in my cheeks. "I . . . ummm . . ." Great, Gloria. Super smooth. Just what you need to say to attract a future husband.

"How about this?" Vincent says, completely ignoring his friend, who's still half leaning on him. He pulls out his phone. "I'm going to get your contact information, then I'm going to go make sure everything is alright with Nigel. No aftermath, no job losses. And I'll let you know the results after everything is cleared up."

"Really? You would do that? I mean . . . I'd rather not have an entire department's TAs on my conscience."

"Consider it done."

He hands me his phone so I can type in my information. I open his contacts and add the name "Pretty girl that is out of Nigel's league Gloria."

As I hand the phone back to him, he kisses my hand like some kind of actual knight in shining armor and disappears into the party without another word.

I'm still swaying in place, possibly staring all moon-eyed after him, when Jimmy's voice breaks the spell on me.

"Who the hell was that?"

I give him my best disapproving librarian look. "That was Vincent Davenport, and don't you dare say any of the things you're thinking right now because I already know I'm not interested in hearing them."

He huffs out an angry breath. "Fine. I'm really glad you're enjoying yourself and meeting nice guys like Vincent Davenport." He says it in a sarcastic voice and waves his hands to show how unimpressed he is with the name. "But your roommate is over there dancing, and I think she would be safer if we all stick together."

I narrow my eyes at him. "Right. You're making a scene because you're worried that my roommate won't feel safe if we're separated at this party."

Jimmy answers me with a glare. Not wanting to make any more of a scene and not really having the energy to fight it out, I let Jimmy corral me back to where Bee and Jeff are still dancing. I would bet money that neither of them actually noticed me being gone. This is all Jimmy being paranoid.

Whatever. I roll the tension out of my shoulders and join back in the dancing. Jimmy's smile and laugh come back out, and things actually start feeling more enjoyable again. I just hope Vincent decides to use my contact information. I allow myself a little daydream as I dance. It involves finding an apartment to rent with one Vincent Davenport while we both finish college, followed by a trip to Paris and a romantic engagement, then a beautiful, lily-scented wedding and a glamorous, lily-scented life together. Yes, that would fit very nicely into my plans for myself. I smile as I dance. To think, this party might be the moment that changes my entire life.

Chapter Ten

JIMMY

I'm two weeks in, and is it too early to say that college is killing me? All of these classes I signed up for to try and get close to Gloria are so stinking hard, and trying to survive them along with the steady stream of parties, late-night gaming sessions, as well as a whole manner of "bro bonding time," as Jeff calls it, has me at the very end of a very frayed rope.

"Okay, I didn't want to resort to this." I'm trailing after Gloria like a hungry puppy. "But I am begging you. Do you hear me? I will get down on the floor and kiss your feet if you agree to this, full-on desperation, begging you right now."

She doesn't even turn to look at me, just keeps walking, knowing I'll follow. "Jimmy, I get that you're desperate to pass the classes you shouldn't have signed up for. That's not in question. The question is, what's in it for me? I'm not trying to be cruel or anything, but it doesn't seem like you have . . . anything, really, to offer me."

"My undying love and affection."

She cocks an eyebrow but continues walking. "Hmm, it looks like your love has already died to me. Sorry, not interested."

"You can use my body. You can have my babies."

"Oh, you would be willing to gift me with the opportunity to have your babies?" Gloria finally stops walking and turns to face me. I can tell by her tone that I've hit an unexpected nerve and she's about to say something hurtful, but I can also see a smile tugging at the corners of her mouth, so my heart soars. "You would graciously let me give up my body to house your babies for months and months? Would you also let me change all of their diapers and wake up in the middle of the night to feed them?"

"Okay," I admit, "I can see how I didn't really think that offer through. But please, Gloria, just give me a chance. I know I'm not that good with all this classwork stuff, but if you agree to be my study partner, I swear, I will work so hard for you. Just tell me what to do, and I will be all over it. Carrying books in the library? You got it. Making a slideshow? I will animate every slide myself. Dressing up in a costume to present? I'm there. Please, please, please help me out here."

She huffs out a breath and rolls her eyes. "Fine. Mostly because you're really pathetic and annoying when you whine, but also because there's no one else in history that I want to be partners with."

"I'll take it!" I cheer and sweep her up in my arms.

Oh. Bad idea. Her whole front is pressed against my whole front, and my body seems to have a hair-trigger response anytime it touches her body.

I set her down and try to act casual about stepping backward. "So, yeah, just say the word. Let me know where you want to get started."

Gloria clears her throat and looks at the floor, face bright red. God, I'm such an idiot. I can't believe how quickly I made things uncomfortable between us. One step forward, two steps back, I guess.

"How about we take a look at the topics and decide what we want to do our project on?" she tells the floor.

"Yeah. That sounds best . . . good thing I found such a smart person to be my partner, right? I would have been lost otherwise."

That gets a low chuckle out of her. She gives her head a little shake, then turns and starts walking again. It takes me a second to get my brain function back online and follow her to the library.

"Think again," Gloria says, throwing an eraser at me. I snatch it from the air and pocket it like some kind of love token. No, desperate probably doesn't look good on me. She continues. "Henry VIII is easy and obvious. Everyone will want to do their project on him."

I spread my hands. "I'm sorry. I have been described as both easy and obvious, and I don't see what the problem is."

She groans and throws another eraser at me, which immediately gets put away in my pocket with the other one. "We don't want our professor and everyone else in class comparing our presentation to every other presentation. If we choose a topic that no one else chooses, we avoid that comparison and make our own lives easier."

She makes a good point.

"And if we do it your way, we don't have to work as hard, but we still get the grade?" I confirm as I lean forward to show her that I'm paying attention. "Is this how you got through high school?"

"I got through high school with a lot of hard work." She playfully snaps back as yet another eraser zings toward my face before I snatch it from the air and put it away for safekeeping. How many of these things can one girl have, anyway? "This isn't some big strategy. It's just common sense. Church music under Henry VIII's reign is much more niche and therefore not already done to death by every other freshman history student."

I grin at her. "You're the expert, but you do realize I know nothing about churches, music, or Henry VIII, right?"

Her lips twitch twice before she gives in and smiles back at me. "I guess it's good you chose someone so smart to be your partner. Also, let's not forget who it was that promised they would do whatever I said when it came to research and presentations."

I let myself get lost in her smile—bright white with canines visible—and eyes—the deep black of seawater right before a storm hits it—before catching on to her words.

"Wait, what's that about a presentation?" Thinking back, I realize it wasn't that long ago I promised to dress up and make a fool of myself if it would convince her to be my partner.

Gloria gives the fakest innocent look I've seen in my entire life. "Well, if we're doing a research project about music, don't you think it would make sense to actually add some music to the presentation?"

"Gloria, I'm going to share something with you that I haven't told anyone before. I don't sing. I can't sing. If you have some idea that I'm going to suddenly gain musical abilities through will alone, you should realize that's not reasonable. It's not going to happen."

"Don't worry about anything, Jimmy." She pats my cheek and gives me a smile that has me frantic with worry.

The worst part is I'm not sure if I'm more worried about

what I might have to do in front of a huge history class or how Gloria is going to respond when I end up disappointing her with my contributions.

I turn my attention to the book she hands me, hoping that we can still survive it when I let her down eventually.

GLORIA

I wish I could say absolutely that my reasons for agreeing to this study partner thing are selfless and noble, but, well. One of my reasons—that Jimmy looked so desperate and pathetic—can maybe be considered selfless. All of my other reasons—that his ass is very easy to look at, that I know I can decide exactly how I want to do this project and not worry about him arguing, that he smells like sex in the best possible way, that he promised to carry books for me and wear a costume for our presentation—are decidedly not noble or selfless. I'm not admitting those reasons to anyone, though. I'll take them to my grave.

But now, I'm looking across a huge pile of books at him and wondering what I can possibly do about the wretched and confused look on his face. I knew going in that I would be doing the heavy lifting with this project, but I truly underestimated how bad Jimmy is at research.

"What am I looking for again?" he asks, maybe for the tenth time since we sat down at this table.

I stifle an annoyed sigh as I close my own book. It's not his fault that no one ever taught him how to research. "How about you take the sticky notes and mark all the pages that mention William Byrd." Even he can't go too far astray with that, right?

"Okay. Yes. Sticky notes. William Byrd. Bird, bird, bird." His voice trails off, but not enough that I can't hear as he starts chanting, "Bird, bird, bird. Bird is the word. Weird name. B. I."

He's flipping through a glossary, trying to find a name that he's misspelling. Oh, god. I really need to do something about this.

Nope. I stop myself from intervening. If he marks every single page that mentions birds with feathers, I still won't be any further behind than if I really was working on my own. If I take the time to set him straight, I'll fall behind in my own research.

"B-b-b-bird is the word."

"Do you think you could do it without making any noise?" I break into his musical masterpiece.

His eyes go wide with hurt, and I immediately feel like a puppy kicker. "Oh, yeah. Sorry," he says and hunches back over his book.

Not only am I a puppy kicker, but I am the queen of all puppy kickers, the ultimate thief of all joy, and the worst kind of ice bitch to ever walk the planet.

"I'm sorry," I say. I find his foot under the table and give it a playful nudge with my toes. "I'm sorry I snapped at you. You can make noise. Whatever helps you work."

Jimmy's face lights up with hope and relief. "Really?"

"Yeah. You . . . do your thing. I'll be okay."

It might kill me, a misanthropic voice at the back of my mind mutters, but I'm pretty sure that his kicked-puppy face will kill me more painfully.

But Jimmy has already moved on. "Bird is the word," I hear him chant as he starts flipping through pages again.

* * *

It takes two hours of "study session"—in which I struggle to pay attention to anything in the books in front of me and Jimmy struggles to remember that William Byrd is the name of a person, not an actual bird—before Jimmy agrees to call it quits and start up again tomorrow.

I groan as I—finally—flop down face-first on my bed.

"Research project getting you down?" Bee asks sweetly from her desk without looking away from whatever she's working on.

"I knew it was a mistake to work with Jimmy, but I had no idea how bad of a mistake," I grumble through my pillow.

Now she does stop working and turns to face me. She stares at me, deep in thought about something that I'm not privy to, for long enough that the silence between us gets awkward.

"Okay, I think I have to tell you something," she finally says. "But I can't tell you the full thing because it involves a secret that isn't mine to tell, but I think you need to at least know some of this."

I prop myself up on my elbows. I'm sure my confusion shows clearly on my face. "Huh? What are you even talking about?"

Bee comes to sit on her bed so she can look me in the eye. Why do I get the distinct impression I'm about to get bad news about the death of someone I care about?

"The thing with Jimmy," she starts, "is that . . . ugh, there's no good way to put this!"

She tugs her fingers through her hair in a show of frustration I don't often see from her. She's normally either so dreamy I have to roll my eyes or so peppy and happy I feel sick. I don't think I've ever heard this harsh tone from her since we met.

"Okay, let's try this again. The thing with Jimmy is that not a lot of people have really held him accountable up to this point in his life. It's not that everyone makes excuses for him or that his parents don't want him to be successful. It's just . . . impossible for me to explain without me betraying a confidence." Her face sinks down into her hands, and she lets out a groan to rival the one I gave earlier. "Just . . . I think he needs someone to kind of push him, and it seems like you might be the person the universe has volunteered to do that pushing."

I sit, stunned into silence for a beat. "So." I take another moment to think it through before starting again. "What I'm understanding is you want me to give Jimmy more of a chance?"

"No! Yes? Hell, I don't know. I want someone to hold him accountable for his actions since no one else will."

"I don't want to promise you something I'm not sure I can do." There is a moment of silence between us. I really like Bee, honestly more than I like Jimmy at this point, or maybe different? I look back at her. "He was so obnoxious today! I think he has literally never researched anything, and he's making this project twice as hard as it would be if I could just do it on my own."

"But?" Bee gives me the stern-mother glare, which has the inconvenient power of bringing all of my honesty to the surface.

"Not to gross you out or anything—I know you two are childhood friends—but . . ." I can't hold back anymore as I tell her. "He smells delicious, and no matter how terrible he is at research, the real thing distracting me from my research is the fact that I want to lick him all over, maybe even bite him a bit so that everyone can see that he's mine. Okay? Happy now?"

She snickers at me. "Well, I'm happy that you've admitted it, at least."

I throw my pillow at her. "Admitting it doesn't change anything. I have plans for my life, and they absolutely don't involve the babies of some no-name, no-pack, man-child of a wolf shifter. And one thousand percent not during my freshman year of college."

"Does his pack or his name really make that much of a difference to you?" Bee tosses my pillow back to me. "Just don't do the babies part. You can still have fun with him, can't you?"

I sigh and try to shake off the sick, trapped feeling I get at those words. "It's not that easy for wolves," I explain. "I don't know how much you already know. I don't want to seem condescending by telling you about something you already understand . . ."

"How about you assume I know nothing, and I won't get offended if you say something I already know," she assures me.

"Yeah, okay." I give my shoulders another roll. I'm a little nervous about letting an outsider in on wolf secrets, but I have to talk to someone, and I'm cut off from all of my usual friends right now. "Heat is . . . it's different from regular human ovulation and fertility. It can't be controlled by the same hormone pills—or any hormone pills that have been discovered yet. For us, it's like, your body decides it's baby time, and that's it. No more choice in the matter."

Bee's eyebrows look permanently stuck to her hairline. "I didn't realize that about hormonal birth control. I always thought it was basically the same for all of us."

I sigh. "Nope. Wolves are super fertile at certain times, at least compared to humans. Even when we're not in heat, we can get pregnant, but at least condoms usually work then. During heat, basically being in the same room as a potential mate's semen is enough to get you pregnant. And the fact that I feel physically attracted to Jimmy? Pretty much a sure sign that our genetics are compatible."

"Wow." Bee blinks at me. "Wait, but . . . heat isn't all the time. I know that much. Can't you like . . . you know . . . get it out of your system when it's safe and then promise not to go near each other when the risks are higher?"

A giggle bubbles up from deep inside me. "You want me to try and bang Jimmy out of my system?"

"I mean, I'm sure he wouldn't mind." Bee stares at me with a serious expression before we both fall back on our beds in an uncontrolled fit of giggles.

"Well?" she eventually asks, wiping her eyes.

I wipe my own eyes, a little surprised that I'm able to laugh about this stuff at all. "No. It really doesn't work that way.

First, even condoms aren't perfect, and I absolutely cannot afford to make any mistakes in that department. Second, sex only strengthens any potential mate bond. If I didn't feel any attraction to him, ironically, I wouldn't be having this problem. Every guy I've slept with before, I chose because we didn't find each other attractive. It was just a matter of taking care of a basic physical need, and then we never really wanted to talk to each other again. But if I have any feelings to begin with . . . I can't afford to let myself be tied down like that."

Bee lets out all of her breath in one loud gust. "Well, that sucks," she proclaims, and that simple pronouncement makes me feel a thousand times better.

"Yeah. It really does."

Her eyes slide over to look at me. "So, tell me if I'm being too intrusive? It's just that I've got so many questions right now, and no one has ever been willing to tell me about this stuff."

"Really? But didn't you grow up with Jimmy? I would have thought at least some of this would come up just from being near shifters," I ask her.

"No. You're right. It's kind of weird. But Jimmy's family, his pack, they are just . . . a bit different. And it's not like I was going into heat or hooking up with anyone. Let's just say I've been pretty sheltered." She looks away, and I realize that we're back in uncomfortable territory for her.

"Hey! We're going to be sharing a room all year. You might as well know what's going on with me." I decide to shift the conversation back to safer things. I have all year to learn more about her. "Ask away. I'm an open book."

"Okay, first question. How often do you . . ." Her face turns bright red before she can even finish the question.

"Go into heat?" I take pity and finish the question I think she's asking.

Bee nods.

"It depends. How old you are, whether you're around a potential mate or not, and genetics play a role. Some people spend most of their twenties either in heat or pregnant. I've been lucky so far, averaging just once a year since my first one. I imagine it will pick up at some point, but it hasn't been too bad yet."

"How long does it usually last?" Her eyes are wide.

I shrug. "Until you get pregnant or convince your body that it's satisfied in other ways."

A confused look crosses her face. "Other ways? Like, you can fake a pregnancy to trick your body into moving on?"

I can't help it. I cock an eyebrow at her and say in a suggestive voice, "You can't fake a pregnancy, but if you're sufficiently satisfied . . . physically . . ." I trail off and wait for understanding to dawn.

"Sufficiently satisf—" Her eyes get huge. "Like, sexually satisfied? Are you telling me that you masturbate until your body doesn't care about babies anymore?"

I burst out laughing. "Actually, that's pretty accurate. I don't think I've ever heard it said quite like that, but, yeah, that's pretty much it. It's kind of a coming-of-age thing to give girls vibrators as 'First Heat' gifts."

Bee's jaw drops. "No. You're messing with me. There is no way that is true."

My laughter doesn't ease up at all. "One hundred percent true," I confirm. "But you don't have to take my word for it. I'm sure at some point this year, you'll catch me putting my collection to extra use."

"Wait, wait, wait a second." Bee sits up with a jerk. "Your collection? You have a whole collection?" She's practically shrieking this.

"It's a lot safer than sex with an actual guy. What can I say?"

Fortunately, she seems to be shocked and amused rather

than disgusted. I guess, if she does decide I'm too much of a reprobate for her, I might end up looking for a new roommate for next semester, but that sounds terrible. I hope I don't scare her off.

"Show me!" she demands with a twinkle in her eye. "I need to see this fabled sex toy collection if I'm going to believe you."

Okay. Maybe I have nothing to worry about after all. I think Bee and I are going to be just fine.

Chapter Eleven

JIMMY

"This looks suspiciously like not the giant pile of homework you said you were behind on," Jeff's voice is stern but not too judgy.

I pause my video game and look guiltily up at him. "It was hard."

He raises an eyebrow at me, and suddenly, I get a feeling like it's actually my dad standing there. Even Jeff's ever-present smile and dimples are nowhere to be seen.

"I'll do it tomorrow?" I try.

Jeff doesn't move a centimeter.

"I don't understand what I'm supposed to be doing," I finally admit. "Gloria said to research this guy William Byrd, and I seriously can't even find him mentioned in any of the books she made me look through. And the math is so far over my head that I don't even know what kind of math tutor to get. I'm so, so screwed, and I don't know what I can do to get out of this mess."

Jeff's expression softens, and he comes to sit beside me. "I will help you, but only because I don't want to end up living with a depressed sad sack all year, and that is definitely what you're in danger of becoming if you fail all your classes and don't get the girl."

I tackle him with a hug. "You are my absolute hero right now, dude. You have no idea. Like, a true lifesaver. I owe you so big."

"Alright." He rolls his eyes. "Turn the game off and get your homework out. I'm not going to stay up all night doing this with you."

* * *

It's midnight, and my brain feels like it's been scraped clean like a jack-o'-lantern.

I thunk my head down into the book in front of me. "I can't do any more. Please, have mercy."

Jeff groans and stretches. "If I let you off the hook now, are you going to be able to pick this back up tomorrow?"

"I don't know, but I can't do any more tonight. Like, seriously. I don't think I can even still read. Please, don't make me try to keep going."

"Okay, buddy. Maybe it's best if we both get some sleep," he concedes. "But if you embarrass yourself tomorrow because you've forgotten everything, don't tell anyone it was me helping you. You're on your own."

"Promise," I mumble, face still in my book.

Jeff gets an arm around my waist and a shoulder under my armpit and hoists me up. "Come on. Bedtime. All of the benefits will be lost if I let you fall asleep at this table."

"You're a good friend, you know that?" I mumble, eyes barely open, as I let him steer me toward my room. "Like, maybe one of the best friends I've ever had."

"Yeah, yeah. See how you feel in the morning after not

getting enough sleep because I made you stay up so late studying."

I stop and turn to face him. I try to convey how serious I am through sleep-filled eyes. "I mean it. You really helped me out tonight. No one's ever sat me down and made me work like you just did. I think . . . I think maybe it's what I've been missing, so I owe you one. For real."

"Okay, pal, time to get some sleep." He pats my shoulder and gives me a gentle shove toward my door. "I'll put it in the register. You owe me one. But right now, we both just need to sleep."

I'm already halfway there by the time my head hits the pillow.

* * *

"This . . ." Gloria lets a long pause hang in the air as she goes over my notes. "This actually isn't too bad," she admits. Maybe I should be hurt at her lack of expectations, but mostly, I'm overjoyed at the compliment.

"Yes!" I give my fist a celebratory pump in the air. "I'm wearing you down, one research project at a time."

Gloria's eyes narrow at me, the only warning I get before she lands a solid punch on my shoulder. "I said it isn't too bad, not that you're suddenly my dream partner. You've still got a lot of work to do."

All I hear is she'll probably be wanting my babies by Christmas. Excellent.

"Be honest," she continues. "You got help with this?"

I wilt a little under her continued glare.

"Okay. Yes, I got a little help last night. Jeff said he didn't mind helping me out. It's not like we're going to fail because I got help from someone."

"That's not what I meant. I just meant, if he was able to

help you before, maybe he could help you again. God knows I wasn't making much progress." That last bit is muttered almost too quietly for me to hear.

"In that case, yes. I think he probably can help me some-times. He's a good guy like that." I hope I'm not overselling him to her. I only want her in the market for me, and I'm all too aware that she doesn't currently see me bringing much to the table.

"Okay. So, you've got some William Byrd information. Let's start organizing how we're going to present it."

She keeps talking like she's truly not interested in Jeff beyond his ability to help me study. I keep watching the way her mouth moves as she shapes each word. My mind wanders, imagining what shape her lips would form if she kissed my neck, my shoulder, my knee . . . and I let her scent wash over me too. Nothing fancy, just simple and delicious. The slightly sweet, almost but not quite vanilla of hand soap, plus the heat of her blood pulsing through her veins, the slightest hint of sweat gathered from a day of walking to classes and sitting in lecture halls. I would dive in and eat her out right now if she would let me. But she's talking about Henry VIII and church music. Somehow, I think she would stop me before I got her jeans unbuttoned.

Damn, I want to taste her so bad that I'm getting hard under our shared table in the library just from imagining it.

And she's staring expectantly at me, like maybe she just asked me a question, but I was so busy imagining the taste of her pussy that I completely missed it.

"Sorry. Can you say that last part again?"

Gloria rolls her eyes. I am so busted.

"How about you get Jeff to help you organize this William Byrd information, and I'll research some more about how the church was affected by Henry VIII. And while Jeff is helping you with this, he can also help us find a good party to go to and celebrate the progress we've made."

Well, that deflates me pretty damn quick. "Yeah, I can do all of that," I say, even though what I want to do is drag her across the table, knocking every single book off it in the process, and fuck her right there so she can't talk to me anymore about William Byrd.

Chapter Twelve

GLORIA

Vincent Davenport Jr. is grinning down at me. I have to take a moment to pinch myself.

"I wasn't sure if I would see you again."

Some part of my brain that must be correct at all times gives me a tug at that. Of course he would see me again. It may have been Marcus who got me through the door, but it was definitely Vincent's text on my phone that gave me the original invitation.

Whatever. I need to learn to get past these things.

Ducking my head, I try not to make it too obvious that I'm checking for Jimmy across the room, where he's finally giving me a little bit of space while still insisting no one should go anywhere alone at a vamp party. "Well." I try for my most girly, casual shrug. "Here I am."

"Here you are," he agrees, eyes raking hungrily over me. I wonder if I'm under—or over?—dressed, but he pulls me toward the center of the room without questioning my fluttery, cropped top, floral blouse, and high-waisted jean shorts.

"So, how is your semester going so far?" I ask, hoping I can get some real conversation going.

"My semester?" He looks confused by my question, which has me second-guessing what I asked him. With his fingers on my elbow, he leads me toward the bar at the other end of the room.

"Umm, yeah, like, do you like your classes so far?"

Vincent gives me a look like I've sprouted an extra head. Great. This is all going exactly as planned, obviously.

"I guess they're fine," he says finally, letting it fall halfway between a question and response. "Just the same old. I mean, I guess now that I've been here a few years, I've settled in. How about you? Is everything about college still fresh and exciting, or are you jaded like me."

I don't want him to think I'm just some dumb freshman. Or maybe I don't want to feel like a dumb freshman anymore.

"Well"—I aim for light and flirtatious—"maybe I'm not quite as jaded as you, but I suppose some of the shine has started to wear off."

He gives me a real smile, reminding me that he has sparklingly white teeth and eyes a girl could easily get lost in. "You want a drink?"

I look down at my still mostly full cup. "Sure. Why not?"

He disappears for a minute and comes back with full shot glasses. Okay. No. This is not going exactly as planned. I mentally rearrange my plans for tomorrow in case they have to accommodate a hangover, reminding myself that it will be worth it if I manage to snag Vincent Davenport for myself.

"You're really in the party spirit," I say, taking the shot glass and putting my best game face on. "Well, cheers, I guess." I toss back the shot.

"To not being entirely jaded yet," he adds before downing his own shot.

It doesn't go down smooth. It goes down like the cheapest

vodka to ever cross my gums. And it's not chilled. It tastes like oil straight from an engine and makes me cough and gag.

"Not a fan?" Vincent is still grinning down at me, but the oiliness of the vodka seems to have transferred to his smile.

"I can safely say that's the worst shot I've ever taken in my life."

"If you want to party with the big kids, you'll have to get used to drinking the real stuff." He pats my shoulder in an annoyingly patronizing way.

I'm reassessing my belief that Vincent Davenport might be worth it. Bad liquor is one thing, but I am really not into being talked down to like this.

I take a swallow of beer to try to wash the horrible shot flavor from my mouth. Cheap beer is better than that cheap vodka any day. I notice that Vincent is staring at me with a weird look on his face, and I suddenly don't want to be anywhere near him.

"You know, I think I just saw my friend from math class over there. I think I'll see if I can catch up to him."

I turn to go, but Vincent has his hand around my wrist, and I can't walk away without it getting awkward.

"If you'll just—"

"You can catch up with him later." Vincent is still grinning down at me, but that oiliness has spread, and his eyes are ice-cold.

My wolf senses prick up on high alert. Analyze the threats in the room. Map the possible escape routes. Do I call for help now? Ideally, I'd like to get away without making a scene, partly because if I can't trust Vincent, I can't trust any of his friends to back me against him.

But even as I plan, the room starts to spin and tilt sideways. I tug my arm. I should be able to break his grip without much trouble, but I can't seem to connect my thoughts to any actions. My arm hangs limp as everything continues to turn around me.

My head weighs a million tons as I try to turn toward where Jimmy was last time I saw him. Where was he, again? And why did I let myself be led so far away from where it was safe? I try to Call him—or even just say his name—but all that comes out is a croak. That can't be my voice, can it?

A noise reaches me from down at the end of a long tunnel. A flash of movement, a Jimmy-shaped voice, and something moves my arm. I'm pretty sure it's not me that moves it, but something does. I manage to focus my eyes for just long enough to see Jimmy looming above me, feel his arms cradling me, and then the world goes dark and quiet around me.

Chapter Thirteen

JIMMY

I want to kill somebody. The only reason I haven't already killed somebody is that my need to get Gloria to safety trumps my need to take revenge on every filthy, would-be-rapist frat boy in that place. But now I'm stuck pacing her room ineffectively and wishing I had taken five minutes to burn their whole fucking house down.

"What's going on?" Bee's voice is scared and small in the doorway. "Is she alright?"

"That fucking asshole piece-of-shit vampire gave her something, and now I can't get her to wake up." I can hear the panic rising in my voice but can't do anything about it. I can feel the tears prickling close under my eyelids, but I can't do anything about that either. In fact, there is literally nothing I can do at all right now.

Except imagining what I'm going to do when I can get my hands on that piece-of-shit asshole of a vampire fucker.

"Okay." Bee's voice is blessedly calm, and it instantly

brings my turmoil down a level. "Do you know what he gave her?"

I shake my head helplessly. "I was watching them from across the room. It looked like they were just talking, you know? And I'd promised to give her some space, so I was trying to be okay just letting her talk to someone a little way off. But then he seemed to be leading her farther away, and he gave her something to drink, and I could see something was wrong. She was just standing there, like, swaying in place, and I saw him grab her wrist, and I just lost it. I wasn't really thinking clearly. I just pushed past him and grabbed her and carried her here. But she hasn't woken up or moved or anything since I grabbed her. Did I do the right thing? Do you think she's going to be okay?" I'm pacing, feeling my panic rise again. "Should I have taken her to a hospital or something? Would they even know what to do with a wolf?"

Bee kneels beside Gloria, pressing her fingers to her neck to test for a pulse—*Idiot*, I berate myself. I was too panicked to think of checking her pulse—thumbing back her eyelids and poking and prodding her in various places.

"I'm sure he wasn't trying to kill her or anything like that," Bee says. "I mean, I guess we could take her to the clinic, but she told me before that she doesn't go to doctors."

I tug at my hair, trying to get myself to calm down and focus. "Right. What would a doctor even know about a wolf that wolves don't already know?"

"Do you think . . ." Bee trails off and looks back at Gloria with a worried expression.

"What?"

"Do you think we should tell someone? Call the police or something?"

Shit. I don't know. I'm never going to forgive myself if I made the wrong choice here tonight.

"No." I shake my head. "Think about it. A rich vampire

like this, with a whole fraternity to back him and probably more money than I can imagine? For all we know, he does this all the time, and the cops are happy to look the other way. We deal with this on our own."

"I guess you're right. If a vampire can do this"—she waves a hand at Gloria—"in a crowded, public place, there's probably a reason he thinks he can get away with it. Besides, I hate to put her through the whole ordeal of getting her blood tested and making a statement to the cops when I can't even ask if that's what she wants to do, you know?"

I heave out a sigh. "I just wish she would wake up already. It's really freaking me out that she hasn't even moved since she blacked out."

"I know," Beth reassures me, "but wolves heal fast, right? Probably the best thing we can do for her right now is keep an eye on her until she wakes up. Here, sit on my bed, and I'll put on a movie to distract you while we wait."

I slide my shoes off and follow her instructions. I try to look at the TV, but I can't even pay attention enough to know what she puts on. My eyes keep sliding back to Gloria, lying completely still on her own bed.

* * *

Bee has put something new on the TV twice already by the time Gloria jerks awake, thrashing her arms and legs like she's trying to swim against a riptide.

I'm there in a moment but afraid to touch her in case she sees me as a threat.

"Gloria! Gloria? It's me. Jimmy. It's just me and Bee here."

In the midst of her panicked thrashing, she ripples and shifts to her wolf form, then stands on her bed with hackles raised and teeth bared, her dark fur seeming to suck all the light out of the room. She looks like something from someone's nightmares. She looks beautiful.

I can see her eyes are still somewhere else. Definitely not safe to touch her.

"Bee, I need you to get out," I say in my calmest voice.

"But—" she starts to protest, but I slam a hand over her mouth without taking my eyes off Gloria. Rather, without taking my eyes off feral wolf Gloria.

"Get. Out. Not. Safe."

Thank god, she finally understands what's happening and eases out of the room without turning her back on Gloria. Bee can be innocent and naive and sickeningly optimistic at times, but she's not stupid, that's for sure.

"Gloria, I'm going to shift, okay? I think it's better if we're both wolves right now." Of course, she doesn't respond. Her eyes still have clouds of panic and madness in them.

I shift but stay back. I probably can force her to submit if it comes down to a physical fight, but that's the last thing I want to do to her after what she's just gone through. Instead, I flatten myself to the floor, submissive as I can make myself, sending every signal that she's the one in control here.

After what feels like an eternity of her staring at me without seeing me, she lets out a howl of anger and defeat. She's still furious, but she knows I'm not the one she's mad at. She hops down from the bed and gives me a lick on the face. A hello lick. Also a comfort lick. I'm not sure if she's comforting herself or me more, but I'll take it either way. I return the greeting and stand so she can sniff or lick as she wishes. She takes two turns around me, licking my face, sniffing my ass, bumping me with her shoulder each time she passes, and all of my tension dissipates. She puts me at ease like she's a pro at this sort of thing, like it wasn't her who was almost violated just a few hours ago.

Having gone through the necessary greetings, she flops

down on the floor beside me and gives me a look, inviting me to join her. I don't need a second invitation to do what I've been dying to do since the first time I met her. I lie down beside her—apparently, we're still doing wolf form, and I won't complain about that—and curl my body so I can touch her without invading her space.

That's how I fall asleep, and I'm pretty sure it's the best sleep of my entire life, with my tail resting lightly on top of hers and our noses snuffling breaths into each other's faces.

GLORIA

I wake up with dog breath in my face.

And my first instinct is to breathe it in deeply and lick the nose and mouth it's coming from.

Shit.

The events of the night before come back to me in pieces before knitting themselves together to form a whole picture, and suddenly, I'm having to stop myself from a rampage.

Well, at least that explains why Jimmy and I are all wolfy and sleeping together.

Shit.

There will be no getting rid of him now since his overprotective instincts were obviously proven right.

I ease my wolf body away as carefully as I can, tiptoe into my closet, and shift where he won't be able to see me. I also can't see, now that I'm in a dark closet and only have human eyes. It's times like these that it would be really useful to have one of those wardrobes that you could grab any two items and have a guaranteed outfit for the day. I, of course, do not have that kind of wardrobe. I slip on the first pair of pants I find— sweatpants, by the feel, but no idea what color—followed by what I hope is my least sexy sweatshirt.

Okay. Deep, non-sexy breaths before I go out.

"Gloria?" Jimmy's voice is panicked.

"I'm just here." I stick my head out of the closet. Jimmy is standing stark naked in the middle of my room, every muscle tensed like he's on the verge of springing into action. "I'm okay."

He relaxes some. "Do you . . . remember what happened?" Wariness replaces the panic in his eyes. The poor guy looks like he's had a worse time than me.

"I remember." I come out and put a hand on his arm. "I'm okay. You saved me."

Jimmy melts into my touch, then closes the distance between us, wrapping his arms around my waist and burrowing his face in my neck. I'm pretty sure I feel tears. Probably not the right time to point out that I'm not super comfortable with him hugging me while he's naked.

"I was so scared," he mumbles into my shirt. "You wouldn't wake up, and I wasn't sure if I'd done the right thing, and then you did wake up, and it got even worse."

My whole body is shaking as I rub his back. "It's all okay. You did the right thing. I'm alright."

"Fuck." He leans back to look at me. "I should be the one comforting you right now. Shit. What can I do? What do you need?"

I need so much right now, but what can I tell him when I haven't had a chance to sort it all out in my mind? "Well, I might find it comforting to have, like, another layer of clothes between us?"

He takes a step back, wiping his face on the back of his hand. "Shit. Yeah. I guess, maybe I should try to find some clothes or something."

"It wouldn't be the worst idea," I hedge.

"Do you . . . do you want me to leave you alone?"

Recognizing the desperation in his eyes, I lean forward and rest my head on his shoulder. "You can stick around if you put some clothes on. As long as it's okay with Bee. Who is where, by the way?"

Jimmy looks around like he's just noticed her absence. "I told her to go when you wolfed out, and I guess she just never came back?"

"Well, I'll let her know the coast is clear and ask if she's okay with you hanging out for a while. Sound good?"

Jimmy nods and wipes his eyes again. He kneels down to sort through the remnants of his clothes, which did not handle his quick shift well. They're in tatters in a sad pile on the floor.

"I might have something baggy enough to fit you," I say. I can't handle being in the same room as naked Jimmy for much longer. Apparently, coming way too close to being date-raped by a vampire does not actually have a cooling effect on my libido. My body knows exactly what it wants, and what it wants is currently squatting down in front of me without any clothes on.

I hurriedly dig through my pajama drawer to find my baggiest sweatpants and T-shirt, then turn all of my attention to finding my phone and letting Bee know it's safe to come back. I wonder if she's been filling out a roommate change request already or if she's going to wait until tomorrow. I really hope I didn't scare her off.

* * *

I shouldn't have worried. Bee comes barreling into our room less than five minutes after I text her and wraps me in a smothering hug.

"Oh my god, you can never scare us like that again!" she practically shouts while attempting to squeeze me to death. "And if you want to go to the police and report that douche canoe, I will be right by your side and hold your hand if you want me to."

Tears prickle at my eyelids, and then the dam bursts without warning, and I'm flooding, overflowing with tears and racked by sobs, so all I can do is cling to her while the storm passes through me.

"I just can't believe it," I finally manage once the tears have calmed and we're all sitting together on the floor. "It never occurred to me that someone would actually try something like that. And that it would happen to me? I can't wrap my head around it."

"Why wouldn't it happen to you?" Jimmy looks adorably confused.

I look to Bee for confirmation, but she's also giving me a quizzical look.

"I mean . . . it's just me. Just Gloria. Why would he be interested . . . I mean . . . it's not like I'm anyone special or anything . . ." I trail off because both of my friends are tilting their heads like I've stopped speaking English.

"Hey," Bee says, putting a hand on my knee and squeezing, "I don't like hearing you talk about yourself that way. You aren't 'just' anything. You're amazing, and important, and way better than that asshole piece-of-shit vampire could ever hope to deserve. Do you hear me?"

"I . . ." I mean, I hear her, but I can't say I believe her. I'm stupid, small-town Gloria, who was idiot enough to think the heir to a pharmaceutical empire might actually be interested in me. But Bee is looking into my soul with the most intense expression I've ever seen.

Jimmy puts his hand on my other knee. "She's telling the truth. I know it doesn't mean much, coming from me, but you're way better than that fuckwad. You deserve better than him, even before he drugged you. You're so much better than him."

"But I'm literally nobody." I curl in on myself, trying to protect my tender bits from exposure.

"Not to us, you're not," Jimmy says firmly, and something cracked inside of me starts to mend.

Bee looks like she's mulling something over and can't decide whether to bring it up.

"What are you thinking about so hard over there?" I ask.

"I was thinking . . ." She heaves a sigh. "I was thinking that he's probably done this before, and he'll probably do it again, but we can't really go up against a guy like that, whose parents probably paid for a library or something, but we should try to do something to stop him, but even if we don't do anything about him, there's a chance he'll still try to retaliate against you, so I really think we need to strategize and figure out a next move."

"Shit. You're probably right," I admit. "You might be safe, Bee, if he doesn't remember that you're my roommate, but something tells me Vincent is going to at least do something against Jimmy and me. He seems like the kind of guy to throw a tantrum if he doesn't get what he wants."

"But what can we even do?" Jimmy sounds worried. "The police probably aren't on our side. Who else could we talk to?"

Bee nods. "I wonder if there's a good way to kind of get the word out. You know, like, be on the lookout for predatory rapist vampires?"

Jimmy gives me a questioning look, and I nod my agreement. "So we find a way to warn people about Vincent," he says. "If we do that, you're both going to need protection. Now I'm thinking it's a good thing we happen to have the same class schedules." He nudges me with his elbow. "I really don't think it's a good idea for you to go anywhere alone while Vincent might be looking for revenge."

Bee claps her hands and jumps up with a smile. "What about your roommates? I'm sure Jeff will want to help, and the other two—aren't Devon and Marcus vampires? They can help protect Gloria."

Jimmy looks skeptical. "At least Devon and Marcus seem like good guys. It feels wrong to trust any vampires after what happened last night, though."

"Oh, come on. You can trust your roommates. It's not fair to lump them in with someone horrible like Vincent," Beth argues. "Maybe Gloria can stay in your suite until this blows over? Safety in numbers?"

I have to put my foot down. "No way. I'm angry and I'm scared, but I'm not imposing on Jimmy and his roommates like that. Besides, we don't know for sure that Vincent won't come after you too, and there's no way I'm leaving you vulnerable like that."

"Exactly," Jimmy surprises me by jumping on my bandwagon. "I would never leave either of you in this dorm alone, without anyone to watch your back. You should both stay in my suite until we figure something out."

"That's even worse!" I protest. I am not letting stupid, rotten Vincent push me out of my own dorm like that.

"I can't watch your back if I'm there and you're here. I suppose I could stay here and watch your back, but your bed is awfully small. I don't think that's going to be very comfortable for either of us."

I snort my disagreement. "You were just fine sleeping on the floor as a wolf. Are you too good for that now?"

"Are you prepared to see me naked every morning and night when it comes time to shift?"

"I wouldn't see you naked," I grind out, "because I obviously am an adult in control of myself and have the ability to look away when you shift." I mean, I didn't have the ability to look away this morning, but . . . we'll call those extenuating circumstances.

Bee snorts. "Well, that's nice for you two, but I'm not interested in sharing my space like that, whatever you decide to promise."

A look passes between them that I can't decipher.

Jimmy looks away first. "I mean, I suppose I could shift in the closet, but that would mean getting wolf hair all over your clothes. I still think my suite is the better option. There's more room for privacy, more people to potentially watch out for each other, and the bathroom is only shared with the suite, not the entire dorm floor. I'm just trying to make sure everyone stays safe."

Bee and I both blow out frustrated breaths.

"I hate to admit it, but I think Jimmy makes the best points," she says.

"Yeah, fine. But you and I are not, under any circumstances, sharing a bed," I argue.

Holding up his hands, Jimmy looks both hurt and guilty as hell all at the same time. "I will be a perfect gentleman. You don't have to worry about me at all."

"Right," I mutter, but I think we all know that it's not Jimmy I'm really worried about here.

Chapter Fourteen

JIMMY

Stay. Cool.

It's no big deal that I finally managed to get Gloria into my dorm. Never mind about how it happened or the fact that Bee is here too. Let's ignore the part where I've promised to not sleep in the same room as her and she doesn't even want me to touch her. The important thing is that I'm making progress.

The other important thing is that our little three-person circle has been expanded. I had to explain to my roommates what was going on if I wanted them to agree to two extra people staying with us, but all of them immediately agreed to help protect the girls against whatever Vincent the asshole vampire might send.

Marcus and Devon both seem to have taken particular offense that it was one of their own kind who drugged Gloria, like they have to prove that honorable vampires exist since Vincent obviously isn't it.

It's not helping that Marcus and Devon have some weird

argument going between the two of them, which pretty much prevents both of them from staying in one room together for more than five minutes. That doesn't seem like it bodes well for us all working as a cohesive team against vampire frat boys, but what do I know, anyway?

"Remind me again why you guys don't want to share a room now?" I gently inquire as I help Gloria haul in her heinously ugly flower suitcase. I make a mental note to figure out her birthday and replace all of her luggage for her.

"Why would you think we would be okay with sharing a room at all?" Marcus casually responds, staring pointedly at the opposite wall. Devon shoots him a look full of daggers before stomping to the coffee maker and starting a new pot.

"Well, I thought after the last couple of parties that you two . . . were kinda . . ." Before I can finish my sentence, Devon jumps in to end the conversation.

Devon lets out a humorless snort of laughter. "Apparently, things that happen at parties don't count in the real world. Apparently, if you say something enough times it makes that thing true. Apparently, whatever you thought you saw was entirely in your head, and you should keep it to yourself."

Marcus finally looks at Devon again. "And apparently, complaining enough about the reality of a situation will change the reality of that situation."

Jeez. Sorry I asked.

We finish moving all the girls' stuff in as I mentally take stock of what my options are for protecting Gloria and Bee.

There's Jeff and his friend Gabe, and while I'm happy to have the extra numbers, I can't imagine how two humans with zero fighting experience whatsoever are going to be much help. They're eager, though, so I guess that counts for something.

"We're sleeping in your room, so you've got about ten minutes to put away anything incriminating before we go in there and start getting ready for bed," Bee announces while

I'm still wrapping my head around the idea that Gloria is staying here tonight.

"Incriminating?" I ask, completely lost.

Bee gives a significant look that I should probably under-stand—all raised eyebrows and unblinking eyes—but I don't.

"You know, anything that you might prefer your female friends didn't stumble upon by accident? Anything that you might keep in your bedroom, which is a little too personal to share with the average buddy?"

What is she—? Oh shit. It hits me like lightning, what she might be referring to, and I make a scrambling, completely undignified dash for my room to clean things up before the girls go in there. It's not like I regularly keep a stack of porn by my bed or anything, but there are definitely a few things in this room that I would prefer to keep private, at least until Gloria and I have gotten to know each other better.

"Okay, the coast is clear," I announce when I get back to the common room. "Not that the coast wasn't clear before," I backpedal. "I mean, everything was fine before. I just wanted to make sure everything was tidy enough for company. You know?"

Gloria bites her lip to stop the giggle that is very obviously fighting its way out of her. "Okay. Whatever you say, Jimmy."

"Yes, I'm sure the coast was very clear a few minutes ago before you went in there," Jeff the traitor chimes in.

"Yeah! And besides, didn't you just do the laundry? All of the incriminating evidence should be squeaky clean." Devon winks at Bee and Gloria.

Lovely. I guess he still has his sense of humor.

"Wow. Thanks, guys. Who knew you could both be so helpful?" I say through clenched teeth.

Even the guys look like they might break something if they have to keep in their laughter much longer.

"Fine, I had to do a little more than tidying," I admit. "But

I refuse to apologize for living my life the way I want to. So there."

Everyone bursts out laughing at once. Feeling all sorts of annoyed and grumpy, I stomp over to our shared minifridge and grab one of the beers that we've been stocking for just such an occasion. I glare around the room over the rim of my can at everyone.

* * *

I know the couch won't be comfortable to sleep on as a human or a wolf, so I opt for the floor, which is only comfortable if I'm a wolf. That's okay. I feel more confident as a guard in wolf form anyway.

I just wish I didn't have my heightened senses being filled so thoroughly by the off-limits, out-of-reach, untouchable, completely delectable girl on the other side of my bedroom door.

I can hear the girls whispering to each other and giggling long after everyone else is asleep. You'd think they didn't spend every night sleeping in the same dorm already, the way they apparently need to catch up on every bit of gossip. And, yes, some of what I overhear is about me, and no, I don't love what I hear.

And then there's the fact that Gloria's scent has already infused the entire suite. I can hardly smell anything else, now that I've got her in my nose. What I want is to have her on my tongue, on my fingers, on my dick. But all I get is her soap and her musk and her sweat—nothing heavy, just the natural scent of her after she took a shower in my bathroom—and it's driving me crazy.

I roll on my back, trying to get comfortable and scratch that one random itch on my back at the same time. The girls' giggling picks up volume, and my ears prick in their direction involuntarily. I kind of hope they're giggling about me. At least then I've made Gloria laugh. That's a good thing, right? But I can't make out any words, just tone as they keep talking. What the hell am I gonna do? Keep torturing myself on this living room floor. That's what I'll do. That's all I can do, short of bursting in there, taking Gloria by the throat, and . . . well, all of that would be pretty damn counterproductive, wouldn't it?

"I didn't think wolves had trouble sleeping." I jerk around as Marcus steps out of the shadow of his doorframe and heads to the kitchen.

I stare at the vampire as he moves around the kitchen, grabbing things. I get up off the floor and shift into my human form.

"What are you doing up?" I ask as I grab my sweatpants off the ground and slip them on.

"I thought I might prep some things for breakfast tomorrow since we have a full apartment. What about you?" he asks without looking at me.

"What do you mean? I'm cool." I wander over to the kitchen and sit on one of the wooden barstools.

Marcus stops what he's doing and turns around to look at me, an accusing look on his face. "So, that's how you're playing it? You have zero interest in that female shifter in your bed right now and have not been spending all evening thinking about her? That isn't the girl you've been jacking off to in the shower every morning and think we haven't noticed?"

I go still for a moment. Did I tell him all of that? Or any of that? I didn't really think he was the type to pay attention to that stuff, and honestly, confiding in Marcus of all people seems a bit surreal. But, hey, we're here. Why the hell not? It all just tumbles out of me.

"Why can't she just admit that she's attracted to me the

same way I am to her? Why does she keep insisting on chasing after these rich assholes when I would obviously treat her so much better?" I get up from the stool and start pacing, unaware that Marcus has put down what he was doing in the kitchen to give me his full attention.

"Maybe after this whole Vincent disaster, she'll realize that she doesn't actually want a guy like that," he tells me in a placating voice, but I am still in my head.

"I hope. But she could also realize that she doesn't want any guy at all after going through this shit. Or she could decide that she wants a guy and go out to find some regular guy who isn't me." My heart stutters at the thought. I really might die if she moves on and finds some perfectly nice guy who isn't me.

"Would it really be so bad if she met someone who could give her what she wants? Are you really feeling like you can't give her up?" Marcus asks me as I finally turn around to look at him.

"Fuck. You're right. I'm acting ridiculous and lovesick and utterly pathetic. I guess I am ridiculous and lovesick and pathetic, though, so what am I supposed to do?" I say as Marcus gets back to his work in the kitchen.

"I wish I could tell you. Hell, I wish I knew the answer for myself as well," he mutters as he continues preparing something for breakfast.

I take a minute to look at Marcus, really look at him.

"Devon would be a lucky guy to have someone like you."

Marcus pauses from what he's doing, and his shoulders draw up with tension.

"You have no idea what you're even talking about," Marcus says so quietly that I wouldn't have heard it without my wolf hearing.

"I'm gonna try to sleep for a bit. Sorry if I snore," I say as I wander back into the living room, hearing Marcus snort behind me. "Thanks, man."

"For what?"

"You know. For hearing me out. For not busting my balls too bad," I say before shifting back into a wolf. I turn around three times, hoping to magically make the floor more comfortable, then lie down again and continue to fail at sleeping.

Chapter Fifteen

GLORIA

Bee and I peek out of Jimmy's bedroom to see his wolf self sleeping in the center of the room. I would be lying if I didn't admit to certain parts of me perking right up at the sight of him.

Which is bad and unacceptable if I want to live my life and follow my dreams and not drop out of college to have babies.

Ugh, what is wrong with me? I breathe deep and try to get a grip before striding across the room to the kitchenette with my head held high. If I don't get some coffee, I'm going to start committing violent acts.

Of course, Jimmy is lying on his back with all of his wooly goods on display.

Not gonna look. Not even looking in that direction. Besides, I've already seen it. I am not going to check out the guy that I am hard-core lusting after. Nope. Not happening.

Bee snickers from her place behind me in the dorm room, and I shoot her a death glare. Sure, she can laugh all she wants while not actually leaving the room.

As I reach for the coffee maker, I notice that it is already full of hot coffee. A full pot. It looks like one of the guys was up early. I also smell something else in the oven and notice a full tray of cinnamon rolls baked fresh. I didn't think Jimmy could cook, let alone bake something from scratch. I wonder which roommate has the cooking skills. I make a mental note to buy some more coffee for the guys as a thank-you for letting us stay here.

Halfway through pouring myself a cup of coffee, I sense movement behind me, and Bee's pretend vomit sounds from the doorway tell me exactly who it is.

Jimmy leans against the counter, grinning at me, his entire naked body on display.

Well, there go all of my good intentions to not look at him. And damn it if he doesn't look even better than I remembered.

"Good morning. Can I help you with anything over there?"

"I'm doing just fine, thank you," I promise him. "Maybe you could, you know, get some clothes on? Or something?"

"But Bee is in my room with all my clean clothes, and I wouldn't want to terrorize her by swinging anything too close for comfort," he says with a look of absolute innocence on his face.

I have to shoot another death glare at the now closed door, behind which I hear Bee actually cackling. I'm going to murder my roommate.

Devon joins us—thankfully clothed—and rolls his eyes at Jimmy. "I'd heard rumors about werewolves having absolutely no concept of shame or modesty, but I never really believed them until I started living with this guy."

"Don't even pretend you don't enjoy the view. I am providing a great, free service here, a feast for everyone's eyes!" Jimmy teases.

Devon rolls his eyes again. "Have you ever heard the phrase 'no mystique, big mistake'? I've seen the view"—he waves a hand at Jimmy's crotch—"and am pretty sure there's no more view to see. You should keep something back if you want anyone"—now he twitches his eyebrows significantly in my direction—"to ever stay interested."

"He has a point, you know," Bee says, walking out of the room as if she wasn't being a complete traitor less than two minutes ago. "You might want to try leaving something up to the imagination sometime. Girls like having a little mystery to solve sometimes."

Jimmy's smug look drops from his face, but he plasters it back on before turning back to me. "I don't know what these guys are talking about. I'm just hanging out in my own dorm doing the things I normally do in my own dorm."

"Well, that actually is true," Devon concedes.

At the same time, Bee mutters, "Emphasis on the 'hanging out' part of your statement."

I crack up at that and can barely put the coffeepot back because I'm laughing so hard.

Jimmy gathers up what little dignity he can muster and saunters toward his room. "Fine," he says. "I will put on some clothes since everyone else is so uncomfortable with a little nudity."

"Who made the cinnamon rolls?" I ask after him.

Jimmy turns back and gives a look at Devon before continuing to walk to his room.

"No clue. Maybe, you know, Devon?" Jimmy says over his shoulder before closing the door to his room.

"Cinnamon rolls!" Bee squeals in delight as she dives for the stove. I look over at Devon, who has gone kind of still.

"Probably Marcus. He likes to use the kitchen."

Bee and I both turn to look at Devon, concern on both of

our faces. He shakes off his mood and plasters a fake smile on his face.

"I may not be able to eat them myself, but they do smell amazing. Let's crack into these suckers," he says as he grabs the oven mitts.

"You know we're here if you need to talk to someone, right?" Bee says, patting his shoulder maternally. Devon nods his thanks at her before pulling the cinnamon rolls out of the oven.

* * *

The guys have all agreed to take it in turns to make sure Bee and I don't have to go anywhere alone. I appreciate them being so protective, but I also can't help feeling like it's a little overboard. I mean, when I haven't been drugged, I can protect myself. And, shitty as it is, I'm not the first girl to have something like this happen to her. In the light of day, after a full night of sleep and recovery, it seems a lot more likely that Vincent will go looking for easier prey now that I got away from him once. But when I tried to tell that to Devon, he just raised his eyebrows and asked how many vampires I'd really known. Apparently, once a vampire chooses its prey, it doesn't give up. It's like a matter of pride or some bullshit.

Oh joy, to have the honor of being this particular vampire's chosen prey.

Jimmy seems way too pleased with himself for his trick at the beginning of the year, switching his entire schedule, because now it means he gets to be my bodyguard for the foreseeable future while the vampires rotate who's watching Bee depending on when they have classes. Jeff is a little upset that he isn't on guard duty, but he admitted pretty quickly that a human couldn't hold his own against a vampire. Instead, he's trying to think of long-term solutions to stop Vincent from pulling this bullshit on anyone else.

"What do you think?" I hear Jimmy ask and realize he's probably been talking to me for a long time, and I have no idea what he was saying.

"Think about what?" On a normal day, I could probably fake it until I figured out what I'd missed, but today is far from normal. I just don't have it in me to pretend I was listening.

"We should go back to the dorm for lunch and to check in with the others, but stopping for a coffee won't keep us out too long," Jimmy says without complaining that I was ignoring him. "Is it alright if I buy you a coffee?"

I half turn to stare at him as we walk. "You . . . want to buy me a coffee?"

"Yeah. Or a tea? One of those really sugary frozen coffee drinks? If you'll let me, I want to get you something."

"But why?" I blurt out before I realize what I'm saying. Real nice, questioning the guy who seems to want to do something nice, but I guess that's just who I am.

Jimmy shrugs. Does nothing ever get to this guy? "I like you. I like seeing you happy. I thought coffee might make you happy."

Everything inside me melts into a puddle of mush on the sidewalk for a moment. This guy.

"Sure. You can buy me a coffee, but not another sugar bomb nightmare," I say and silently promise I'm not going to choose based on the price of the drink this time.

JIMMY

Okay, I can admit that just hanging out naked in my dorm was never going to be the most effective tactic to convince Gloria to give me a shot. I can't say I would do it any differently, given a second try. I mean, eventually, it has to pay off, right?

But buying her a coffee does seem to thaw some of her ice princess armor. She's smiling as we walk back to the dorm, and she talks about our history project without rolling her eyes once. Not even when I ask her to explain again who Tallis is and why he's important. And everyone is back at the dorm by the time we make it back, which means most of the people most important to me are all in the same place together, which I always find comforting. I don't know if it's a pack thing or just a me thing, but having the people I care about gathered with me is one of the best feelings in the world. The only reason I would want them gone is if Gloria suddenly changes her mind and wants to hook up with me, in which case I probably still wouldn't really mind all of my friends being there with me. Gloria might mind, though, and I'll kick them all out in an instant if she asks me to.

"We've only thought of one solution so far," Jeff announces as soon as we walk through the door.

Way to break up my daydream.

"Solution?" I ask.

"Let's hear it," Gloria demands.

Jeff and Gabe have some kind of silent conversation with their eyes, making me wonder if humans also have secret ways of communicating with each other that they keep under wraps, before Jeff turns back to Gloria.

"I think we have to cancel him."

Now it's Gloria's turn to be confused. "Cancel?"

"I think we need to publicly shame him for his actions, you know, warn people away from him and prevent him from being able to victimize anyone else. It's risky, and there are still a lot of kinks to work out, but it's the best option we've come up with so far today."

Bee leans forward to join the conversation. "I agree, partly because I think we should try to stop him somehow, but also because I suspect there are a lot more people with similar experiences—not necessarily all with a positive outcome like yours—that haven't had any way to share what happened to them. If we could find some way to get the word out about all of these predatory guys and also give victims a platform to share their stories, it could be really empowering."

"But," Jeff adds, "like I said, we still haven't figured out a way to do it safely. We need to find a way to promise at least some anonymity to anyone who shares their stories because if we're worried about Vincent retaliating right now, it will only get worse if he finds out we've made his life harder."

"But we definitely want to make his life harder, right?" Bee looks around the room, and every one of us nods in agreement. Even Devon and Marcus, who are still having their weird argument, have come out to the common area for this conversation. We're all in this together, no backing out.

"We want to make his life miserable," I confirm.

All too soon—because I'd happily spend all day every day hanging out in the dorm with my friends, especially if Gloria is there—it's time for class again. My least favorite part of college. At least Gloria is on board with me sitting with her and walking her to and from classes, at least for the time being.

I just want to be as close as I can to her, but I feel like she's taking every chance she can get to put as much distance as possible between us. I'm sure she's got her reasons, but the possibility of Vincent coming after one or both of us trumps those reasons. At least, in my mind, that's the way it works.

It's not like I can hold her hand or anything, though, which is exactly what I want to do, and I know she won't let me.

I settle for giving her what is probably the most pathetic, lovesick look in all of history as we walk to class.

"What do you think about Jeff's idea?" I ask, trying to multitask by watching her, holding a conversation, and not tripping over my own feet. It half works. I keep having to do a funky little skip to make sure I keep up with her and don't walk into anyone.

"I think . . ." She really does look like she's thinking hard about her answer, so I don't interrupt. Besides, this may be the most beautiful she's ever looked, lower lip clenched between her teeth, eyebrows drawn down as she thinks Very Important Thoughts. "I think that I like what he's trying to do, but I hate feeling like I'm putting other people in danger. It would kind of be easier to corner him in a dark alley and just tear his throat out and have it all done with, right? But I know that it's not that simple."

"Definitely not that simple," I agree. "But you know none of us think about it like that, right? It's not you putting any of us in danger. We're in danger because someone else is being a villain. He would be a villain no matter what. I'm just happy I got you away from him before something worse happened."

"I'm also happy you got me away before something worse happened," she agrees. Gloria stops suddenly and grabs my arm, turning me to look into her eyes. "Look, Jimmy." She swallows a few times, like this is some really awkward conversation that she would avoid altogether if she could. "I really do appreciate you rescuing me like you did. It's just . . . I don't know, actually. I don't have a lot of words to describe this, but . . . I hate feeling like I need to be rescued or that I need any help at all, for that matter. But you did rescue me. And I did need help. So . . . I guess what I'm trying to say is . . . thank you."

I manage to listen through her declaration without doing something completely idiotic, like declaring my own undying love, but I am completely unable to respond when she turns and starts walking again.

Chapter Sixteen

GLORIA

"We've got it all set up," Jeff announces the next time I walk through the door.

I'm afraid to ask. "What's set up?"

"The website for people to report when douchebags do shitty things like try to rape people."

Jeff is looking at me like this is all as obvious as can be, but I still don't know what he's talking about.

"Um." I pass my helpless look on to Jeff's neighbor, a giant, completely jacked vampire with—relative to him—the tiniest laptop in the world settled on top of his legs.

"Whatever it was required yet another person to help out?"

"'It' encompasses the entire Vincent incident," Jeff says defensively. "'It' is a pretty big thing we're dealing with. By the way, this is Taylor, not that you thought to ask, and he's going to be helping out with some things. Yes, he's another vampire, but I swear he's on our side. One of the good guys. I hope that's okay?"

Great, just what I wanted. A pea-brained, fanged meat-head underfoot all the time.

But he does have a certain draw, I admit to myself as I watch the muscles in his forearms shift each time he types.

Part of me wants to go full after-school special with the problem. Part of me is absolutely terrified but wants to do something anyway.

"I'm sorry. It's just that this is all . . ."

"Difficult and overwhelming?" Taylor supplies, glancing up from his laptop for just a moment to make eye contact with me before going back to whatever he's working on.

"Um. Well, yeah, that's exactly what it is," I admit.

"That's why I brought Taylor in on this," Jeff says as he plops down next to him on the sofa. "It's going to be tough to share your story."

"It's going to be difficult to go about your life wondering if that asshole vampire is going to retaliate against you," Taylor says quietly while continuing his typing. Everyone in the room stops to look at him.

"Sorry . . . it's not my first time dealing with this kind of thing. My mom . . . well, she wasn't as lucky as you." Taylor looks up from his laptop to meet my eyes.

"I'm sorry to hear that," I say, and I mean it. He's right. We have to do something, not just for any future women but for all the women who never had anyone before as well.

"But at least you won't have to do the work of setting this up or managing it. I'm going to take on all of the aspects of this that I can so you don't have any extra workload. But there is still something that I can't do for you."

Okay, so maybe not so pea-brained after all. I mentally kick myself for making that kind of assumption.

"Okay. What is it that you're actually doing?"

Taylor looks up at me again with a serious look on his face. "We've created a website to host people who want to anonymously post their experiences of rape and sexual assault here on campus, with the hope that, if enough people share their stories, some of these guys will eventually face some real consequences. Of course, the more people we can convince to speak out, the more powerful it will be, but we really can't ask anyone to speak out unless we can guarantee their anonymity absolutely. That's the part I'm currently working on, the anonymity aspect, and then I'm going to work on finding people willing to share. I'm hoping you'll be willing to share once we get it up and running."

That's a lot more than I had imagined. In my mind, there would be some strategic social media posts to reveal Vincent as the villain he is. Failing that, maybe a bucket of pig's blood as a viable alternative. But what Taylor is describing sounds a lot more effective than my vague ideas.

"Wow. That's like . . ."

"Difficult and overwhelming?"

"Yeah. Really fucking difficult and overwhelming. You said you want me to share my story on this?"

He nods. "I think it would really help out. Like I said, that's the part I can't do, but I'll cover everything else so you don't have to."

I take a deep breath and nod slowly. "Okay. I'm in."

The guys on the couch let out a cheer in unison, jumping up to surround me and hug me.

* * *

I can't get past the feeling that someone is watching me. There's a spot between my shoulder blades that keeps itching like someone's laser eyes are boring into it, but the lecture hall is full, and I don't even know a tenth of the people in this class.

I look around once again, trying to be subtle as I turn to

look behind me. I don't see anyone that I recognize from Vincent's fraternity, which I take some comfort from, but I can't delude myself into thinking I know everyone he's connected to.

Jimmy and I are in the least conspicuous spots we could find: middle row and off to the side. The instinctive, animal part of my brain can't stop mapping every exit and counting out the potential steps it would take to escape, in case some shit goes down. But that's idiotic because I know Vincent isn't going to send thugs into a math class to beat me in public. No, it's entirely possible he's sent someone to keep an eye on me, report back to him about anything and everything I do, maybe even jump me in a dark alley if the opportunity arises, but I can't imagine a situation in which I'll need to make a run for it during a lecture. This knowledge doesn't stop me from counting and recounting the steps up to the nearest exit, calculating how many people I would have to jump over to get out to the other aisle and the second nearest exit.

I try to be subtle as I side-eye a girl a few rows behind me who I don't remember seeing before. Though I was never trying to memorize every face before.

Fucking Vincent has basically managed to ruin my life for the foreseeable future, and I need to accept that. I can't accept it, though. My anger over the situation cooks down into a goopy, smelly desire for revenge. God, I want to make him pay so bad.

* * *

The feeling of eyes on me continues through class and on as Jimmy and I go for our now expected post-class coffees.

Am I imagining things, or did that girl across the room look away a little too quickly when I made eye contact with her? Or maybe it's the guy at the next table over, seemingly absorbed in his laptop, but it's not like it would be a stretch for him to shift his gaze a few inches higher to watch me over the screen.

"Do you get the feeling we're being watched?" I ask Jimmy as quietly as I can.

He frowns and looks around the room as if he might actually catch someone staring at him. "Why would anyone be watching us?"

I stifle my sigh. Of course he hasn't noticed anything. It's probably all in my head. I'm getting paranoid and jumpy over nothing.

"I don't know. Never mind, I'm probably just being crazy."

"Oh. Okay." His baffled frown stays put, but he doesn't say anything else, so I assume he's just going to drop it. He surprises me, though. "There must have been a reason you were thinking about it, right?"

"Huh? A reason?"

"Like, instinct or something. If you think someone is watching you, they probably are. Or maybe it's something else that's off. I think we should trust your instincts. You want to go?"

Yes. I want to be back in my room. Better yet, back at home where it's safe. Stinky and boring and absolutely stifling, yes, but at least it's safe there.

"Do you mind? I've been getting this weird feeling ever since we left your dorm. Like I said, it's probably just in my head."

"Well, it's a pretty smart head. I trust you." He stands up without inviting further discussion and waits just long enough for me to gather my stuff up before walking out the door.

* * *

JIMMY

I don't want to worry Gloria, but her suggestion that someone is watching her has me freaking out more than a little. She just confirmed that she's feeling the same thing my instincts have been screaming at me all day. Someone's eyes are on us, but they're always just a little too quick for me to catch them looking.

"I think we need to get you away from campus for a while," I tell her on our way back to the dorm. My protective instincts are raging right now, shouting that I need to drag her away to live with my pack so my whole family can help protect her. But I know she'll never agree to that. And my parents wouldn't be too happy about it either, come to think of it. While I'm more certain by the minute that Gloria and I are meant to be together, the idea when they sent me off to college was not for me to fall head over heels for the first girl I met. Add to that the fact that my pack is close enough to school that she wouldn't really be any safer from Vincent than if she stayed here, and I'm back to square one, trying to keep her safe.

"I can't. I've got classes," she says, like I care about that when all I can think of is her possibly being in danger. "You've got classes. I'm not letting Vincent Fucking Davenport scare me out of school so I have to run back home without a degree. Besides, where would I go? It's not like I can hide out in my old bedroom, tell my parents, 'Oh, by the way, you'll be seeing more of me for a bit because a wealthy, deranged vampire is after me.' No, I'm staying here and facing my problems. I am not going to run away."

"But it's not like you get any award or anything for staying here and being a target. What if we just took, like, a weekend away or something. Just a little bit of time to regroup and think of some better ways to keep you safe. Please?"

Her shoulders slump a little, and I'm not sure whether to feel hopeful that she's about to agree with me or heartbroken that she looks so fucking defeated.

"Fine. A weekend, if you can think of a place we'll be safe. Just because I'm so sick of looking over my shoulder, and I can't function because I'm so tired right now."

"I can find us a safe place," I promise her, already grinning from ear to ear. There are a few possible places I can think of. I'll have the arrangements made before I go to bed tonight.

* * *

Devon looks over at Bee with serious eyes. "We'll keep an eye on things here while you're gone," he says.

"Yeah?" I breathe a sigh of relief. "I wish we knew for sure what Vincent was planning. If I knew he was planning on coming after Bee too, there's no way I'd leave her here alone. But I don't think I can protect both girls at once without help, no matter where we go."

"It's no big deal," Devon assures me. "Bee won't be alone. She's got us watching out for her, just in case. But . . . you're not . . ."

"I'm not what?"

Devon glances around the room to check that everyone else is still preoccupied with other conversations. "You're not just doing this to have a run at Gloria without the rest of us getting in your way, are you?"

"What?" I shout the question, causing everyone in our cramped dorm to turn and look at me immediately. "Why would you even say something like that?" I hiss once the gawkers have turned back to their normal conversations.

"Because it's really obvious that everything you've done since school started was to try and get in her pants. It's not so far-fetched to recognize that this situation is an opportunity for you. I hope you're not the type of guy who would take advantage of a situation like this, but I had to ask."

"Oh. My. God. I hadn't even thought of it like that. Seriously, who do you think I am? I just want to keep her safe. That is all I have been thinking about for three days straight."

He holds his hands up defensively. "Okay, your intentions are honorable. Good. I just thought I would ask."

But now the idea is in my head, and it won't go away. Gloria and I are going to spend a weekend together. It might not be a particularly romantic weekend, considering the reason behind it, but the fact remains, we'll be alone, just the two of us, for forty-eight hours. And it will probably kill me to respect her personal space and keep my hands off her when all I want is to mark her as mine and claim her, over and over, in the most fundamental way possible.

* * *

Gloria snores. Loud. I turned off the radio thirty minutes into our drive because her snoring is the best entertainment I could hope for. She is cracking me up. Every few miles, she half wakes herself with a little snort, then snuggles back into her seat and goes back to sleep. I enjoy this little show for the entire three-hour drive to the pack cabins.

When I park and try to wake her up, Gloria gives an adorable little whimper that makes me want to cuddle her close to me and never let go. Well, I can do the next best thing. I unhook her seat belt and gather her up in my arms to carry her inside without waking her up. She's been through a lot recently. I don't want to interrupt her sleep if I can help it.

The cabin is cozy, just a single bedroom, a bathroom, an open kitchen and living room area, and a couple of closets. It's usually used for newly mated pack members who need to get away and, well, you can imagine. The people staying in it usually only need a bed and a kitchen. But I double-checked, and no one in the pack is expecting to use it this weekend, and there's no way a vampire would think to follow us here. This is going to be the perfect place for me to keep Gloria safe and for Gloria to get some rest.

I slide her onto the bed without waking her up and go out to the car to unpack and get everything settled for our weekend getaway.

Chapter Seventeen

GLORIA

Too many. Too much.

These are my first thoughts as I wake up.

Too many layers. Too much clothing. Too hot.

And that last thought is what brings reality slamming into me. My heat is starting. I should have realized it when I couldn't keep my eyes open on the ride here. Heat is often preceded by a period of energy storing. But I also wasn't expecting my heat to come on for at least a few months.

If it was regular, and if it wasn't disrupted by college stress, and if I wasn't spending all my time with someone that my hormones apparently think is a perfect match.

I groan in frustration—and desperation, because now that my body's decided it's doing this, it's really going for it. I don't have a single sex toy with me either. I wasn't planning on needing any for a short weekend trip.

"Are you okay?" Jimmy bursts in, wild-eyed, ready to protect me from whatever tries to come at me.

But he can't protect me from this.

"Where are we?" I grind out, already writhing on the bed with the need shooting through me.

"My pack keeps this cabin for new mates. I thought it would be perfect since only wolves know about it, and no one would be using it otherwise . . ."

That explains why this room smells like sex. It probably isn't what set off my heat, but it's definitely not helping it now.

"You look . . . Are you alright?"

"Heat," I groan, twisting the covers between my fingers, trying to find any kind of purchase to keep myself from doing what my body wants, which is to tear off my clothes and then his and then ride him until we're both half-dead from it.

"He—" Understanding dawns on Jimmy's face. "You mean, you're in heat?" Is it my imagination, or does hope flash across his face for a moment? "What do you . . . I mean . . . do you need me to get you anything? Or do anything? Or . . ."

If I had any kind of control over my actions right now, I might take pity on him with his half-panicked, half-bewildered expression and let him know it's nothing to worry about. I don't, though.

"Get. Out."

He leaps backward through the doorway and shuts the door without questioning my order, which is good because it's all I can do to hang on to the bed and keep myself from jumping on him.

"Your bag is just out here if you want me to give it to you," he says through the door. "I don't know if you . . . umm . . . brought anything . . ."

Oh, god. He's asking if I have a vibrator with me. Even through my haze of sexual desperation, I can feel embarrassed about that.

"No. Nope. There's nothing like that." I'm tearing my clothes off as I answer him. The heat of them, not to mention the sensation of them against my skin, is way too much to handle. "Just. Stay out of here, okay?"

"Yeah. Of course. Whatever you want from me, just say the word."

Some of the panic has left his voice, at least. I wonder how many females in heat he's had to deal with in the past. If he lives in a big, close-knit pack, maybe he's seen this plenty of times before. Or maybe he's got a small family, and his only experience with heat is his parents periodically disappearing into the woods to deal with it without kids getting underfoot. Maybe it's weird that I know nothing at all about the guy I've been spending so much time with and who I've now gone into heat for.

Weird or not, it's happening.

Free of my clothing, I rest one hand on my breast and trail the other down my body, taking in every shiver-inducing sensation along the way. My own fingers are a poor substitute for what my body is actually demanding, but I refuse—abso-fuckinglutely refuse—to be the dumb country wolf who gets pregnant her first semester of college because she couldn't handle her first heat away from home.

I can barely touch my clit I'm so sensitive. I slide a finger next to it, dipping lower to use my own wetness, then sliding up the inside of my labia. With my other hand, I pluck at my nipple and am rewarded by a zing of electricity that shoots through my body. It feels just like a plucked guitar string vibrating through me, anchored at each end by my fingers.

I can't help the noise that escapes me in response, and Jimmy lets out his own groan on the other side of the door.

My inner muscles tighten, almost painful with nothing to tighten against or around.

I squeeze my breast, reveling in the satisfying weight of it against my palm, tweak my nipple again, making my back arch up and up until I'm practically bent in half, and let out a moan of desire and frustration and absolute desperation.

Jimmy echoes me with his own moan, which sets the guitar strings inside my body to vibrating so fast I think I might snap.

One more slide of my finger is all it takes to topple me over into a gasping orgasm.

And five seconds is all the relief I get from my body's demands.

"Jimmy?"

"Yeah, I'm still here." His voice sounds strangled. I wonder what he's going through right now. I'm sure the pheromones are rolling off me in waves, and there's no way a male wolf won't feel some kind of effect from that. I've never seen a male have this kind of reaction to a female in heat, though.

"Do you think . . . I mean . . . I think it might help if you . . . talk to me?"

"Talk to you? About what?"

"Umm." God, I'm going to die of embarrassment. "Like, if you could say maybe what you would do if you didn't have to stay out there?"

There's a choked-off gasp from the other side of the door before he speaks. "Like, you mean, what I want to do to you?" he asks.

"Yeah. But I understand it—"

"No. I mean, yes. I can." He takes a slow, shaky breath. "I can do that."

My hand settles back in its place between my legs, by finger sliding up and down my cleft, gathering wetness on each trip down and swirling just above my most sensitive part on each trip up, almost hypnotic as I wait for Jimmy to start talking.

"I want—" Another shaky breath. "—I want to taste your neck first. I would start by just barely licking you on the spot right behind your ear, just above your jaw. And then I would taste from there, down along your neck where your artery is, because I want to know if it tastes any different from one spot to the next. And I would take my time because I want to feel your pulse against my tongue."

My hand drifts up from my chest to my neck of its own accord, and I scrape my fingernails lightly against my skin there, imagining what I'm actually feeling is the scrape of Jimmy's teeth as he explores my neck.

"Then I would move lower. I want to taste every centimeter of your body, but I would probably get stuck for a while on your nipples. I've imagined them so many times, you have no idea."

That surprises a laugh out of me. "What do you mean? You've seen them before."

"Barely. It was dark, and you were so fast about shifting that I barely saw anything. I could have stared at them for hours without even blinking, but instead, I just got a few seconds in the dark. If I ever get to see them for real, I'm going to spend as much time as possible touching them and tasting them and feeling them, and then maybe I'll die happy."

He sounds more relaxed, and that helps me relax. I increase the pace of my finger as I trace my clitoris and labia.

"So what else are you going to do before dying happy?" I ask, amazed that I can joke at all with my body wound so tight.

"I'm going to lie down on my back and let you ride my face. That way, I wouldn't have to worry about going too fast or too slow because you would set the pace."

That image definitely does something for me. The curse I almost let out is broken off by a moan and muscles that I thought were tight enough to snap drawing up even tighter inside of me.

"Fuck. Gloria. Fuck," Jimmy gasps, and then I hear a movement like scrambling footsteps, followed by a tortured groan. A toilet flushes in the next room, followed by a sink coming on and what I have to assume is Jimmy washing his hands.

"Umm, Jimmy?"

"Yeah. Sorry. I really tried not to do that."

He sounds so guilty.

"Not to do what?"

"I didn't want to make this about me," he explains. "I wasn't going to let myself come until you were through this."

Oh. I never expected him to be a gentleman in that particular way.

"It's okay. As long as I'm not in any danger of getting pregnant, it's okay with me if you come."

"Are you sure?"

"I'm sure. Now, tell me more about me riding your face." Good god, I want to do that in reality, but imagining it will have to suffice.

"I want you to ride my face, and I don't think I would be able to close my eyes while you were doing it because I wouldn't want to miss seeing your body above me for even a second. And I would taste you as you rode me. I've probably imagined what you taste like even more than I've imagined your nipples."

His words—and the image he paints with them—send me gasping into another climax. My whole body bows as wave after wave of pleasure crashes through me, and then I lie there, panting and wrung out and happy, while I try to get my bearings again.

JIMMY

The sound of Gloria's orgasm sends relief washing through me. Even though I'm painfully hard—again—just from hearing her get off.

"Are you . . ." I'm pretty sure she's not done, and asking her before she's through it could be dangerous. "Are you okay in there?"

"I'm okay for now," she pants.

"You want me to get you anything?"

"You can't come in here."

Right. Because the thing that would easily be the best thing to ever happen to me would also be the worst thing to happen to her. She doesn't want a mate and babies, and as much as I want to dive in and start forever with her, I need to respect what she wants.

"You want me to take a walk and give you some space for a little bit?" God, it hurts to ask that. But it's the right thing to ask, I'm sure of it.

She puffs out a long sigh. "Would you? If you could just give me, like, thirty minutes, I think that would be enough."

"Yeah. No problem. I'll get out of your hair for half an hour. Or an hour, if you want. Do you want to eat something?"

"I don't think I can. Thirty minutes is enough."

"Okay." I press against the door as I talk to her, willing all of my feelings through the thin wood toward her, hoping she feels how badly I want to care for her. "I'll be back in thirty." And hopefully, that thirty minutes is enough to take care of the painful erection I'm sporting.

I strip down out of sight from the house and shift. Sometimes just shifting is enough to get rid of an unwanted hard-on, but not this time. I'm every bit as keyed up and ready to go in my wolf form as I was before. It makes it harder to run, but

I have to put some distance between Gloria and myself. For my own sanity, I need some time away from the cloud of hormones she's filled that house with.

Choosing a direction at random, I start running, nose twitching for any hint of prey I might catch for dinner. With Gloria in heat and taking over the cabin, I'm not expecting to cook anything anytime soon.

After ten minutes of running, with no promising scents to chase, I shift back to my human form to address my issue that hasn't dissipated at all since this whole thing started. Even after I came earlier—and I'm still kicking myself over that—I didn't feel any relief at all. Well, if at first you don't succeed . . . keep jacking off until your dick literally can't take it anymore.

I steady myself against a sturdy tree and start stroking myself, hard enough that I hope my cock will get the idea. I'll abuse myself if I have to so I can focus on taking care of Gloria. As my hand slides along my length, I can't help but relive the scent and sounds as Gloria got herself off. I want to be the one who takes care of that for her, but getting to be there, getting to smell her arousal thick on the air, getting to be the one talking her through my horndog imaginings, will stay with me for the rest of my life.

As I wrap my fist around my cock and thrust into my hand, I imagine what it would feel like to be rutting into her right now. I can practically feel her slick heat all around me as I slide in and out of my clenched fingers, and that's what causes my balls to tighten and pump stream after stream of semen onto the bark of the tree in front of me.

I groan with the momentary release, then realize I'm still as hard as before. I tighten my grip and pump harder. If I can't take care of this right now, how am I going to take care of Gloria later?

This time, I imagine she has her mouth around me, and the simple thought of her smiling up at me, then wrapping her lips around my cock is enough to send me painting the tree bark a second time.

And I'm still impossibly, painfully, irrationally hard.

I let out a sob of frustration, shift, and run back to the cabin. My thirty minutes are up, and I'm still as desperate for her as I've ever been.

Chapter Eighteen

JIMMY

I put my clothes back on, careful to not rub my still-hard and extremely sensitive cock on any more clothing than is absolutely necessary, and wash my hands carefully in the kitchen sink to make sure none of my semen can come within touching distance of Gloria. I've heard too many stories about wolves getting pregnant to take any chances. If it was just about me, I'd be happy to take any chance as long as it meant being with Gloria. But she says she doesn't want babies right now, so I'll do whatever I can to prevent pregnancy.

"Jimmy?" Gloria's voice is tentative, calling out as soon as I turn the water off.

"Yeah? I'm here."

I'll do anything for you, I think but don't say out loud.

"I think . . . Look, I know this is way too much to ask, but I'm going to ask it anyway, okay? Just know that you can say no, alright?"

I'll never say no. "Of course. Yeah, what is it?"

"I think I need . . ." I wait through the longest silence of my existence. "I think I need you in here. I don't think I can take care of this myself."

My stomach swoops like the first big drop of a roller coaster. Is she asking what I think she's asking? "Do you mean . . . um . . . you want all of me?" I hold my breath, waiting for her answer.

"I think I need you physically," she says. "Don't read too much into it, okay? I would just be using you to get off. And you would have to wait until later." She huffs out a breath. "You know what? Never mind. I know it's way too much to ask. Just forget I said it."

"What if I can't forget about it?" I ask.

"Then pretend you forgot about it so we won't have to be embarrassed every time we see each other."

"What if I don't want to forget about it?" I trace the wood grain of the door, silently begging for her to tell me it's okay to open the door and come inside.

"Of course you want to forget about it," Gloria mutters.

"No, I don't," I breathe. "I want to help you. Whatever you need. Even if it's letting you use me." I can't do much more to lay myself bare for her. If she won't let me in now, she must really mean it.

"Even knowing that it's just my hormones speaking? It doesn't mean anything, and I still don't want to risk getting pregnant?"

"I'll do everything I can so you won't get pregnant," I promise. "Just let me try to help you through this. I want to be the person who helps you, and it's not like I can help you with math. Let me prove I can do this for you."

She makes me wait another eternity before responding. "Okay. Whatever I try to do, keep your clothes on, okay?"

"I promise to keep my clothes on. And try not to come until I'm far away from you," I add before opening the door.

God, nothing could prepare me for the sight that greets

me. Gloria is lying in a nest of rumpled bedding, skin flushed, hair tousled and spread out around her head, wearing floral cotton panties and a neon pink sports bra. All it would take to have her completely naked for me would be a swift tug at both garments. But I have to resist that.

"Can I come closer?" I ask, feeling shy now that I'm actually finally at this point. What if I'm not good enough for her? What if I can't satisfy her after all?

She nods. "Come lie down," she demands, patting the bed beside her.

"I've never—" I start to say, but she interrupts me.

"Neither have I," she says. "At least, not like this. I mean, never while I was in heat before."

"Yeah, that's what I meant. I've been with people before, but never like this."

She takes a long breath in and out. "I guess we'll both be figuring it out together, then," she says.

I turn to face her, waiting for an invitation to go further. She's already doing more than she wanted, I know, so the least I can do is go at her pace.

"I think, maybe if you get on top of me," she says, almost as if she's asking a question. "I think I want to feel you on top of me."

I take a slow breath, knowing that doing that and not letting myself come is going to be a special kind of torture. "Okay. Yeah. I can do that." I rest a knee between her legs and hold myself up above her. Then something occurs to me. "Is it okay if I kiss you? Or is that too . . ." I'm not sure how to finish my sentence. Risky? Intimate? Too much like real feelings instead of the physical release she's looking for?

"Not on my mouth," she answers before I finish my question, "but you can kiss me other places."

I try not to let my hurt show. I get it. She's not in love with me, and she doesn't want to be in love with me, and kissing her on the mouth might bring her closer to those feelings. But, damn, I want her to fall in love with me more than I've ever wanted anything in my life.

"Okay. Not on the mouth," I confirm, then lower myself over her until every bit of me is pressing down into every bit of her. My lips find her ear, her jaw, her neck, and I let myself explore every precious inch of skin. I taste the sweat drying on her skin and the physical heat rolling off her in waves that comes along with her body's arousal. I nibble at each place I can find her pulse pumping and relish each twitch and groan I elicit from her.

And she tortures me in turn by rocking her hips up so I can feel the heat and wetness of her core against my thigh. I can tell she's trying to get more pressure, more friction, there. But I know I'm a goner if I let her rub herself like that along my dick. I made a promise, and I intend to keep it. Shifting lower so she can grind herself against my hip bone, I capture her nipple in my mouth through the sports bra. She groans as I bring it to a hard point, then again as I move to the other one.

Her hips rock faster. I have to think of spiders and maggots to keep myself from coming in my pants every time her leg shifts against my hard cock, but I keep working her nipples all the same. When she hooks her free leg around my hip and I put my hand on her ass to help her keep her rocking motion, I have to bite my cheek and focus on the pain so I don't give in to the pleasure of feeling her against me like this. If it's this good when we've still got clothes on between us, I can hardly imagine what it will be like someday if she decides to give herself to me all the way.

Gloria makes sounds that might be for pleasure or maybe frustration. I answer them by matching her hip movements with my own. Gloria stiffens in my arms, her back arched back, eyes closed, biting her bottom lip so hard I can see a bead of blood well up under her tooth, and lets out a moan that lasts as I rock her through the waves of an orgasm, and she collapses back on the bed, completely boneless.

She doesn't say anything. All she does is blink up at me a few times, slower each time, until her eyelids slide closed and she falls deep asleep. I wait about three seconds before running to the bathroom, where I can come without any risk to her and without getting my pants dirty. She's still fast asleep by the time I come back, so I lie down next to her and allow myself to drop out of consciousness.

GLORIA

I wake up to the glorious realization that some of my heat has passed, followed by the terrible realizations that I am still very much in heat and Jimmy is in bed next to me. Maybe, if he were in the other room, or even just across the room, I would be able to think for a moment and resist my current urge.

But, no.

I turn over and straddle him. It only takes one grind of my hips before he jerks awake with a confused look in his eyes.

"G-Gloria?" he gasps as I roll my hips again.

"I need you," I groan. "Is this okay?" I don't know what I'll do if he says no. I don't think I can stop unless he stops me.

"Okay. Yeah. Do what you need to."

I feel him harden against me as I grind, but it's not enough. I grab his hands and put them on my breasts, hoping he'll figure out what I need like he did last time.

Jimmy lets out a groan that could almost be a sob. "Gloria," he gasps, "I really don't think I can hold off like this."

"Okay. What should we do instead?"

He groans again, tipping his head back and letting his eyes roll back. Jimmy grabs my hips in both hands and holds me still for a moment.

"You're going to make me come if you keep riding me like that. I want to help you, but I just don't have that kind of control."

"So, maybe if I ride you in a different way?"

His eyes darken as he looks up at me. "Move up here," he growls in a voice that goes straight to my core.

I want to ask if he's sure, make sure I'm not overstepping or forcing myself on him, but the hunger in his eyes shuts me right up.

I crawl higher until I'm straddling his face, and he uses his hands on my ass to press me down onto his mouth.

Jimmy devours me through my panties like I'm the first meal he's ever eaten and the last one he expects to ever get. The heat of his breath hits me and heats me from the center out. All I can do is grip the headboard until my knuckles are white and hang on for the ride. He rocks my hips like he was born knowing the exact speed and rhythm I need to feel good. His lips are exactly as soft as I need them, with the perfect amount of firmness pressing between my labia and onto my clit.

For the first time in my life, I actually want my heat to last. I never want to stop feeling these heightened sensations, never want to stop riding Jimmy's face as he groans in satisfaction against me.

It's over too soon. I feel myself climbing higher and higher, hear myself calling out, and can see my orgasm wash over me, as if I'm out of my body, watching from the ceiling somewhere. Then I slam back into myself and am shuddering and spasming uncontrollably as each fresh wave of pleasure washes through me, crashing into my nervous system until I slide off of Jimmy and lie in a quivering puddle, unable to move or speak. Unable to let him know that I can feel my heat washing away and the urgency to mate—the danger—has passed. He did that for me.

* * *

I swim through a hazy awareness for the next few hours. I vaguely notice Jimmy leaving the bed, hear the shower running, feel cared for and comforted when he tosses a sheet over me and tucks it in around me. I notice these things with a detached interest but have no energy or strong desire to respond to them. The world washes past me as I allow the hormones of my heat to wash out of my bloodstream. The house is dark when I return fully to consciousness, and all of the desperate needs my body ignored through the heat cycle slam into my awareness at once.

I disentangle myself from the nest of wadded-up sheets and blankets around me and stumble to the toilet just in time to relieve myself without making a mess. With one urgent need taken care of, I turn to the next. I duck my head under the faucet and suck down tap water as fast as it will come.

"Gloria?" Jimmy's sleepy voice behind me is a mix of worry and confusion.

"Thirsty," I gasp through swallows of water.

"I left some water by the bed for you. I guess you didn't notice," he yawns. "Why don't you lie back down, and I'll bring it to you? And maybe some food?"

My stomach lets out a loud gurgle just at the mention of food. I'm too tired and hungry to fight his offers of help, so I nod and let him lead me back to the bed.

After he puts a glass of water in my hands, he asks, "Are you . . . through it now?"

I nod and gulp the water down. It's the best thing I've ever tasted. "Thanks to you, yeah. I think it's passed. Not exactly how you expected to spend your weekend out at this cabin, right?"

Jimmy's eyes gleam in the moonlight coming through the window. "Honestly, it was an honor. To know that you trust me like that, to know I could help you out. I wouldn't change anything about this weekend." He looks down shyly. "I mean . . . unless you regret it. You would let me know if I messed things up between us, wouldn't you?"

I grab his hand and tug him down so he's sitting beside me on the bed. "You were amazing. Nothing you did could mess things up. And the fact that you respected my wishes, didn't just take it as a sign from the universe and try to get me pregnant? I'm really grateful to you. Not every guy would have done that for me."

"Yeah?" he breathes, his eyes hopeful. "Because in case you didn't figure it out before, you should know that I would do anything for you. I want to be there for you. I want to be the guy you turn to. For anything."

I pat his hand in what I hope is a reassuring way. "I get that. I really do. It's just . . . you have to understand something about me. I've got goals and hopes for the future and things to get done, and . . . best-case scenario, I spend the next four years in school, and then I might consider something more than regular friendship with you. I'm not looking for a mate anytime soon, and I can't promise you I'll ever take anyone— including you—as a mate. I don't want you hanging around on the off chance that this could become something in four years. Do you get what I'm saying?" The furrow between his brows makes me think he really doesn't, but I have to give him a chance to respond.

"I know what you're trying to tell me is I shouldn't hope for anything, but all I can hear is you saying that there's a chance, so . . . get used to me because you're not getting rid of me that easily. Now, let me get you something to eat."

He stands up and is out of the room before I can argue. Which is probably for the best. I need to wait for the light of day, and a good night's sleep, before I try this argument again. Even though I know I'm in the right from a logical standpoint, all I want to do is curl up in his arms and let him take care of me.

The morning will make everything clearer. For now, it's all I can do to stay awake as Jimmy feeds me canned soup, then snuggle back into my nest and fall asleep.

Chapter Nineteen

JIMMY

Gloria is pretending everything is the same. She has been since she woke up after her heat passed.

Well, that's fine. I'm pretty sure she knows the truth, that every single fucking thing has changed between us. It may be way, deep down that she knows it. But she knows it, I'm certain.

"Did you miss us?" I call out to the dorm at large when we get back.

"How could we have a chance to miss you?" Jeff calls back. "You've barely been gone."

I put on a hurt and offended expression. "I can't believe what I'm hearing. Your roommate has been gone on an epic quest, and all you have to say is that it wasn't long enough?"

Jeff rolls his eyes and throws a pillow at me. The whole group is there, piled on top of each other on the couch like a pile of puppies.

"We were just about to draw straws on who should get your bedroom," Gabe volunteers.

"Nope," Jeff says. "He's lying. Nobody was willing to venture into your stinky room. In fact, we're kind of confused at how the girls survived in there."

"My room is not stinky." I turn to Gloria for support. "Tell them my room isn't stinky."

She just gives me a bland smile and says nothing. Okay, maybe not every single thing has changed between us.

It suddenly occurs to me that Bee has been notably quiet for this discussion. "Bee? You want to back me up here? I can count on your support, can't I?"

She doesn't even acknowledge that I said anything. Her gaze keeps shifting back and forth between me and Gloria, and then her eyes pop open wide, and she climbs over the couch to grab Gloria by the wrist and drag her into my bedroom.

Well, shit. There's no way that's going to be good for me.

"Looks like the girls have important stuff to talk about?" Devon says with a bewildered look.

Marcus, who I notice is in the room this time but sitting as far from Devon as possible, rolls his eyes. "Isn't it obvious that Jimmy and Gloria hooked up this weekend?"

I gape for a moment at him. "Hey! It's not like that!"

I'm not sure what it is like, but saying we hooked up makes it sound dirty and shameful, and I am anything but ashamed.

"Oh?" Marcus grins at me, taking some of the sting out of being outed like that. "Did you, or didn't you?"

"I mean . . . yes, I guess we did. But I don't think she wants anyone to know about it, so maybe you can all just . . . keep it quiet?"

"I was going to have posters made up, though," Jeff says before turning back to the TV.

I'm pretty sure he's just joking. And I'm pretty sure they'll make fun of me if I ask him if he's serious. God, I hope he's not serious.

Devon pats the couch cushion beside him. "We're here if you need to talk about it. In the meantime, take a seat and rot your brain with TV."

I squeeze into the spot that Bee was sitting in and let myself melt into the cushions, not paying any attention to whatever is playing on TV and letting my mind drift.

GLORIA

Bee drags me into Jimmy's room, and I can already tell by the look in her eyes that I'm busted.

"Spill it," she orders, pushing me down to sit on the bed.

"I don't know what you're talking about." I try to look innocent, but I can feel the heat in my face giving me away.

Bee waggles an admonishing finger at me. "Oh, no, no, no, missy. I don't need a wolf nose to smell the sex all over you two. Tell me right this instant what happened between you, or I swear I will never forgive you."

I flop back on the bed with a sigh. "Jimmy took me to this official honeymoon cabin couples from his pack use all the time, and it smelled like all of the sex everyone had in it over the years, and it helped to set off my heat."

"And?"

"And I wasn't planning on going into heat, so I hadn't brought anything to help me . . ." I raise my eyebrows suggestively. "You know, get through it."

She sinks down next to me on the bed. "You didn't have your vibrator, so you let Jimmy do it for you?" I can't tell if she's incredulous or judgmental or some other thing entirely.

"I mean, if you want to be crude about it, yes, I guess you could put it that way. I tried other alternatives first, just so you know, but they just weren't working, and I was desperate."

"Oh, I bet you were," she interjects with a grin.

I give her a shove, then smack her with a pillow for good measure.

"It was actually . . . I don't know. Jimmy was actually really sweet about the whole thing. Like, I never expected to be able to describe someone as a perfect gentleman while he was also eating me out."

Bee gasps, her eyes huge. "Oh my god. I'm so torn between wanting every detail and already having an image in my mind that I'll never be able to unsee. Ugh." She presses her hands into the sides of her head. "Nope. No more details. I've already heard too much. Just—" She sobers suddenly. "Wait, you said that it's ridiculously easy to get pregnant when you're in heat. Does that mean . . ."

"No. We were careful. His sperm never came near me. I should be safe."

The relief on her face matches my own.

"Like I said, he really was the perfect gentleman." I jokingly nudge her with my elbow. "He made sure the lady came first."

Bee can't stop the snicker that bursts out of her, and pretty soon, we're both sprawled on the bed, laughing uncontrollably.

* * *

We wait until all the giggles are out of our system before rejoining the others on the couch. Well, on the floor, actually, because the couch is too full unless we sit on people's laps, and that would be counter to my quest to keep things platonic with Jimmy.

Do Jimmy's roommates look at me differently than before? If Bee figured out just by looking at us that Jimmy and I hooked up, it's not a stretch to think they could jump to the same conclusion. I stare straight ahead at the TV and hope nobody sees my cheeks turning pink. Hopefully, Jimmy at least has the decency to not go bragging about it, but how well do I actually know him, anyway? I'll just have to assume everyone knows and hope nobody says anything about it. I might just die of embarrassment if they ask for details.

Gabe taps me on the shoulder. "Hey, since you're back, I wanted to let you know that I think we're ready to go live with our plan. Only if you're ready, though. Just say the word and we'll hit publish."

"Really? I thought we were still stuck trying to find a way to make sure it's anonymous, weren't we?"

"Yeah. So, the problem is Vincent is going to know who it is no matter what we do. There's always going to be a risk of that. But it's not like he has any proof of who's behind the story unless he comes forward and actually admits that he was the one who drugged you." He pauses, and I get the feeling he's debating how he should break bad news to me.

"What is it?" I ask, feeling nervous.

Devon slides off the couch to sit beside me on the floor. "So, this isn't good news, but it's helpful for what we're trying to do. We found some more of his victims and convinced them to share their stories too."

"More? How many more are we talking about?" A pit of acid churns in my stomach. When he says victims, I get the sense that they might not have been fortunate like me. Believing that I came close to something worse than a bad drug experience is completely different from having solid proof of what that "worse" might have been.

Devon rubs slow circles on my back, and Bee tucks me in against her side and squeezes me close to her.

"The guys found two girls based on reports from people who were at other parties, and one came up to me yesterday and said she'd heard about what happened and wanted to share her story. So right now, we have four stories about him, including yours, but we think there will be more people who come forward."

I swallow the bile fighting its way up my esophagus. Three other people aside from me. Probably more. Probably less fortunate in friends who were available to rescue them.

I stand up suddenly and run to the toilet to throw up.

Chapter Twenty

GLORIA

I start in surprise when a girl I vaguely remember seeing in class before plops down beside me. Weird how quickly I've gotten used to always having Jimmy on one side and not looking for someone else to sit with.

"You're Gloria, right?" she whispers.

All systems immediately go on high alert.

"Um . . . who's asking?"

Jimmy presses his fingertips against my arm, a comforting reminder that he's there if I need him.

The girl lets out a low chuckle. "I'm not someone you have to worry about. I heard about what you're doing from one of my friends, and I wanted to add my story."

"Your . . ." I turn to look more closely at her. She's tatted and pierced like no wolf I've ever met, and I notice for the first time that she has the low body temperature and slightly metallic smell of a vampire. "Your story?"

"You didn't think you were the first, did you?" she says with a sardonic grin. "I had my own run-in with our mutual friend V. I wish I'd had someone in my life at the time who could help me get my story to the right people. Instead, I was stupid and thought going to the cops would help bring me . . . I don't even know. Closure? Justice, maybe? I ended up having to take a semester off and change my major when I came back. So, yeah, when I heard that someone was trying to do something about V, I knew I had to jump on the wagon when I had the chance."

I'm pretty sure my jaw hit the floor a minute ago and I just haven't felt it yet. "I . . . That's . . ."

"Thank you," Jimmy jumps in, saving me from having to come up with a more eloquent response. "Can we get a good number to get in contact with you?"

Jimmy might not be the best at classroom and book intelligence, but I have to admit, he's not stupid.

The girl jots some numbers on a sticky note from her backpack, then disappears into the higher rows of the lecture hall before I've even sorted out what I should say to her.

JIMMY

"Gloria is a rock star!" I announce, waving the sticky note at everyone in the dorm with pride.

And everyone in the dorm right now turns out to be . . . nobody?

"While I appreciate your support," Gloria says drily, grabbing a soda from the minifridge, "I'm not the one who should be getting credit for this."

I wave the sticky note at her since there's no one else around to appreciate its significance. "What are you talking about? You're getting more people to come forward. You're helping uncover just how horrible Vincent really is. Why shouldn't you get credit?"

Gloria gives me a pitying look and flops down on the couch. "The only thing I've done is have some friends willing to support me. Besides, hearing all these stories of people who weren't as lucky as me just makes me hate the whole situation more and more. I feel gross being praised for something I didn't have any say in when a lot of these people have had their lives totally fucked up by Vincent and his buddies, and they aren't getting praised for it."

I sit down beside her on the couch, and she jumps up and starts pacing the dorm using fast, tense steps.

"I have to do more." Pace pace pace turn. "I have to do . . . something." Pace pace pace turn. "I don't know what to do, but I have to do more."

This doesn't seem like progress. I stand up and intercept her.

"If you want to do more, we can figure out a way to make that happen." Her eyes are pleading, and my gut responds with a pang of desperation. I want to do something to make this better for her, but what can I do? Aside from asking my friends to help out, which I've already done. "I promise, we'll figure something out."

I'm probably not thinking clearly. It's definitely not the best idea I've ever had. I slide my hands to rest at her hips. She would tell me if she wanted me to stop, right? She doesn't say anything, so I pull her closer and wrap my arms around her waist. "We'll figure something out later," I promise, then slant my lips over hers for a kiss.

It's sweet and tender. Everything that we didn't have when we were at the cabin and she was in heat and we were both desperate. This kiss is different. It's everything I need. Like water or air or food. Kisses like this rocket to the top of my list of things necessary for survival.

"Is this okay?" I murmur against her lips, terrified that she might say no and push me away.

She nods, so I keep kissing her.

The taste of her mouth when she's angry and worried—or whatever this emotion is—is completely different from what I've imagined. It's completely different from the taste of her pussy through her underwear when she's in heat and panting in desperation to get off, that's for sure. But it's also different from what I imagined it would be like to kiss her this way, without the desperation and excuses in the way.

A very pathetic moan escapes me, and I can't help but tighten my hold on her and deepen our kiss.

Without warning, Gloria pulls away from me. "What are we doing?"

"We're kissing." I think over the past few moments, trying to figure out what she has a problem with so I can fix it. "Is it bad? Do you want me to do something different? I can try—"

"No, it's not bad," Gloria cuts me off before I can completely spiral out of control. "It's really not bad. It's just . . . not in my plan."

"Plan?"

"Yeah. My plan. To be somebody and do something with my life."

"So . . . kissing me goes against the plan?"

She takes a shaky breath. "Kissing you goes so far against the plan that I don't really remember what the plan is."

"Oh." I force myself to loosen my arms from around her waist. "I just thought . . . I mean, you just seemed . . ." There's no possible good way for me to finish those statements, so I just trail off and let them hang awkwardly in the air.

Gloria huffs out a breath of air that sends her bangs flying away from her face, and I wonder all sorts of things that I shouldn't. When was the last time she got her haircut, and would she possibly consider letting me cut her hair, mostly for the purpose of being there for moral support, but also because I think I might actually be dying with the need to wrap my fingers around the silky, brown curls.

"I know." She pats my shoulder in a painfully friend-like way. "Jimmy, if my life was different, or if my goals were different, maybe I could let myself get caught up in whatever these feelings are. If I was a different person, it wouldn't bother me to do the college werewolf cliché and get pregnant before winter break and drop out before summer break and spend the rest of my life raising babies."

"Wait a second." I hold up my hands to stop the high-speed train of her words coming straight at me. "I don't want you to get pregnant and drop out and all of that stuff either. I never said I wanted that, did I?"

She rolls her eyes and gives a frustrated sigh. "You don't have to want that. It's just what happens. And when it happens to guys, they shrug and say it's meant to be and go on living their best lives. If it happens to me, it will be the end of every one of my dreams. Please, don't make me explain this any more. If you don't get it, you're not going to get it."

I risk coming close enough to touch her but think better

of actually closing the distance between us. "You don't have to explain it to me. I know there are plenty of things that I need help understanding, but this isn't one of them. You say getting pregnant would end your dreams, so we'll make sure you don't get pregnant. I can be careful. Wasn't I careful enough at the cabin? We won't do anything risky. Just, don't just shut me out because you think you can't trust me. Please, Gloria. Let me try to prove that you can trust me."

Her shoulders lower. I'm not sure if it's defeat or agreement, but I take a risk and slide my hand into hers.

"Just let me know if you want me to stop, okay? Anytime. Whatever we're doing. I'll stop if you say stop."

She twines her fingers with mine, and my heart soars up somewhere above the moon.

"Even if that means we never actually have sex?" she asks.

"I'm pretty happy with what we already did. I don't need any more than that," I assure her and am a tiny bit surprised to realize that I mean it completely. If the most I ever get from her is getting to eat her out while I come in my pants, I think I might still die happy.

Gloria rolls her eyes again, but this time, a smile tries to twitch on the corner of her lips.

"I mean it, Jimmy. This is a nonnegotiable for me. If it's going to be too hard for you to only have part of me and know that you don't fit into my life long term, we should quit while we're ahead."

What she doesn't understand is it was too late for me to quit while I was ahead the first time I saw her.

"I just want to enjoy whatever you're willing to give me."

"Well." The twitchy not-quite-a-smile at the corner of her lips bursts out for real. "There was this thing you did with your tongue that I wouldn't mind trying again now that I'm not too desperate to think straight."

I respond immediately, sliding my hands back to their

home on her hips and walking her toward my bedroom door, kissing her all the way there. A soft, rumbling growl fills the room, and it occurs to me in a distant kind of way that the sound is coming from me.

Everything we did at the cabin was desperation and necessity. This, right here, right now? I want it to be completely different. I want her to want this because she wants it, not because her body demands it.

My own body is feeling pretty damn demanding right now, though.

I kiss my way down her neck as I walk her to my bed, savoring every taste I can get of her skin. I lay her down as gently as I can without letting up on my exploration. I add a few little nips against her neck, her earlobe, the slope of her shoulder and am rewarded by a small gasp from her each time. I store the memory of every single response, filed carefully away to be reexamined and enjoyed later.

"Jimmy, what are you doing to me?"

The breathlessness of her voice brings a whole new level of hardness to my erection.

"I'm trying to make this good for you," I tell her. It should be obvious to anyone here, but she did ask, so I tell her the whole truth. "I'm trying to make you want me."

Gloria's fingers tangle in my hair and suddenly pull me back and away from a particularly tasty part of her neck. Her eyes hold a weight that I don't think I've seen in them before. "Jimmy, the problem was never that I didn't want you."

"But what can it be if it isn't that?" I'm no expert, but it kind of seems like everything she's agreed to do with me has been against her wishes. I want her to want me above anything else.

"The problem is that I do want you, but there are other things I want too. The problem is that, even though I want you, I know I can't have you and still have those other things."

I give up on making sense of that and go back to her neck. "Can I take your shirt off?"

Gloria sighs but pulls her shirt over her head without argument. I forget how to speak when I'm greeted with the glorious sight of her breasts in a bra with some kind of cheerful print all over it. I look closer and realize I'm looking at smiling cartoon faces on various types of sushi. It surprises a laugh out of me.

"What's so funny?" Gloria asks.

I respond by burying my face between her boobs and squeezing those adorable sushi bra cups together against my face. A groan of pleasure escapes me. Just barely, I manage to keep from confessing my undying love for her right then and instead lay her down on her back so I can really get to work.

Before, that night at the first party, I barely caught a glimpse of her naked body. She was so quick to shift and run away from me. Later, up at the cabin, we did everything through layers of clothing—which definitely had its own type or sexiness to it—but this is different.

When I unhook her bra and drag the straps down from her shoulders to reveal her body slowly to me, my breath catches in my throat.

"This is the most beautiful thing I've seen in my life," I confess, barely above a whisper. "I want to see this every day for the rest of my life." So much for not confessing my feelings for her right now. Fortunately, she giggles instead of running away screaming.

Emboldened by that giggle, I lean down over her and take her left nipple all the way into my mouth. Her boobs are large and round, with equally large, round areolae surrounding each nipple. I take one, then the other, between my lips, sliding my tongue along the edge, trying to determine if there's a difference in taste or texture or if it's just the color that changes. The nipple itself rolls delightfully against my tongue, a hard, fat bead representing her arousal.

Her needy groan matches my own, shooting straight down to my cock, which was already straining against my fly. I let her hips cradle mine and allow myself to enjoy the heat and pressure of her body against my erection.

She isn't comfortable having sex? That's just fine by me, as long as I can have this with her. I rock my hips toward her.

"Jimmy, fuck!" She gasps. "Do that again?"

I find a rhythm that has her panting and gasping and groaning out curses at me, and I need to make her come fast because I'm about to go over the edge, and I don't think I can keep this up after I come. Keeping my rhythmic hip thrusts isn't easy as I bend to capture her nipple in my mouth again. With each swirl of my tongue, Gloria's voice rises in pitch until she finally squeaks, "I'm . . . fuck, Jimmy, I'm coming," and shudders beneath me. I don't even have time to say anything before my own orgasm hits, pulsing stream after stream of come into my briefs so I'm sure she can feel that wetness through her own clothes. I collapse on top of her, barely managing to hold myself up enough so I don't crush her to death, but I'm not ready to roll off her and lose our physical connection yet.

* * *

GLORIA

My mind is reeling. First, just from the shock of how fucking good that felt. I mean, Jimmy got me off—and not while I was out of my mind, desperate from heat—without even unbuttoning my pants.

How?

Second, from the realization that he seems to have enjoyed himself too. Or else he's a damn good actor, still holding me tightly and panting like he just sprinted ten miles. All evidence points to the conclusion that he came too. Again, without even unbuttoning my pants. And he's the first guy I've been with who didn't at least try to get inside me after I said no.

No arguments about how he would use a condom, or how he's actually an expert at pulling out in time, or how if I actually liked him, I'd trust him enough to let him come inside me. And, maybe most important of all, not a single word about how the universe obviously wants us to reproduce, so we should let it happen.

Shit. I really could fall in love with a guy like this. I had hoped that this was just lust that would pass as soon as my heat was over, but I have most definitely developed some feelings for Jimmy.

But that doesn't change my plans. It can't change my plans. Because even if I do fall head over heels in love with him, I'm not going to allow myself to fall into that "mated" lifestyle, move back to the farm, and raise his babies for the rest of my life.

And it looks like I am going to do that first thing, so I need to figure out what to do to prevent the other thing.

"What are you thinking?" he asks, lifting his head just enough to look me in the eye. "I can hear your brain whirring from here."

"I'm thinking . . ." I search for a plausible—and safe—lie

to tell but come up empty. "I'm thinking that I appreciate you respecting my boundaries."

His face lights with a huge grin. It's like the sun coming out and warming me through to my core. "Glad I could help."

I wrap my legs around him and slide my hands up his back, exploring his muscles and pulling him close simultaneously. I need to let him know how much it means, but I don't want to burst the little bubble of pleasure we're currently floating in.

"I mean it, Jimmy. It's hard to find a guy who doesn't push."

Jimmy bends to give me a gentle kiss, just barely tasting me, nibbling at my lower lip, sharing a breath between us. "I just want to make you happy. Whatever that takes."

That's when we hear the sounds of a suite full of roommates all getting home at the same time.

Jimmy drops his forehead to mine and groans, not in the sexy way he groaned when he was sucking on my nipple. "I don't want to leave this room," he whispers.

"But we have to," I remind him. "We have news to share, remember?"

"Right. News." He inhales slowly, then heaves himself up. "Here." He hands me my shirt and bra. "You get changed first, and I'll be . . . um . . . right behind you."

"After you've changed pants?" I can't help but tease. The thought of him coming just from rubbing his erection against me actually has me more turned on than I ever could have guessed.

Jimmy turns a bright pink. "Yes, right after I change my pants. Now, will you put your shirt on before I realize that I can't let you leave this room after all?"

I grin and get dressed, then saunter out of the room, enjoying the heat of his gaze on my ass as I walk.

I'm greeted by five pairs of raised eyebrows. Well, if they

didn't know about Jimmy and me hooking up before, they definitely know now.

"I was just . . . um . . ."

"Relieving some tension?" Bee asks brightly.

"Blowing off steam?" Devon grins with a very wolfish look for a vampire.

"Oh, I know! Team building," Jeff says ever so helpfully, then taps his nose knowingly.

I can feel blood rushing into my cheeks and can't think of a damn thing to say in response. I have to accept it. I've been made, and in a lifetime of embarrassing moments, this one might just be the worst.

"Speaking of teamwork." Jimmy's voice from the doorway makes me jump. God, I hope he has a distraction for everyone so I can escape this humiliating conversation. "Gloria brought us another one!" He pulls the crumpled-up sticky note the girl gave us earlier from his pocket as if it had been there all along, not recently switched over from a completely different pair of pants just moments ago.

"Another one?" Gabe asks, looking confused. "Another what? And what does it have to do with teamwork?"

Bee saves me from having to explain by snatching the paper from Jimmy's hand and laying it flat on the table for all to see. "Is this another Vincent victim?" she asks.

"Yeah," Jimmy says. "She told us that she had to drop out for a while because of what he did to her."

I'm grateful to be out of the other conversation, but this one is way worse. We all stare soberly at the name and number on the sticky note.

"I think we should go live with this tonight," Gabe says, "if you're ready, that is," he adds, looking at me.

"Yeah. I think I'm as ready as I'll ever get, and the longer we wait, the more opportunity he has to keep doing this to more people. Let's get it done."

Gabe and Jeff take the sticky note into Jeff's room, presumably to see if they can get more information before going live with the site. Marcus disappears into his room, and Devon slumps down on the couch.

Bee slides an arm around my waist. "We're here for you. You know that, right?"

"Yeah, I know that." I allow myself to lean into her, enjoying the different type of comfort from Jimmy that she offers.

"And I'll be sleeping out here from now on," she adds cheerfully. "There is no way I'm sleeping in a bed you just had sex in."

Good thing I'm not drinking anything because I would have absolutely just done a cartoony spit-take at that. Jimmy and Devon both dissolve in laughter.

Traitors.

Chapter Twenty-One

GLORIA

I wear my most comfy, unsexy pajamas possible to bed. Yes, evidence points to Jimmy being attracted to me—for whatever reasons—regardless of clothing or situation or my own perception of my desirability. That doesn't mean I need to tempt him any more than necessary, though.

I'm already snuggled deep into the covers by the time he slips into the room. I insisted he give me plenty of time to get dressed before coming in here. We're in a new phase of our . . . relationship? . . . but that doesn't mean I'm ready to be naked in front of him or planning on actually having sex tonight. Nope. Our friends have insisted we start sharing a bed, but they don't have to know what we do or don't get up to in it. And we are not getting up to anything else.

I planned it out so I wouldn't have to get undressed with Jimmy watching, but now I realize that I didn't make any plans to keep Jimmy from getting undressed in front of me.

He turns to face me with a smile and slowly tugs his T-shirt over his head. Damn, he's earned the right to show off his body a little.

"In case you were worried about it, I don't mind if you watch," he says with a wink and a grin.

I bury my face in the pillow. "That's okay. I didn't let you watch me, so it's only fair if I don't watch you."

"But what if I want you to watch me?"

My head pops up. "What? Nobody wants to be watched."

"What makes you think that?" He pops the top button of his fly open. "I would love to be watched, especially if it's you who's watching."

Well, he's in luck because I can't look away now that my eyes have locked on him. "But . . . why?"

The question encompasses so many other questions. *Why me?* probably being first on the list, followed by, *What could you possibly be getting out of this?* and *Don't you know that I'm just a clueless, awkward mess of a person who isn't worth your time?* But they all stall out in my mind when Jimmy unzips his pants and peels them down his legs, leaving grey boxer briefs with a little dot of liquid where his half-hard dick is rubbing on them.

"Is this okay?" I hear him ask from a distance.

What kind of question is that, anyway? I throw out all of my plans to keep things platonic for tonight. I toss off the covers and climb to the foot of the bed. I don't want to ruin this moment with any of the confused words currently warring in my head to get out, so I don't say anything at all.

Jimmy lets out a needy gasp when I tug him toward me with the waistband of his underwear. Very satisfying that I can have that kind of effect on him.

"Gloria, what are you—" He stops abruptly when I tug his cock out of his briefs and settle it between my lips.

I relish the sound he makes, desperate and filled with pleasure all at once. I relish his sounds, and the weight of his fast-stiffening cock against my tongue, and the flavor of his skin in my mouth, smooth with the slight tang of sweat but still clean from his shower earlier.

Wanting to experiment, I slide the tip of my tongue in a circle around the end of his foreskin, and Jimmy rewards me with a whimper and tangles his fingers in my hair.

"You don't have to," he starts and breaks off as I take him in hand and slide my fist all the way up and down his length, swirling my tongue harder this time just around the tip.

It doesn't take long for me to get more into the act, seeing how much of him I can swallow down, experimenting with the foreskin, which is still supple and stretchy, even now that it's being stretched over an impressive erection.

I can't get enough of him. I want to savor every drop of fluid that drips from him, memorize every bump and vein pulsing in his shaft, see how long he can last and how many times I can make him come.

"Gloria, if you keep doing that—"

"What?" I try to sound innocent but am pretty sure I come off as extremely naughty.

"God. Fuck. You're going to make me come."

"Oh?"

"Is that . . . fuck. Is it okay? If I come?"

I smile at him, then slide my mouth as far down his cock as I can without gagging, making up the difference with my hand.

"Fuuuuuuck," he moans. "Gloria, we have to stop if you don't want me to come."

"I never said I don't want you to come," I tell him. "You can't come yet, though."

Another whimper from him. I feel like the most powerful woman in the world.

"Can you multitask?" I ask.

Jimmy nods. "Whatever you want, I'll do my best."

I scoot to the center of the bed. "Come up here, then. You aren't allowed to come until I do." Maybe I'm power tripping, but Jimmy's eyes light up at my order, so I guess he doesn't mind.

"How do you want me to make you come?"

I slide my pajama pants off, then lie back. "With your mouth."

Jimmy practically dives to reach my pussy, but I snatch a handful of his hair and hold him back.

"I told you you had to multitask, didn't I?"

He looks confused for a moment, and then it clicks, and his face lights up again. This time, he straddles my face before leaning forward and giving my pussy one long, slow lick.

I answer with my own lick along his shaft. His hips jerk, but he keeps his focus on eating me out. And he does that spectacularly. Each flick of his tongue sends a sizzling bolt of pleasure straight through me. He alternates between long strokes and lightning-fast flicks, and every single one brings me closer to the edge.

Not wanting to be selfish, I redouble my efforts, grabbing onto his hips and tugging them toward me. He takes the hint and starts thrusting into my mouth. I moan around him, and he groans against me, and it only takes a few moments before I'm bucking and writhing and coming beneath his tongue. Jimmy tries to back away from me, but I dig my fingers into his hips and swallow him down as deep as I can. I don't want to stop to say anything. I hope he gets the message. This is something I want to do. This is a small thing I can give him after he's given me more than I could have asked for.

"Gloria, you're going to make me—"

I make a grunting noise around his cock, which is completely filling my mouth, and hope he understands that I mean it as consent.

"God, I have to—" Jimmy tries to pull away again, but I

hold his hips in place as he comes, swallowing reflexively as his come shoots across my tongue and down my throat.

Only after he's finished coming do I let him roll away from me.

He's panting, his curly hair plastered to his forehead. He reaches out blindly and grasps my hand, hanging on like it's the only life raft in sight in the whole ocean.

"That was . . . incredible . . ." he gasps.

I'm too wrung out from my own orgasm to respond with words, so I just smile at him and squeeze his hand. Maybe later, we'll both be able to think clearly enough to set up some rules and boundaries for this thing between us. Right now, though, I just need sleep.

JIMMY

I put some clothes on, even though I'd much rather sleep skin to skin with Gloria, because I know she'll be more comfortable that way.

Someday, I promise myself. Someday, she'll trust me, and I won't even have to make promises first. She'll just trust me because I've proven myself enough times. Someday, she'll slip into bed with me without hesitating about which side to take, and it will feel as natural to her as it already feels for me. I hang on to that someday with everything I've got. Because if I don't have someday, I don't have a damn thing.

She turns on her side and curls up as far from me as possible on the edge of the mattress.

I should leave her alone. Let her sleep how she wants and remind myself that someday it will be different.

I turn over and lie with my back to her.

Nope. Not going to work. I feel sick to my stomach being in the same bed as her and so far away.

I turn onto my stomach and try to get comfortable.

No dice. I swear, every nerve ending that isn't connected to her—all of them, at the moment—is burning like I've been dunked in acid.

I flop over to my back and stare at the ceiling. Willing my eyes to close. Willing my thoughts to stop racing. If I tell myself to close my eyes and go to sleep enough times, it will happen eventually. Right?

"Jimmy, what are you doing?" she grumbles, exasperated.

"Sorry. Can't get comfortable."

"Would it help if I go out to the other room?"

I'm turned over, across the bed, and cradling her to me faster than I realize what I'm doing. "Please don't?" I beg once my brain catches up to events.

"Okay, but I can't really breathe," she says from underneath my shoulder.

I draw back a couple of inches. "Shit. Sorry."

"I take it the problem isn't that I'm taking up too much room on the bed?"

"No," I assure her. "That is definitely not the problem. In fact—" I feel suddenly shy but remind myself that the worst thing that she can do to me is say no. And that will feel exactly like dying, but it won't actually kill me. "—do you think it would be okay if I hold you?"

She raises a surprised eyebrow. "You want to snuggle?"

"God, yes. I want that so bad."

With a chuckle, she turns her back to me again.

"Well?" she asks over her shoulder. "Are we doing this or not?"

I slide my left arm under her pillow and wrap my right arm around her, pulling her tight to me. "We are definitely doing this."

Let's never stop doing this, I want to say. *Let me hold you forever, just exactly like this*, I add in my mind but not out loud. Who was the person who didn't believe in mates and thought he could play it cool and maybe have some fun with this girl? He's long gone. Totally forgotten. I will do anything for Gloria, if she'll just let us stay like this forever.

With that thought, with Gloria tucked snugly into the curve of my body, I can finally slow my thoughts enough to fall asleep.

*　*　*

"Are you ready for this?" Devon asks Gloria over a mug of coffee the next morning.

Judging by the antsy tapping of her toe on the floor, I'm guessing she's the furthest thing possible from ready. Ready or not, the site went live at midnight, so we're about to find out if there's going to be any fallout.

Devon is officially on Bee guard duty today, and neither has had to leave the suite yet. Marcus, Gabe, and Jeff are all already set to keep an eye on the other girls who came forward with their stories. We haven't gotten any updates from them yet, which I think is a good sign, but Gloria and Bee have both reminded me several times now that we might not see any carnage right away.

I put my hand on Gloria's knee to calm its jittering, even if I can't calm her at all. "I'll be right there with you. Whatever happens today. You're not facing it alone."

She takes a huge breath and lets it out so slowly I think I can see each particle—molecule? Good thing I'm not actually a science major—as it leaves her body.

"I wish I wasn't facing it at all. I wish none of us were facing this. I want to go back to a few weeks ago when my biggest worry involved which frat boy to try and date."

"Yeah, but"—I nudge her playfully, not at all desperate for acknowledgment—"it's brought us together, right? Silver linings? Or something like that?"

The look Gloria, Bee, and Devon shoot at me withers my soul.

"Sorry. I guess we aren't doing silver linings with this."

Bee rolls her eyes. "Only you would be able to find a positive side to a serial rapist attacking your friends and classmates."

Oof. I really hadn't thought of it like that. "Okay. I can see you're right. But just so you know, that isn't how I was thinking of it at all."

Gloria relents and puts a hand over the one I have resting on her knee. "You know what? It's hard enough to find positives in the world right now, so I'm going to take them wherever I can find them. And try really hard not to feel guilty about it."

"And now that you've both made me want to puke, I'd better get to class." Bee stands up and grabs her backpack. "Here's hoping I can get through today without attracting any notice."

Devon smiles and swings the strap of his laptop bag over his shoulder. "But if you do attract any notice, you've got a scary vampire to back you up."

"I feel better already," Bee says, linking her arm through his and leading them out into the very real and very dangerous world.

Chapter Twenty-Two

JIMMY

It takes all of five minutes to confirm that, yes, there is fallout. Already.

I'm walking with my arm around Gloria's waist and reveling in the feel of her curves under my hand, wondering how long she'll let me get away with it before she gets prickly about being touched or about being seen with me.

And then someone barks. I turn my head, automatically trying to pinpoint the source of the weird sound. Gloria tenses, and I turn back to look at her. Her eyes stare straight ahead, and a muscle in her jaw pumps out and in as she clenches her teeth.

Another bark comes from the other side, followed by a cruel-sounding snicker.

"Are they—?" I start to ask but think better of it when I see her eyes widen a little, and her jaw clenches again.

"Don't react," she mutters, lips barely moving.

I've never been in a situation like this. I don't even know what this situation is. But I trust Gloria, so I stare straight ahead and press my palm into her hip to remind her I'm there with her. She isn't alone.

Unfortunately, we're not alone together. Barking and howling and mocking laughter follow us all the way to class. Maybe the worst part is I can't figure out what their deal is. I was prepared for a gang of vampires to corner us on a narrow walkway, maybe, but this? I have no idea what to do about this.

I slide into one of the uncomfortable lecture hall seats with a sigh of relief. Maybe for the first time ever, I'm grateful class is about to start. No one can bark or howl or whatever it is they're doing while the professor is speaking.

But they can, apparently, hide a "bitch" behind a fake cough.

After the third one—and they're getting worse with each one, I'm sure of it now—I slip my hand onto Gloria's knee and give what I hope is a reassuring squeeze.

"You want to get out of here?"

She glares her disgust at that suggestion.

"I will not give anyone the satisfaction of running away from this. Besides, it's only going to get worse if I don't face it."

I give a tiny nod and hope no one else can see it. With my hand over her knee, I squeeze again, then lean my body against hers to act as much like a shield as possible.

GLORIA

The tension in my fingers and around my heart and in every random place you would never expect any tension eases slightly as Jimmy presses against me. But as awful as it is to have people bark at me and call me a bitch in the middle of class, I know I'm in a better position than the other girls who came forward. Sure, Devon and Marcus and the rest of the roommates are keeping an eye out to make sure they're safe, but I'm the only one who knows with absolute certainty that someone is right there, doing whatever he can to protect me.

I press my hand down on top of the hand he has pressed over my knee and squeeze. It helps to ground me. Gives me perspective about how important it was for me—the person with some kind of protection—to come forward when I know others weren't in a position to do it safely.

Even knowing that, class takes an entire eternity with another half eternity on top, and my stomach is in knots by the time we stand up to leave.

"Watch out, bitch," someone sneers at me as they bump into me on our way toward the door.

"Better watch your back," someone else growls as they bump me in the other direction.

Jimmy looks like he's about to go after one or both of the assholes, but I grab onto his arm and hold him back. I wish I could say it's from some altruistic desire to keep Jimmy from getting hurt, but it has a lot more to do with the fact that there are more assholes, and if he leaves me alone, the assholes might be brave enough to do something more than bump into me and say nasty things.

"Just keep walking," I mutter to him under my breath and do exactly that. I swear I hear his teeth grind together. I want to tell him how much it means to me to have someone looking out for me, but now is not the time or place for it. Especially when a third asshole bumps into me hard enough to knock my backpack to the floor.

I give myself five seconds. Five seconds to feel all of the rage and fear that's trying to overtake me. Five seconds to recognize the adrenaline rocketing through my body that makes it impossible to think clearly. Five seconds to drag Jimmy down to the ground with me to help repack my backpack and be on our way again. In those five seconds, I'm kicked once, my backpack is stepped on, and no less than three people mutter something about bitches going to college.

But Jimmy helps gather the scattered papers from my backpack and hands them back to me without a hint of recognition of what's really happening.

I really worry about what the other girls are going through, considering how bold these assholes are when Jimmy and I are here together, watching each other's backs.

* * *

The suite is full of people when we get back. Taylor is standing at the tiny counter, tapping intently at his laptop keys while Jeff hands out mugs of tea and cans of beer to the visitors in the room. Marcus is leaning up against a wall with a scowl on his face, honestly looking like some kind of grumpy vampiric cliché. Devon is on the couch, patting the shoulder of a girl with red-rimmed eyes and occasionally handing her fresh tissues. Bee has her arms around the girl I recognize from the other day when she gave me her information.

My stomach drops straight to the floor. These are the other girls who agreed to come forward, and they obviously haven't come away unscathed. Guilt twists up all of my insides.

"Shit" is the very clever and articulate thing I manage to say. "What's been happening?"

Devon hands another tissue to the crying girl. "Lydia has been followed by shitheads all day. We finally gave up after her chem class was completely ruined. No one was learning anything in that class today."

"I knew someone would figure out who the stories were from," Taylor mutters, still typing frantically. "I never imagined how quickly they would get organized, though. And, like, really organized. I'm trying to figure out if there are any victims who didn't come forward that have been dealing with this shit today. I still think strength in numbers is our best bet."

"Shit," I say again. I can't seem to come up with anything better.

Jimmy slips his hand into mine and squeezes. And I let him, and I let myself appreciate the comfort he's offering. "I'm so sorry I got you guys into this."

"No way," the girl I remember from before says, eyes flashing in anger. "You don't apologize. Vincent needs to apologize. All of his psycho sycophants need to apologize. No one in this room right now has a reason to apologize."

"I one hundred percent agree," Bee says, standing up and facing me. "You did the right thing by coming forward. You all did the right thing. It's that piss-poor excuse for a vampire who is wrong, and I really don't like seeing anyone else taking responsibility for his bullshit."

I stride across the room and wrap her in my biggest hug—not too difficult, considering she's tiny and waiflike while I'm a big, hulking wolf who happens to be dressed as a human right now.

"I am so grateful you're here," I murmur into the space above her head. "Like, you have no idea how glad I am to have you as a roommate."

I hear her mumble something but can't understand. Pulling away, I realize I've got her squeezed so tight to my chest that there's no possible way she's able to breathe right now.

"Oops, sorry about that." I step back and let her go.

Bee pats my shoulder, coming across as way less comforting than she did with the other girl. Oh well.

"Shit!" Taylor shouts from his position at the computer, then, "Fucking son of a bitch!"

We all turn to him with questioning gazes, but he's completely absorbed in whatever he's dealing with on his computer.

"Um . . . something we should know about?" Jeff asks.

Taylor looks up and blinks around at us like he has no idea where we all came from. "There have been some responses online," he explains.

My stomach, already tied in knots, gives a new twist inside of me. "I take it, not a great response?"

Taylor wobbles his hand in a flip-flopping motion. "Some of it has been the best we could hope for, which is more people coming forward with their stories about Vincent and some of his friends. Obviously, I wish there weren't any more victims, but since we were pretty sure already that there were more, the best thing for our cause is for people to keep sharing their experiences until no one can argue this guy's innocence, right?"

"But . . ." I prompt.

"But some of the responses have been exactly what we were worried about. People defending Vincent and claiming all of these stories are lies told by liars who . . . I don't even know, are trying to get attention? And people threatening legal action, which we expected at some point, but again, not necessarily the same day we went live. But the worst thing . . ." He looks at the floor and runs a worried hand through his hair. "The worst thing is that someone has identified and named every single person who's shared their story. And not just names." He looks around at each of us. "They've shared personal information for everyone. Dorm numbers. Phone numbers. Classes. We're going to have to find these other girls and try to protect them somehow. I don't think any of you can safely go back to class for the time being."

I sink down on the couch, feeling utterly defeated. "This is so fucked-up." I fight back the tears that are welling under my eyelids. Crying won't help anything, and I'm probably the least affected by this situation. How can I justify crying about it when I'm safe here and other people are actively in danger right now?

Marcus straightens suddenly. "We need to track down these other girls right now and bring them back here. Or someplace safe if there are too many to fit in this dorm. But I don't imagine any of them are going to be willing to go with me just based only on my assurance that I want to help them. We probably need at least one of the girls to come along."

I nod. "I agree. And considering I wouldn't trust a guy I don't know coming up to talk to me right now, I think you're right that we need at least one girl to go. I can do it." I feel better already now that a plan is starting to come together.

"No way am I letting you go alone," Jimmy jumps in.

"And too many guys will just seem threatening," Bee argues. "If two guys are going, you need at least two girls. I'll come along too."

JIMMY

I'm grateful for any time I get to spend with Gloria, don't get me wrong. But spending time with Gloria when I'm worried about protecting her from crazy assholes, and also trying to protect Bee from crazy assholes, and trying to find other girls who are also in danger from crazy assholes, is probably my least favorite way to spend time with Gloria. The way we spent time together last night . . . well, I'll be happy every minute I can spend like that with her. Right now, duty calls, though.

Bee breaks into my thoughts. "Poor Kelsey. I think she's taking it the worst in a way because she knew some of what to expect ahead of time."

"Who's Kelsey?" I try to catch up with the conversation that seems to have been going on around me while I was obliviously walking along and daydreaming about Gloria.

"The girl who gave you a sticky note with her information just the other day?" Bee rolls her eyes at me. "The girl who was sitting on your couch crying just a few minutes ago? How do you not know this."

I hunch my shoulders. "I don't know. I didn't get a chance to ask her name before." Jeez. Sisters.

"Anyway," Bee goes on, "her life was basically destroyed by this shit the first time around. She had to drop out of school for a while, then when she comes back, she does the right thing by coming forward, and now she has to deal with this all over again. I feel so bad for her."

I squeeze Gloria's hand, wanting to comfort myself as much as her. I hope her life isn't ruined by this. Whatever happens, I promise myself that I'll get her through it. That thought sparks something in my mind.

"How many people are we trying to find today? How likely is it that we run out of room in our dorm?"

Marcus, who has been broody as fuck throughout this

whole thing, grunts. "If we're able to convince everyone to come with us, we're going to run out of room tonight. Vincent has been at this for three years now, and it seems like this is a regular . . . activity for him."

I shiver at the thought of three years' worth of victims of the same twisted shithead.

"I'm actually more worried about people refusing our help than anything else," Gloria says. "We can squeeze people together in that dorm, have some share beds and others sleep on the floor." She looks at me. "Wolves can bed down together on the floor easily. But how are we going to convince people that we're actually here to help? If they've been dealing with the same shit as me, they're not going to be very trusting."

"The fact that you've been named on the site will help us out, at least," Bee points out.

Ice-cold, acidy fear slices through my stomach thinking about that. I've been trying not to think about it. I squeeze her hand for comfort again.

"Yeah," Gloria agrees. "I'm a lot more likely to trust someone that I know has been through the same thing."

Marcus gives another sour grunt. "We need to prepare ourselves. I think there will be someone we can't help. I don't want any of us getting our hopes up that we can save everyone."

"Well, aren't you just Mr. Positive," I joke, but the pit in my stomach tells me he's right, and I'm absolutely terrified of what we're walking toward.

* * *

We find Selena—the first name on our list of people who came forward after the site went live—in her dorm. And she's just as trusting as Gloria thought she would be.

"Go the fuck away!" she shouts through her door without

even opening it to check who's knocking. "I'm not coming out unless you burn this fucking building down, so go ahead and get on that."

"You don't have to come out," Gloria says, lips practically pressed against the door. "Just hear me out, okay?"

A huffed "whatever" comes through the door, and Gloria takes that as a signal to start talking.

"My name is Gloria. I'm one of the people who shared her story. Listen, I know it took guts to add your story to the site, and I'm sure you're questioning that decision now, based on the fact that you're under siege in your dorm room, but I want to help you. I want to make sure it was worth it for all of us to come forward so that he doesn't do this shit again and also maybe so I can feel like I got my revenge or something. I've got a lot of emotions going on right now, in case you hadn't guessed."

"And I'm just supposed to take your word that you're on my side?"

Gloria sighs and lets herself slump against the door.

"You're not 'supposed' to do anything. If you can't trust me, I get it. I'm honestly not sure if I would trust me either if our places were switched, but you can look me up. I'm named as one of the girls who shared our story on the site originally. I've been putting up with all sorts of name-calling and bullying and bullshit all day, and I want to help you if you're in the same boat. But I can also understand if you can't trust me."

Gloria stumbles forward a step when the door she's leaning on opens unexpectedly.

A girl in all-black clothes and pitch-black makeup around her eyes blinks out at us. "Okay, Gloria. Say I do agree to try trusting you. What do we do then?"

"First, we find the other girls who came forward today. I don't think any of us are safe on our own. Second, we stay together tonight. Again, safety in numbers. Third, we work together to come up with a game plan to get everyone through tomorrow. Fourth, we keep figuring out each day as it comes."

The girl nods thoughtfully, then sticks out her hand. "I'm Selena, and if you had tried to bullshit me about having a big plan to fix all of this, I wouldn't have trusted you, but you seem just as lost as me right now."

"It's a pleasure to meet you, Selena," Gloria says, "though it really sucks that it's under these circumstances. Are you ready to go looking for some others like us?"

"Lead the way," Selena says, and then we're off to the next dorm.

Chapter Twenty-Three

GLORIA

Ten is how many people were on our list from the start. Girls that either came forward as Vincent's victims on the website or got named or outed by someone else. Three is how many we couldn't find at all, and I fully expect to stay awake all night worrying about where they might be. Two is the number of girls we couldn't convince to come with us. Yes, I'll be awake all night worrying about them too.

Which leaves us with five. Five girls to protect as well as we can. Five girls to try and find enough bedding and space for in a four-bedroom suite with shared bathroom and kitchenette. Oh yeah, along with four original roommates, plus Bee and me, plus the victims who came forward originally. And Gabe and Taylor because—as they keep reminding people on repeat —they're the ones putting out fires online, and it doesn't make sense to do that away from the people who are actually affected.

"All I was trying to say," Jeff shouts over the noise of the small army that is currently stuffed in the living room, "is that it makes sense for the girls to share a bed with each other."

I have to admit, he has a point. The beds in the suite are just large enough for two people to sleep very uncomfortably. You can fit two people in them, which I find amusing. Like the original designers knew that people would be trying to fuck in these beds, and they accepted this fact, but they still had to make it as uncomfortable as possible.

"All I was trying to say," Devon shouts back, "is that we should find an equitable way to share the blankets so that people sleeping on the floor don't get cold!"

"Do vampires even get cold? I thought you were room temperature to begin with!" Jeff is still shouting, even though everyone has quieted around their argument.

Devon's nostrils flare in anger. "Don't. Talk. About. Shit. You. Don't. Under. Stand." He punctuates every word by jabbing his finger into Jeff's chest.

Jeff looks like maybe he's regretting—or at least second-guessing—what he just said, and then he huffs and storms out of the dorm. Looking too angry to speak, Devon turns on his heel and storms back to his bedroom, slamming the door behind himself. Most of us swivel back and forth, staring after the two guys with "what the hell just happened?" expressions on our faces. Marcus continues his broody act in the corner before muttering something about finding more blankets and leaving the dorm without making eye contact with any of us.

Bee steps into the void left behind by the argument with her hands raised in a placating signal. "Look, I know it's been a tough day for everyone, but if we can get through tonight and hopefully get some rest, we can come up with some more long-term solutions tomorrow. In the meantime, I know it's not my place to ask this, but someone has to. Can all of the wolves agree to sleep on the floor tonight?"

Jimmy and I nod. I was already planning to, and Bee

knows it. She's smart to only ask when she already knows what the answer will be.

Selena nods her assent as well, so at least that's three people who don't need beds to sleep.

"Awesome," Bee says with a perkiness that I could never have mustered. A wave of thankfulness washes over me that she's taking charge instead of me right now. "Now, I realize it's not really polite to talk about this, but, again, someone has to." She looks around at all the girls. "Can a vampire and a human share a bed without any issues?"

"I'm fine if she is," Kelsey says defensively. "I don't bite." The statement might be sarcastic in any other circumstances, but everyone just nods their acknowledgment of the statement.

Lydia jerks her head in a nod. "I'd rather share a bed than sleep on the floor, and I'm more comfortable sharing with a girl than a boy, so the vampire thing isn't an issue for me."

The room lets out a collective sigh of relief.

"Wait. What about you?" Jimmy asks Bee, and I immediately want to kick his ankle. Everyone was just starting to calm down. Why the hell is he stirring things up again?

She shoots him a killing look, which I find completely understandable. "I haven't had to deal with my name getting dragged through the mud today. I don't need a bed as much as other people do.

"Okay," he agrees faster than I expect him to, "but you sleep in the wolf pile so we can keep you warm."

Bee raises an eyebrow like she's about to argue, then huffs out a breath and starts pulling pillows off the couch. "Fine. You know I love being the weak human who needs the strong wolves to take care of all my basic needs. Wouldn't want me to do anything independent or anything like that, now would you?" Bee keeps up a stream of murmured sarcasm as she arranges the couch cushions on the floor.

* * *

After Jeff and Marcus come back with extra bedding that they got from I have no idea where, the dorm becomes quite a cozy little nest. And I refuse to be jealous of Bee as she snuggles in with the pile of wolves denning down on the living room floor. I will not be jealous of how Jimmy's wolf tail curls protectively over her leg. I will definitely not be jealous of how her hand rests on the fur at his scruff.

Okay. I am actually completely jealous and having to fight to tamp down my rage every moment I see them touch.

God. Fucking. Damn it. Not only am I obviously developing unwanted feelings for Jimmy, but I'm also the worst possible friend and roommate in the universe.

Feeling rotten and dejected, I slink away from the cozy wolf den as soon as everyone else is asleep and curl up in the far corner alone. I want to be a good friend, and I know—at least I think I know—that it's nothing like that between Jimmy and Bee. But knowing it doesn't help me to not feel a sour pang of jealousy in my stomach when they touch casually in their sleep. I squeeze my eyes closed and try to calm my emotional turmoil enough to sleep, but it doesn't work. I'm wide-awake until sunrise.

After the worst night of sleep of my life, I'm woken up by a panicked buzz in my ears. The pile of wolves have all shifted back to their human forms and are waiting on orders. I wonder if I should shift before remembering that I don't particularly love being naked, especially not in front of people, and my dirty clothes are all wadded up in a laundry hamper.

I'm saved from decision-making by Marcus storming into the dorm. "None of her friends can or will tell me where she is," he announces to the group before anyone can ask any questions.

"But were they choosing to not tell you, or are none of them able to tell you?" asks Gabe impatiently.

Marcus shoots his best laser eyes, but Gabe stays standing.

"Don't you think I tried to figure that out? Either they truly don't know where she is, or they really don't trust me and they're good actors. Either way, the only update I can provide is that no one is willing slash able to tell me her whereabouts."

I shift back to human and try to be inconspicuous about showing my private bits while also panicking pretty hard about actual situations that matter. "Who?"

"Cassie," Marcus explains, and the name is all I need. We couldn't find her yesterday, and now it sounds like nobody can find her.

"How long have you been looking for her?" I ask, though the question that's actually trying to press its way out through my skull and eye sockets in the form of a migraine is, why the hell didn't anyone wake me up before now? Why didn't anyone wake me up as soon as they knew there was a problem?

I push my frustration and guilt aside with an angry mental shove. I can't deal with those emotions right now. "Has something changed?"

Taylor turns his laptop toward me. "I thought I would try reaching out to her again this morning since you couldn't find her last night. I thought maybe if she's not feeling too trusting of people randomly coming up and claiming they want to help, she might be more open to a message on social media. But everything from her social media has been completely wiped clean. She no longer exists anywhere on the internet, as far as I can tell, and that is not right. Everyone leaves footprints, whether it's a social-networking site, a dating profile, or the porn they watch, but I can't find a damn trace of her. And apparently, no one can find her in person either."

Gabe spares a glare toward Marcus, who meets his glare with an evil, broody glower. If someone doesn't intervene soon, we're about to have a huge mess on our hands.

"Okay." I hold up my hands in the best peacemaking gesture I can muster. "So we're missing someone, and we can't find her at her dorm, and none of her friends are willing to tell us where to look. Does that sound right?"

"Yeah, that's about it," Gabe mutters toward his shoes.

JIMMY

I am definitely, one hundred percent, no doubt about it, going to hell. Or wherever terrible wolves who can't control where they're looking when the girl they're into is naked go.

I really am trying to focus on Cassie and the fact that someone I promised to protect is missing.

But also, boobs.

Gloria's boobs.

And her ass and her stomach and the crease where her legs meet her hips.

Shit. Focus.

Cassie is missing and definitely in danger, and I am at least partly responsible.

God, Gloria looks good. And it's been hours and hours since I was able to touch her. I'm not sure why she went off to sleep in the far corner of the room, but now I am aching to touch her again.

What the hell is wrong with me? There are other things I should be focusing on.

"I need to get dressed, then we can start searching again," Gloria announces.

I try not to watch her leave. I swear, I try so hard not to stare at her ass as she walks away from us. I don't succeed.

"Dude." Jeff punches me on my shoulder. "Get a fucking grip."

"Yeah. Right. I'm focused." I try not to be too obvious as I wipe away the drool on my chin. Wow, my dad is going to be proud of me.

* * *

Armed with a picture of Cassie and a list of every possible place she might be seen on campus, Gloria, Bee, and I are off on the hunt again. We decided to split our search parties up by quadrants, with our group taking the southwestern corner of campus. Apparently, that's where some of Cassie's classes—along with the special library that only architecture students ever use—are. The fact that there are special libraries for architecture students was news to me, but I guess you learn something new every day.

Bee smacks my arm. "Are you listening?"

I guess not, or I would have realized she was talking to me.

"Um, yeah, totally. What was that last bit?"

She glares at me, then gives up and faces forward again.

"I was saying, having everyone stay in your dorm isn't really a long-term solution. We have to come up with a better plan than just 'wait for this all to blow over,' you know?"

Gloria hugs herself and shivers. I want to stop everything and wrap her in my arms again. Remind her that I'm here for her. But she keeps walking, gaze fixed in front of her like she's on a mission that can't be interrupted. I suppose she is. I try to think of ways to help other than offering her distractions.

"What about getting farther away?" I suggest. "Maybe if we can get everyone away from campus entirely, it will be easier to keep everyone safe, and we'll be able to think more clearly to plan our next steps."

"I'm not going home, if that's what you mean," Bee says.

At the same time, Gloria growls, "You want me to run away and hope my pack can help me?"

"No. I mean, that wasn't really what I was thinking. Would it really be that bad, though?"

I look from one girl to the other and see only stubborn glowers.

Bee breaks the silence first. "I came to college to get the whole college experience. No one is going to force me home before I decide it's time."

Gloria nods in agreement. "It was hard enough to

convince my parents to send me to college. If I go back now, I'll never leave home again."

"What about . . ." I hesitate, uncertain how she might take this suggestion and not ready for the rejection if she hates it. "What about the main pack? They're close to here. Your family wouldn't even necessarily know if you left school to stay on pack lands for a bit, right? And you would have the best protection available." My whole pack would be protecting her, instead of just me, but I don't say that out loud.

She gives me a sidelong look. "That's even worse. Back home, I'm stuck, but I have plenty of freedom as long as I stay there. But the main pack has all of the people in charge who could decide that I need to do something different with my life. The main pack has the pack leader, who I prefer to not have looking over my shoulder or pulling my strings."

I risk a glance at Bee, who has her eyebrow raised in a *what did you expect?* expression.

I hate that they're right, but I don't want to go back there any more than they do. I still haven't thought of an answer by the time we reach the library, where Cassie apparently works three days a week.

* * *

"I think we need to assume the worst possible scenario," Marcus says, thankfully either not noticing or choosing to ignore my behavior. "Someone might have taken Cassie in order to silence her. She might just be holed up in a friend's dorm, waiting for things to blow over, but I don't think we can count on that. So, assuming either Vincent or someone close to him took her, where would they likely take her, and how do we get her back?"

"Cassie is a vampire," Taylor reminds us, "so she wouldn't have been easy to take, especially if she had her guard up."

"But a group of vampires? Or someone with access to drugs to knock her out?" Gabe says. "She would have been a lot easier to take in either of those scenarios." He rakes his fingers through his hair with a grunt. "And we don't even know how long ago they took her."

Marcus paces the room, giving death glares to anyone who meets his eyes. "We should have tried harder to find everyone yesterday. We knew, damn it! We knew they wouldn't be safe, and now it might be too late."

Lydia grabs his arm and matches his angry gaze without blinking. "You blaming yourself and all of us isn't helping anyone right now. Cassie made the choice to come forward with her story, just like the rest of us. I knew it was going to be a risk. She would have known it too, but she still did it. All we can do now is try to track her down and help her. So stop focusing on what you wish you had done and focus on what you can do now."

Marcus's broody, angry eyes don't soften, but his shoulders do slump a little. "Right," he grunts. "Focus on what we can do now. Right now, what we can do is go to the authorities."

"What?" Gloria yelps, popping out of my room fully dressed and looking angry. "No way are there any authorities who can actually take down Vincent. What good would it do to talk to the police, who have already probably been paid off by his family to turn a blind eye? Or the school administration, who all know that his family can donate enough money to open an entire new library or take as much money away in the form of legal fees and other bullshit? No way. It won't be worth it."

Marcus turns to her with a renewed scowl. "You might find this hard to believe, but there are a lot of vampires who don't like it when other vampires make the rest of us look bad. I think if we let the highest-ranking vampires know what's going on, they would be interested in doing whatever it takes to minimize the damage Vincent has been doing."

Gloria huffs. "So, you think they'll help us just to avoid a PR headache? And you're willing to bet everything on that?"

"I think it's a risk we have to take. Do you really want to look back at all this and know that you didn't do everything possible to help someone?"

Bee jumps between them. "While I can see how you both make good points, I think Marcus might be right about this, Gloria. Whether we agree with their motivations or not, the vampires will want to minimize their exposure in all of this. Also"—she gives me an apologetic look—"I think the shifters need to know what's going on too. The Council of Wolves won't be happy if they're blindsided by this."

At that, everything in my stomach curdles in an instant. I stuff my hands in my pockets so no one can see them shaking.

Yeah, the Council won't be happy about any of this. My father is going to string me up by my tail.

Gloria looks confused. "How much do you know about the Council?" she asks Bee.

To her credit, Bee stays cool. She shrugs. "I grew up around Jimmy's pack, remember? And I've studied other races a bit. I'm hardly an expert."

That seems to calm Gloria's curiosity, though my heart is still thundering in my ears. I'm not ready for anyone—least of all Gloria—to know all of my secrets.

"Okay," Marcus says. "I'll go to the Vampiric Enclave and let them know what's been happening here. Who's going to talk to this wolf council of yours?"

I gulp. "I can talk to the Council. I . . . know someone on it." Is that enough information? Is it too much information? Gloria squints her eyes at me like she's trying to solve some puzzle, but she doesn't ask or comment, so maybe I'm safe.

"I'll keep trying to trace everyone online," Taylor volunteers, already hunched over his keyboard in the position I've become accustomed to seeing him in. "There has to be a trace of her somewhere. I just have to figure out where to look."

Jeff looks sideways at Devon. "Maybe a vampire will have some ideas of where another vampire would have taken someone to? If that vampire can think of some places to start looking, maybe that will give us something to do."

Devon crosses his arms and addresses the air beside Jeff's head. "Sure, I'll direct you to all of the sketchy vampire hide-outs where all of the sketchy vampires take their victims to feed on."

Jeff rolls his eyes. "Just a thought, man. I didn't mean to offend you."

"Maybe, just to cross them off the list, Devon can check out any places that vampires are known to gather," I break in before their argument can start again. Arguing is the last thing we need right now, and it seems like the only thing some of our group are capable of.

* * *

In spite of me begging—with my eyes, since saying out loud would raise a ton of questions—Bee to go to the meeting with me, she gives a way-too-cheerful "Sorry, bro, gotta stay here" and sends me on my way. And I still haven't gotten to touch Gloria since I woke up without her this morning. I can hardly imagine this day getting any worse, except I know for a fact it's about to get a lot worse.

The drive home is uneventful, aside from how many times I fantasize about driving myself into a ditch so I don't have to face my family.

Sure enough, their response to my arrival is exactly how I'd imagined it.

"Where's Bethany?" my mom asks less than five minutes

after my tires cross the compound gate. "Why didn't you call ahead? Is something wrong? Is she alright?"

"Mom, Bee is fine. She had other stuff to do today. And besides, can't I just surprise you sometimes by coming home without calling ahead?"

Her eyes narrow to suspicious slits. "Greyson James, what have you done?"

Shit. First and middle named and I barely walked in the house.

"I haven't done anything! Why do you have to jump to the worst possible conclusion every time?"

"Because I know my offspring, that's why. So, if you haven't done something, what's the real reason you're here?"

I deflate under her scrutiny. "I swear, I didn't do anything. But something did . . . um . . . happen."

Now, her eyes are wide with fear, and I have to rush in with reassurances.

"It's not me or Bee. We're both fine. But a . . . friend of mine . . . she kind of got on this vampire's bad side, and Bee thought I should let the Council know so they don't get, like, blindsided by it or anything like that. But we're both fine. Promise."

"Well." She takes a deep breath. "I guess we'd better gather the Council if that's what you think is best."

It's the last thing I want to do. I'd rather wipe my butt with glass shards any day instead of calling the Council. It's what I have to do, though. I nod to give her the go-ahead since I can't bring myself to say it out loud.

If I don't say it out loud, it can't be real, right?

Chapter Twenty-Four

GLORIA

Okay, so Jimmy has some kind of connection to the Council of Wolves. No big deal. Not like they have ultimate control over the choices I make in life or anything.

No. Big. Deal.

Shit, I am freaking out right now.

Add to that the revelation that Bee knows more about werewolf politics than I realized and the fact that Jimmy not only let Bee sleep with the pack last night but explicitly invited her to do so. There is definitely something going on there, and I'm mature enough to admit that I hate it. I'm not, apparently, mature enough to have any control over my emotions or jealousy or anything, but at least I can admit to having those emotions.

I'm so fucked. I can feel myself falling more and more for the guy, and he could cause me so much trouble, way more trouble, I'm realizing, than some packless townie could have. The deeper I get, the more dangerous he seems to me.

"It's been too long since we've been back to our own dorm," Bee tells me, linking her arm through mine. "Let's stop in and see how our room is holding up."

I'm not sure I really want to go back to my dorm. I hate the idea that something could have happened to our dorm while we were out, and by staying here, I can keep imagining everything is safe there. But Bee seems pretty fucking adamant.

"No one is going anywhere alone," Gabe insists. "Anyone needing to go to a different dorm to get personal items needs to go in a group."

I can't argue with him there. Bee gives a mutinous look. If she were a wolf, her ears would be laid back on her head.

Jeff gets a sly grin. "I don't suppose . . . if we did go to your dorm . . . we might run into a certain blonde RA?"

Gabe smacks the back of his head. "You're pathetic."

"Wait." I try to follow this new turn in the conversation. "Are you actually angling to go to MacLennon because you're hoping our stuck-up, judgmental RA will be there? Why?"

Jeff gets a dreamy look and rubs his chest like his heart is literally aching with longing. Blech.

"You wouldn't understand," he says, voice a million miles from us. "The way she looked at me that one time? It was like she saw straight through my soul or something. She might not know it yet, but we're definitely meant to be."

I shake my head. There really is no accounting for taste. "Well, if you really want to come, I'm not going to stop you."

* * *

Our dorm is trashed. Someone broke the entire door off its hinges. Didn't even try picking the lock or asking for a key or anything. The door hangs askew from one sad, bent hinge, revealing the mess someone made inside.

Tears well in my eyes as I take stock of the damage. It's not like I had a lot of stuff—and none of it was fancy or worth any money—but it was still mine. I feel almost as violated by this as the moment I realized I wasn't in control of my own body at that party. That party, the drugging, the attempted assault, they all seem like a lifetime ago. But here, in this moment, this lifetime, I'm staring at a pile of bedding and clothing that have all been ripped to shreds and doused in some kind of foul-smelling liquid that is now permeating the entire dorm floor.

"Oh my god! You're back!" Lacey barges into the room without knocking.

I guess it would be stupid to knock when the door is so obviously useless. I brace myself for whatever she's about to unleash on us. Are we about to get kicked out of the dorms? Put on some sort of probation? The blazing anger in Lacey's eyes doesn't bode well, that's for sure.

"Do you know who did this?"

"No," I mumble to my feet. "We've been away for a few days. We only just saw it like this a minute ago."

"We didn't do this," Bee adds. "I swear, we didn't have anything to do with this."

Lacey looks between me, Bee, and Jeff with an angry, confused look. "Of course you didn't do this. Do I really look stupid enough to assume you'd trash your own dorm? I was asking if you knew who did it because I assumed someone else had trashed your dorm. Someone reported it last night, and paired with the rumors going around since yesterday . . ." She trails off with a glare.

"Rumors?" I ask. The only reason I'm still standing is I don't want to risk getting any of the rancid mystery fluid on my clothes and skin. Otherwise, I would be huddled on the floor sobbing right now.

Lacey's gaze softens. "Rumors that you were one of the girls named on that Davenport site that went public yesterday."

My stomach knots and unknots itself. I want to be sick. I want to run away and never face another person again. Is this going to be the rest of my life? Dealing with the aftermath of this one shitty thing that happened to me?

"Right. Those rumors," I manage to say.

Lacey looks me up and down, assessing but not openly judging like I expect her to be.

"Look." She leans back as if to signal she's done with her assessment. "For what it's worth, I think everyone who came forward with that was really brave. It just fucking sucks that now I have to figure out what to do about this mess."

My eyes jerk up to meet hers in disbelief. "You're mad about having to deal with the mess someone else made of my dorm room? Unbelievable!"

"I didn't say I was mad at you! I'm just pissed about having it happen under my watch!"

"Yeah, because it's an inconvenience for you to clean it up! Well, don't worry. We can clean it up ourselves." I don't want to clean it up myself. But I want to get her pinched face out of my room as soon as I fucking can.

Jeff slides himself between us, facing Lacey so I can't see his expression. I would put money on him grinning like an idiot at her.

"Lacey, right?" He holds out his hand as if to shake. She gives it a disdainful glance, then ignores it. "I'm Jeff. We didn't get to talk properly after orientation, and I have been dying to get to know you."

"Lovely," she says with her fakest of smiles back in place. "And I suppose there's something I'm supposedly going to get out of this getting-to-know-you-better bullshit?"

Jeff sucks in a breath that sounds like a moan. "You would have to be the judge of that. What is it you want? You name it, and I will try to make it happen for you. That's something you'll learn about me. I am a guy with connections. You would be amazed at the kind of connections I have. Just say the word. I'm on it."

"And in return, you would get . . . ?" She leaves the question hanging in the air.

"How about if I can get you what you want, you take it on yourself to find some people to clean up this mess so Bee and Gloria don't have to?"

Did I think Lacey's smile was fake before? I was wrong. There's real happiness there, gleaming in her eyes and her sharp teeth. It's not a fake smile so much as a predatory one.

"So, I arrange to have their room cleaned, and you'll give me whatever it is I want?"

"Yes," Jeff sighs.

Lacey steps back suddenly, that triumphant predator look sliding right off her face to be replaced by anger and maybe exhaustion. Her voice is cold and steely when she says, "There's nothing I need from you. Just promise to stay away from me, and we'll call it even."

"But—" Jeff protests.

"I told you. There's nothing you can offer me." She looks past him to me and Bee. "Make sure you get out anything you think you can salvage because anything left here this afternoon is going to the dump." With that, she turns and stomps away.

She's halfway down the hall before she turns and trudges back to us. She looks like someone shoved a lemon in her mouth and she's regretting every choice that led up to that moment.

"There might be something you can do for me." Her gaze flits from Jeff to me to Bee and back.

Jeff steps toward her with a grin. "Name it."

If anything, Lacey's expression gets even more sour. "Just for the record, I was going to get the room cleaned no matter what, so it's not like you could have bribed me into doing it."

Jeff nods eagerly while Bee and I share a wary look.

Lacey holds out her phone. "I have a friend in the same kind of trouble as you." She gestures to the ransacked dorm room to make her point. "She won't talk to me, but maybe she'll talk to you."

I lean toward the proffered phone and snatch it out of her hand when I see the contact Lacey's opened it to. Cassie's now familiar picture grins at me from the same picture we've been showing around campus.

"You know Cassie?" It's too easy. Too good to be true.

Lacey plucks her phone from my hands with a scowl. "I know Cassie, and I also know that the only person who might have a chance at talking sense into her is someone who's been through the same thing. That is the only reason I'm letting you know where to find her." She directs her scowl at Jeff and doubles down on it. "So don't get any ideas about anyone owing anything." Holding out the phone again, she taps the side of the screen, indicating an address with the mysterious but also ominous label of *Safe House 3*. Because not only having a safe house but having multiple safe houses is totally a normal thing that normal people do. "She's there now." Lacey taps her phone impatiently. "Try to convince her to leave the house."

Then Lacey is gone again—for real this time, it would seem—and we're left to collect our jaws from the floor.

With Lacey gone, Bee and I both turn in a circle, taking in the destruction again. Tears spill down Bee's cheeks as she looks around the room. "It's all destroyed. There's nothing at all that I can save."

I rub a comforting hand up and down her back. She hasn't told me much about the life she comes from—I suppose I never asked because I didn't want to share back—but I'm sure she's just like me. There's probably something sentimental in this pile of trash that she knows she'll never see again. I can see that whoever did this tore out the pages of the journal I kept by my bed, shredding all of my personal thoughts and the family pictures I liked to sleep near and scattering them with a carelessness that makes my heart clench.

"There's nothing worth saving," I confirm and pull Bee toward the door. "We'd better get back so we can let the others know about this and try that address Lacey gave us."

Chapter Twenty-Five

JIMMY

"We hereby call this meeting of the Council of Wolves to order."

Jacob's voice rattles through me and leaves my teeth chattering in its wake. It's always been like this with Jacob. Even when I was a kid and he was a slightly older kid, he insisted on being called "Jacob." Never Jake or, heaven forbid, Jay. You had to call him Jacob or risk his wrath. And the guy has a lot of wrath. I honestly have no idea how he keeps up with that much emotion. His "give a shit" is through the roof, off the charts, and, well, completely toxic. But nobody can tell him that. I stopped trying to tell him anything years ago.

"What order of business is being brought before the Council of Wolves?"

His voice seriously belongs in some old-school, low-budget, black-and-white movie. That guy who played all of the creatures in all those old monster movies could have played Jacob, and then it would have at least been entertaining to watch him. As it is, every word out of his mouth makes my

"

teeth grind down harder. I'm going to crack a molar before this meeting is done.

"I stand before the Council to make them aware of an issue that pertains to the pack." I don't stutter, thankfully, but my voice sounds wobbly in my own ears. Not the impression I'm trying to make. You would think I'd be used to this kind of shit by now, but somehow, it never gets any easier.

The pack leader—and of course he's looming over me now as pack leader rather than father—leans forward in his overly ornate, completely hand-carved from a single fallen tree throne. And I have to gulp down the little quiver of panic that's inching its way up my esophagus.

"What issue?" he growls, narrowing his eyes at me in accusation.

"Honorable L-leader," I do stammer this time, "some friends and I have discovered a predator on our college campus. He's a vampire who regularly drugs and assaults other students. We revealed his actions publicly, and he has since retaliated against those who outed him."

He doesn't budge, but I can feel his temperature rising from across the room.

"It sounds like what you're telling me is that you do not, in fact, have everything under control at college as you claimed?"

The question mark he adds to his speech is entirely for show, to remind the pack that he's the wise, good guy and I'm the foolish, bumbling heir. I wish it didn't work so well to put me in my place, but, well, he's been honing that tactic for decades now.

"Everything is under control. There's just this one thing that we agreed the Council should know about."

"And 'we' pertains to? Is Bethany part of this 'we'?"

Damn Bee and her making me do this on my own. "She's

the one who suggested coming to you about it, but she's not in any danger."

The pack leader—never to be referred to as anything other than "Honorable Leader" while in this official capacity, like acknowledging he's my father would undermine his authority or something—raps an angry rhythm with his knuckles against the arm of his throne. The official pack throne, which, to everyone's horror, I am supposed to inherit someday.

"You say that Bethany is safe, that you have everything under control, but you're coming to us for help, and Bethany is nowhere to be found. What evidence do you bring that anything you say is true?"

I should have planned this out better. Maybe made up some note cards.

"Couldn't you just, I don't know, trust me? After all, you are—" I stop myself before the disastrous words slip past my lips. The oxygen in the room is still sucked up as every Council member gasps in unison.

I just fucked up, and I know it, and they all know it too. I was probably going to be murdered by my dad before. Now, I'm going to be murdered by my dad in front of an audience while knowing that I failed and fucked up every single thing I was trying to do.

Great.

"I trust people who have proven themselves worthy of my trust." His voice is quiet but still somehow manages to thunder through the room. "You have proven time and time again that you are not worthy of my trust. This little 'experiment' of leaving the pack to go to school has very clearly failed. You have once again managed to disappoint me, and I assure you, I had the bar set incredibly low."

He takes a break from tearing into me, but I can tell by his long, slow inhale that he's just getting started.

"Here is what will happen." His eyes bore into me,

pinning me to this spot so I can't even wiggle my toes or shift my weight. "This thing with the vampires ends now. It was none of your business to begin with, and you had no right to drag the entire pack into it. I'm sure it never occurred to you that anyone beyond yourself would be affected by your white knighting, but you've put us all in a precarious position with the Vampiric Enclave.

"Furthermore, your stint at college is over. You and Bethany are both to report back here as soon as you can help her pack her things and drive her home. You will stay where you can be protected, whether from vampires, your own stupidity, or some other danger. You will not leave the pack grounds again without an escort until you ascend as my heir. I pray that you gain some level of sense before that time.

"As for these others who need protection because of your ill-thought-out actions against a vampire, they'll come here to live with the pack. They'll abide by pack rules while under our protection. Going back and forth to school will not be an option for them."

I take shallow breaths around the ball of puke that's trying to crawl up my throat. I'm pretty sure this is the worst possible way he could have reacted. I knew this wouldn't be good, but I hadn't imagined it being quite so terrible.

And it's about to get worse too.

"It's not just wolves who have been victims of this guy," I say, trying to sound brave. Trying to sound like I know what I'm doing and like I belong here and like I'm not the worthless fuckup my father thinks I am.

His eyes, which haven't left me yet, narrow to angry slits. "Humans are always welcome guests in our pack. You know that. I can't order them back here, but they're welcome to the protection we can offer."

Of course I know that. That's how Bee and I basically

grew up together. "And what about the vampires?" I ask, despite knowing exactly how he's going to respond.

The pack leader's lip curls up in a sneer. "The blood-suckers can take care of themselves." It's a flashing, neon warning sign that he just used that slur out loud in front of the whole Council. Usually, he keeps his bigotry a little better hidden. "We're not wasting time and resources on them when they have their own people to turn to."

I just hope their own people are more helpful to them than my father has been to me.

"I will pass on your words, Honorable Leader," I say with a bow, then turn to walk out before things get any worse. Though I don't know how things could get any worse.

"Oh, Greyson," he says as I touch the door handle, like he's just thought of something. Some sudden realization that he needs to get off his chest before he forgets. "The girl? She will come back here with you."

Shit, shit, shit. How could he have heard about Gloria? How much does he know? What does he want from her? The thoughts all fly through my head at once, colliding midair like a flock of drunk pigeons. I refuse to turn back and ask him what he knows, so all I can do is push open the chamber doors and keep walking away.

$$\textit{Chapter Twenty-Six}$$

GLORIA

All of the girls are cozied up in a pile of limbs and blankets and pajamas, with the boys banished to the farther edges of the room—on the couch—when Bee, Jeff, and I get back. They're in the middle of some girly movie when we come in, and it almost feels like everyone's managed to forget about Cassie's disappearance. Not that we want to forget she's gone, but living with the constant weight of worrying about her is just too much to keep up. None of us has that kind of stamina.

I'm surrounded by these friends I've been forced to make and feel grateful for every one of them, but I can't seem to feel happy. Jimmy hasn't come back yet or sent any news about his visit with the Council of Wolves.

And I miss him.

There. I admitted it. I feel like a complete idiot, but at least I'm an honest idiot. I miss Jimmy when he's not around, and lean on him for support when he is here, and am actually grateful for everything he's done for me. I'll even admit that I miss touching him and will probably crawl all over him as soon as he gets back.

Now, where is he?

But aside from missing the doofus I'm falling for, it's actually really nice and cozy with everyone gathered around me like this. It feels a lot like the family I grew up with, but no expectations of cleaning sheep pens or taking care of nieces and nephews in diapers. Despite worrying about Cassie, and worrying about what else Vincent might do, and worrying about whether Jimmy is going to come back safe and soon, it feels like home right now.

Marcus comes back moments after us. "Still no sign of her," he tells everyone as he stomps into the room.

"Actually." Bee turns to him. "We may have a lead on that. Our RA gave us an address and hinted that Cassie might be willing to listen to one of the other victims."

Marcus gives a surprised grunt. "So what are we waiting for?"

Devon turns to him with a scowl. "No one is waiting for anything. They just got back. The information is new to us too."

Not wanting to let that argument escalate again, I step between the two guys. "So, who should go to check it out? I think a small group is best. And only one guy at the most."

"I'm ready to go now," Marcus says before anyone else can answer, "and you should be the one to talk to her since you're one of the original victims named."

"And I still have my shoes on," Bee says.

I give her a tight smile. It's nice knowing she's got my back through all of this mess.

The address Lacey gave us turns out to be a small, run-down trailer in a trailer park a few miles from campus. Every window is covered by particle board, and I wonder if that's specifically to keep the sunlight out or if it was simply cheaper than replacing broken glass. The rest of the trailers don't look that much better, with a mix of broken lawn furniture and trucks without tires filling in the spaces between trailers. The closest thing to pavement in the entire trailer park is the cinder blocks holding the trailers up. Everything else is pitted gravel road or knee-high weeds.

There's no answer when we knock on the door. I can't smell any signs of life, but I wouldn't be able to smell a vampire even if my nose wasn't overwhelmed by stray dogs and loose trash nearby.

"We're looking for Cassie?" I call out, hoping I sound friendly and non-threatening.

"Who the fuck wants to know?" a feminine voice growls from the other side of the door.

If I was expecting a warm welcome, I was way off the mark.

"My name is Gloria. From that website about Vincent? I was one of the people he—"

"And, if that's true, what the fuck are you doing here with a human and a vampire in tow?"

I glance at my companions. Marcus has a hat pulled low over his ears and is leaning against the wall in order to stay in the shade, and Bee is nibbling her lower lip with a worried expression. It strikes me that we probably look like the least threatening trio to come through this place, and for Cassie to have her guard up like this doesn't bode well for us getting through to her.

Bee leans toward the door. "I'm just here for moral support. I can wait in the car if you prefer?"

"And I'm here for protection," Marcus adds. "We want to help you."

There's a snort from the other side of the door, followed by the scrape and jangle of multiple dead bolts and locks being undone.

"It's really amazing how many people want to help me now when no one would help me when it actually mattered," the pretty but tired girl who opens the door tells us. "Come inside and tell me what you want. It's annoying to talk through the door like this."

She turns and walks away like she doesn't even care anymore who might be at her back.

"How many other people have wanted to help you?" Bee blinks as she steps into the trailer. Not only are the windows boarded up, but there are no lights whatsoever.

Cassie sprawls on a beat-up sofa in the living room and picks up an already open bottle of wine from the floor beside her. "Well, there's you." She swings the bottle in our direction, then takes a swig. "There's my old roommate. My parents." A twisted look and another swallow of wine straight from the bottle. "And some sketchy lawyer claiming he could help all of us." She drinks again. "It's funny, because when I was actually going through this, the only people who cared only cared about whether I was going to tell everyone and embarrass them. So, what is it that you think you can do for me that no one else could?"

I look down at my hands and try to figure out the right words to say. I can't really blame her for being skeptical, if that's the kind of support she got whenever Vincent hurt her. "We've been staying in this one dorm together," I tell her. "Strength in numbers, you know? We thought if we could find everyone whose identity was exposed, we could protect each other until something can be done about Vincent." I shrug, knowing she has no reason to trust me. "It's not a perfect solution. It's not permanent or anything, but it's nice. I mean, it feels safe, being close to other people who have gone through the same thing."

"Sorry if I'm not that interested in blindly following a group of people whose brilliant plan is to hang out in a dorm together until their problems magically disappear," Cassie says with a derisive snort.

Bee raises her hand like we're in class. "What was that you said about a lawyer?"

Cassie finishes off her bottle and strolls across the room to a counter that divides the living room and kitchen. There's a row of empty bottles on one side and unopened ones on the other.

"I would offer you some, but I've kind of got this 'lurking in the shadows and avoiding everyone' thing going on, and having visitors kind of ruins it." She makes quick work of opening another bottle and comes back to the couch. "Yes, a lawyer contacted me the same day that my information got leaked from that site. He said he's had an eye on Vincent and others like him for a while now and thought my story could help build a case or something. It sounds like as solid a plan as hiding out in a dorm room until everything blows over, so I told him to fuck off. Now that I know the brilliant alternate plans available—" She waves her bottle to indicate us. "—I'm wondering if I should have taken him more seriously."

She slumps, like saying it out loud has highlighted her lack of options. I feel a prick of hope, though. Maybe someone is willing to go to bat for us. Maybe someone other than us is working at fixing things.

Marcus stands up with a resigned grunt. "We won't waste any more of your time, then. Just remember that our doors will stay open for you. I bet that lawyer wouldn't be mad if you changed your mind either."

Cassie's eyes narrow at him.

"Just think about it, okay?" he says, already ushering Bee and me out to the rocky driveway.

* * *

"We're at a dead end," Marcus groans into his hands, showing more emotion than I'm used to seeing from him.

"If she doesn't want our help, we can't force it on her," Jeff says. "We need to find a different approach."

Marcus bunches his shoulders, tugs at his hair. "We haven't talked to his father yet," he finally says after a long internal struggle.

"His father?" I ask. "Whose father?"

Marcus looks like he's trying to swallow a bug. "Vincent's father," he explains, "who runs the pharmaceutical company where most of their money comes from. And I might have an in with him to let him know what Vincent has been up to. But he might not care what Vincent is up to. I just don't know, but I think we need to try it."

I'm curious about the story he seems to be not quite telling, but it's more important that we try to help Cassie, so I let it go for now. "How soon can you get in contact with him?" I ask.

He stomps toward his room and throws, "I'll try right now," over his shoulder before disappearing and slamming the door behind him.

Okay, so Jimmy has some mystery connection to the Council of Wolves. Marcus apparently has some kind of connection to Vincent Davenport Sr. What the hell is going on right now? And where the hell is Jimmy, anyway? The main pack is not far from here. How long is it taking for him to meet with his connection on the Council and convince them to meet with him?

Before my speculation gets too far away from me, Marcus comes out looking like he just saw a ghost.

"I'm going to be out for a while," he says, voice shaking. "I . . . I guess I'm going to have to go meet them in person."

Again, what the actual hell is going on here?

"Do you want someone to go with you?" Bee asks, and my respect for her just skyrocketed if she's offering to be that person.

Marcus shakes his head, nods his head, looks around the room like maybe there's a hole he can crawl into, and generally looks like he'd rather die than do whatever he's about to do.

"No," he finally answers. "This is vampire business. I need to do it myself."

Bee breathes a relieved sigh, and I squeeze her hand to try to communicate how impressed I am with her for even offering. I'm so glad Marcus didn't decide to bring her with him, though. The way he's pale and shaking just thinking about it, I can't imagine he's heading into happiness and safety.

Chapter Twenty-Seven

GLORIA

Everyone is snuggled together and sleeping when Jimmy gets back. I wake up when he tries to squeeze into the sleep pile next to me.

"What time is it?" I whisper, shifting back to human when my wolf eyes register the look of worry on his face.

"Don't worry about it," he whispers back. "Let's just sleep now and deal with things in the morning."

That wakes me up better than a shouted order to get out to the milking shed ever has. I sit up and practically drag him to his room, which is currently empty because all of the girls were more cozy sleeping in the pile, and all of the boys are either in their own rooms or sharing the other boys' rooms.

"Okay, out with it," I order.

He sighs heavily, puts his hands on my hips, and rests his forehead on my shoulder like I'm the only thing keeping him standing.

"Please. Let's just have tonight together. I'll tell you everything in the morning. I promise."

His voice plucks at my insides, setting me to vibrating with sympathetic longing. Longing to just have tonight. To just have uncomplicated. To just not worry about councils or enclaves or corporations or frat boys.

"Okay. Tonight." I tug his hair, pulling his face so I can reach his lips.

He responds immediately, pulling my body flat to his, wrapping me in his arms, and deepening the kiss so I can barely breathe.

And I kiss him right back. I rock my hips toward him, grind against where he's already hard, and take immense pleasure in the quiet groan he lets out.

"Gloria," he groans, then, "Gloria," he hisses as I stroke one hand over the front of his pants.

His skin and abdominals shudder as I slide my fingers under his shirt, tugging his button-down shirt out of his belted suit pants and trying not to think about how these are the clothes he dressed up in today to visit some very important shifters. I scrape my fingernails up his ribs and over his pecs, enjoying every shiver and tremble and groan he gives me along the way.

"What do you want me to do?" he asks, sounding breathless and desperate, his pupils blown wide from lust and his lips and tongue swollen from kissing me so desperately. "I need you to tell me what to do."

And I'm not sure if he's talking about just this moment, just the ways I want him to touch me and get me off, or if he's talking about something else. Asking a question that he doesn't quite know how to voice yet.

"Take off your clothes," I command and hope I don't sound silly, which is kind of how I expected to sound but not exactly how I think I actually sound. "Take off your clothes and kneel in front of me."

He doesn't hesitate for a second. A few of the buttons

from his shirt go pinging around the room because he doesn't bother to undo them before whipping the shirt off over his head. He toes off his shoes while unbuttoning his pants and slides everything—pants, boxer briefs, shoes, and socks—off at once and kneels down in front of me, completely naked.

"What now?" His words and his eyes plead, and my body answers before my mind has a chance to interject.

How did it not hit me until now that I'm still naked after shifting? Usually, I would be hyperaware of my naked skin with a potential mate in the room. But Jimmy just bites his bottom lip and looks up at me with trust and expectation and lust in his eyes as he slowly, slowly trails his fingertips up my outer thighs until his hands rest gently on my hips. This may be my new favorite pastime, watching Jimmy as he savors me.

"Kiss me here," I tell him, pointing to a nondescript space beside my belly button.

Instead of asking why, or pointing out the stretch marks that I know gather at my hips, or laughing because I'm too ridiculous to be giving him orders like this, he does it, swirling his tongue around the spot for good measure before looking up at me expectantly for his next assignment.

"Kiss me here." This time, I point to my hip, the place where red lines lie like zebra stripes along my flank to remind me of the summer when my body filled out and my skin couldn't keep up.

Jimmy doesn't notice the stretch marks. Or, at least, he doesn't say anything about them. He stays there, worshiping the skin of my hip with his teeth and lips and tongue as if it's the greatest thrill of his life. And that sends a thrill shooting through me. The knowledge that he's enjoying this and I'm the one in charge of him enjoying this.

I indicate the crease between my hip and my leg. "Kiss me here."

Without question or comment, he moves to the spot and begins teasing me even harder.

I step back from him and can't help grinning when he makes a needy little whimper and tries to follow me with his mouth.

"Patience," I admonish him with a wag of my finger. "Good boys know how to wait." Something unreadable flashes in his eyes, making me wonder if that was taking this too far, but he settles back on his heels and watches as I walk to his bed and kneel on it, ass in the air, inviting him in so many ways.

Jimmy stays put, eyes locked on me but not moving his body so much as an inch.

I wonder again if this is going too far, but he hasn't stopped me or seemed uncomfortable with anything so far.

"I guess you are a good boy after all," I say in my sweetest voice. "That means you get a treat." I reach behind myself—questioning for a moment where this brazen new Gloria has come from—and dip a finger inside my pussy before sliding my now wet finger forward through my labia and pulling the stretchy flaps of skin apart like I'm displaying a butterfly—wings spread—for him. "Kiss me here."

With a groan, Jimmy launches himself across the room and does exactly what I tell him and more.

JIMMY

I feel like every wildest dream I've ever had is coming true right at this moment.

The taste of Gloria on my tongue, the smell of her filling my nose, the way she's offering herself up to me is intoxicating. Euphoria races through me. The only way she could possibly taste or smell better is if she were in heat right now. The only way this could feel any better is if I were actually mounting her to mate right now.

But I'm not going to fuck this up. She's inviting me to do everything I've ever wanted minus one thing, and I will happily take only what she's offering and count myself the luckiest guy in the world.

She quivers with need or maybe nerves or anticipation as I kiss her pussy, gently at first, then deepening my kisses. Burying my nose at her entrance and swirling my tongue between her labia and over her clit.

Gloria bites back a curse, and I take that as a good sign to keep going. She's so wet that her fluids drip down my chin and neck, making a delicious mess of the bedspread beneath us.

"Jimmy, I need—" she groans but cuts off as my tongue takes another tour of all her bits.

What does she need? I should pull back. Ask her what she wants. But I can't stop eating her out with the desperation of a starving man. And what if she decides what she needs is for me to fuck her? If I do that, she'll never forgive me later, when she's thinking more clearly and dealing with the consequences. I don't know how likely pregnancy is when she's not in heat and if we use condoms, but I don't think it's a risk she's willing to take.

So what does she need? And can I give it to her?

Hoping I'm making the right choice but too deep in the moment to figure out how to stop and ask, I slide my face farther back. I draw S shapes over her with my tongue as I slide backward. My goal is to lick every single beautiful, delicate fold of skin until she screams my name and wakes up everyone in the dorm.

My tongue wanders over her entrance and then farther back. She gasps—in surprise? In disgust?—when I gently spread her ass cheeks apart with both hands.

"Can I?" I can barely remember how to say the two simple words, much less voice exactly what I'm asking.

"You don't have to," Gloria says. "I've never . . ."

"But can I?" I ask again, struggling to not just dive in right now and bury myself in her scent.

"Yes. But you'll stop if I decide I don't like it?"

I squeeze the perfect globes of her ass in each of my hands. "I promise. I'll always stop if you ask me to." It might kill me to stop once I get started, but I made a promise, and I will keep it, damn it!

"Okay. You can do it, then. If you want to."

She can't know how desperately I want to, so I set out to show her.

I drag a finger from her front to back, gathering all of the moisture I can, then rub that moisture across her asshole. The puckered skin feels delightful under my fingertips, and Gloria gasps and bucks as I work my finger over her.

"Still okay?" I ask, and she answers with a moan that I'm a little worried will wake everyone in the dorm.

I won't lie, I'm not that worried. I'll buy everyone doughnuts to make up for waking them up, and I will probably strut like an arrogant peacock anytime someone admits they heard me getting lucky.

I focus my fingers on Gloria's clit and my mouth on her hole. I've never done this before, but somehow, it comes as the most natural thing in the world. Like my tongue was made for her. Like this is what I was really born for, not any of that bullshit with the pack and the Council and the politics.

Gloria's moaning increases in pitch and volume as my tongue slides along her crack, exploring every bit that I can reach. I love the way she tastes here, similar to her pussy, because it's still all her but subtly different too.

I work my tongue at her hole, enjoying how the texture changes there, and she rewards me with a "Fuuuuck, Jimmy" that I will probably store in my spank bank forever.

"Still okay?" And my own voice is breathless and raspy.

"Keep going," she whimpers.

That makes me grin. I'm glad she's back to telling me what she wants. I'm realizing that nothing much in this world is sexier than Gloria knowing what she wants and making me do it. I like knowing how I can please her.

I keep my tongue working at her, keep my fingers working at her clit, and bring back the finger I already touched her hole with. I use my spit to lubricate as I work my finger inside of her, and she makes a sound like a teakettle about to burst, but she also rocks her hips back onto me, so I think it must be a good sign.

The way her muscle pulls at my finger brings me almost to the brink of coming. I can feel a bead of precome already sliding down the tip of my dick. Gloria isn't helping my situation much either. She rocks her hips back and forth, fucking herself on my finger and making all of the sexiest sounds in the world while she does.

"Jimmy, I want you to fuck me," she gasps.

"But you said—"

"I need you in me. Like this. I won't get pregnant if you fuck me in the ass. I just. Need you. Please."

I'm about to come from those words alone, but I try to focus so I don't embarrass myself. "Are you sure? It's not too risky?" God, the hope in my voice sounds pathetic in my own ears, but I can't make myself care.

"Not too risky. Wear a condom."

I gulp. Push down my desire so I can last a little bit longer for her. Slide my finger out so I can reach for the drawer I keep condoms in.

My hands shake as I tear the foil. I almost drop the condom before I even get it over the end of my dick. "Are you really, really sure about this?" I grit out, focusing on not noticing how amazing her ass looks in front of me. I try to brace myself in case she does tell me to stop.

Damn, I do not want her to tell me to stop.

"Yes. Jimmy. I need you now." She punctuates the statement by lifting her ass ever so slightly, and I am a hairsbreadth from coming before I even get inside of her.

I gather up a finger full of her natural lubricant and smear it over my latex-covered cock, then gather some more to help me press my finger back inside of her.

There is no way anyone sleeps through the needy groan she lets out, and sure enough, I hear a giggle from the living room in response. Good. Let them listen. I can't feel shame over what is by far the best thing that's ever happened to me.

Finally, finally, I have her opened up enough that I think she's ready for me. I rest my dick at her hole and say a silent prayer.

"Last chance to change your mind about this," I say, and my voice comes out as a desperate rasp.

"Do it, Jimmy," she whispers.

Sliding into her is heavenly.

"Fuuuuck," Gloria groans.

At the same time, I groan, "Yessss."

She's tight and hot around me, and the sight of her, bent over and on display just for me, is absolute perfection. I have to hold still for a moment so I don't come too fast.

"Jimmy?"

"Yeah," I gasp, praying again that she doesn't ask me to stop.

"Fuck me."

My hips give an automatic jerk at her words, and then instinct takes over. I anchor her with one hand on her hip and reach around with the other to find her clit again. She meets every one of my thrusts with one of her own, her voice growing louder and more desperate as we move together.

"I can't hold on much longer," I warn her.

"Good," she says. "Fuck, I'm so close. I'm—"

On instinct, my teeth latch onto her shoulder as she groans out her orgasm. I can feel her muscles tightening and pulsing around me, and I'm going over the edge too. I manage to tug my dick away from her before I come, not wanting any risk of my semen touching her at all, and nearly collapse as I watch my come fill up the condom. I clamp my hand around the base, and some still manages to pump out around the edges. Good thing I pulled out in time. This condom was not designed with wolf orgasms in mind.

"I'll be right back," I tell her once the room stops spinning. Then I step out to get cleaned up, naked except for the condom, and am greeted by a chorus of snickering, cheering, and catcalling. I gather what dignity I can to walk across the room to the bathroom. At least everyone who could hear us fucking could also hear that I made sure Gloria was satisfied, and that's something to be proud of from where I'm standing.

* * *

GLORIA

Well, I guess if I die of embarrassment, at least I'll die thoroughly satisfied.

Jimmy strides back in—looking pleased as can be and still completely naked—and carefully cleans me up with a warm washcloth. I never pegged myself as a girl who would want that, but I guess here we are. I let out a contented sigh as Jimmy wipes the places between my thighs where my own sticky fluids dripped down and made a mess on me.

"Is this okay?" he asks, still looking all too pleased with himself, but there's a hint of worry in his eyes.

I tug him up toward me on the bed and kiss him slowly, letting myself enjoy the taste of him and the sensation of our tongues tangling lazily together. "This is perfect," I tell him once we come up for air again.

What I don't tell him—because he either already knows and isn't any more ready to talk about it than I am, or he doesn't know yet and I'm not ready to be the one to explain it —is that I could feel our mate bond solidify the instant he bit my neck. He's stuck with me now. And I'm stuck with him. For better or for worse, whether we decide to say the ceremonial words or not.

Fuck. I'm not ready for this. I'm not ready to be mated and popping out babies and giving up all my dreams.

I know what the next step is. We'll move back to be with the pack. Maybe his, because they're close to school and he could theoretically keep taking classes, or maybe mine, because my family will expect my mate to pitch in on the farm to support me once pups are on the way.

Not that either of those possibilities is particularly appealing to me. Not that anyone will ask me what I want to do, now that I'm mated.

Jimmy slides my still-wobbly body under the covers and

then slides in right next to me, curling protectively around me like we're two spoons slotted into the drawer. Except I feel more like an awkwardly shaped soup spoon to his properly proportioned teaspoon. Nobody ever fits with me.

But that thought doesn't stop me from drifting off to sleep, feeling warm and snug in his arms.

Chapter Twenty-Eight

GLORIA

I wake up still wrapped in Jimmy's arms, but I can sense tension from him that wasn't there while we slept.

"Is something wrong?" I whisper the question, not wanting to pop the bubble from last night's mating.

"No. I mean . . . shit." Jimmy breathes deep and squeezes me tight to him. "I should probably just tell everyone at once, but I really don't want to go out there and face the real world. I just wish you and I could stay here forever and not have to go out there for anything."

I bump my ass back toward him and meet his very sizable morning wood. "But we do have to go out there, and it's probably best to get it over with sooner rather than later."

"Just a few more minutes. Just let me keep you here a little longer?" He nuzzles into my hair and breathes me in like I'm the drug he's addicted to.

And I have to admit I love the feel of it. I love the feeling of him needing me like this.

I reach over to my phone to check the time. "Sorry. It's

time for reality." I hop out of bed and start hunting for a wearable outfit before he can argue with me. It wouldn't take much argument to get me back into bed, but I know I have responsibilities to deal with.

Everyone else in the dorm is already up and about by the time we leave the room, offering us a mixture of tired eye rolls, joking innuendos, and wry headshakes. The general consensus seems to be, "What are you going to do? Werewolves are gonna werewolf."

I hate that I'm now living the cliché like that. But I also don't feel like I really have any control over it, which I also hate. I'm just grateful the current roommates are pretty understanding. I hate when I have to explain this stuff, and I'm still having some trouble even explaining it to myself.

Bee is the first person to bring up the real business at hand.

"What did the Council say?" she demands as soon as everyone is seated with coffee in hand.

Jimmy wilts under her gaze, and I have no idea what that's all about. "Mostly, they said that vampire business is vampire business and to stay out of it."

A chorus of "What?" and "Are you fucking kidding me?" erupts around the room. My voice is in there with the rest of them. I didn't expect a huge amount of help from the higher-ups, but I also didn't expect to feel so completely betrayed by them. I thought—whatever else happened—they were on my side. I guess not, though.

Jimmy rubs nervously at his knees, still not breaking eye contact with Bee.

"Yeah. They really don't want to get involved with such a powerful organization or such a powerful family. Something like that. They said to walk away from this whole thing and, like, basically pretend nothing happened and hope things go back to normal."

"Well, that's easy enough to say when 'this whole thing'

isn't actively ruining your life!" Kelsey shouts, pacing the room.

I'm right there with her. The only thing that keeps me in my seat is that Jimmy looks like there's more bad news to tell.

"What else did they say?" Bee's level voice doesn't match my internal turmoil, but her eyes are flashing pure fire.

Jimmy gulps and finally breaks eye contact with Bee. "They said that pack members need to go home, that letting anyone off pack lands was a mistake and a failed experiment. And they also said that any shifters involved have to go back. For protection, they claim."

Bee and I explode out of our seats at the same time. I'm not sure what she's so upset about, but I don't have the brain space to worry about it right now.

"Is that order for all of the pack families or just the local pack?" I demand. "I am not going back home without a fight." Not after all the shit I've already dealt with just to get where I am. There's no way I'm giving up all of my dreams just on the stupid pack leader's stupid orders.

"Actually—" Jimmy's eyes meet mine, then dart away, ashamed. "—they're calling us all back to the central pack. No exceptions."

My jaw drops. They aren't even talking about sending me home. They want me to go to the main pack, where I don't know anyone and I don't have any standing. And for what? So they can keep an eye on me and make sure I don't post any more embarrassing stories on the internet?

To my surprise, it's Bee who has something to say while I'm still trying to work my mouth into any kind of coherent speech.

"No. No way. Absolutely not. He can't make me."

Jimmy stands up and grabs Bee by the shoulders. A twang of jealousy jolts through me before I remind myself that Jimmy and Bee's relationship is not the same as Jimmy's and mine. And it's not like I've talked to Jimmy about the mate bond, which I feel loud and clear right now but he seems blissfully unaware of.

"You know he can," Jimmy says, completely bewildering me again. Who the hell is this "he," and what does "he" have to do with Jimmy or Bee? "I swear, I tried to talk him down, but he wouldn't listen to me. You know how he is."

"No way. Uh-uh. I don't need protecting anymore! Definitely not like this!" Bee is shaking. I can't decide if she's shaking with rage or fear, but I'm certain it's one of those. "I am not giving up on all of this just because he gets scared."

"What do you want me to do?" Jimmy practically shouts back at her. "You know I don't have any actual say in this!"

Bee pokes a hard finger into his solar plexus. "What you can do is go back there like a good little boy—without me— and tell him to fuck himself. I'm not going back."

Okay. So there's more to unpack with every single word she says. Now is not the time, though. I'm not going to question an ally. "I'm not going either," I announce, then amend it to, "At least, not until things are settled with the current situation." After all, I already knew that being mated would mean going back to my mate's pack and dropping out of college, right? I wish I didn't want so badly to sit down and bawl my eyes out right now.

Jimmy sits down with a grunt, looking even more wilted and defeated than before. "That's actually not all of it," he admits, talking to his toes once again.

Bee and I round on him together, having forgotten about everyone else in the room.

"They say they'll offer protection to anyone living on pack lands."

"But?" Bee says through gritted teeth.

"But . . . well, they would be brought into the pack, which would mean staying on pack lands. So . . . you know . . . no more college or anything. Not for the wolves they're ordering home and not for anyone else who goes back with me."

A dazed look passes around the room. It's one thing for the pack to control the pack members. It happens all the time, for big and small things. But trying to control humans and vampires in the same way? Someone high up has lost their mind.

Bee's eyes narrow even further, and she regards Jimmy through the tiniest of angry slits. "There's something else." She says it. She doesn't have to ask.

"Remember that this is the pack speaking, not me, okay?"

"What else did he say?"

Jimmy gulps and gives an apologetic look around the room. "They said . . ." Jimmy looks absolutely miserable. I wonder if I should grab the trash bin in case he pukes. "They said that wolves and humans are welcome to take them up on their hospitality and join with the pack full-time but that vampires have their own systems for dealing with these situations."

Now it's Kelsey's turn to jump up in an outrage. "They're not willing to help us at all? Why?"

Jimmy shrugs. "I don't get any say in it. I swear, if I had any more control, it's not the way I would have done it, but I have absolutely no control here."

"Well, that's bullshit," Kelsey announces to all of us before setting out on a race walk circuit around the room.

JIMMY

If I could disappear into this sofa, I would have done it ten minutes ago. I knew no one was going to take this well. I knew there was no good way to break this news to them. It sucks even worse than I imagined. I should try to explain that I understand that it's bullshit.

But what good will that do?

I should try to explain that my father is just—straight down to his core—a plain old bigot. He's scared, but how will it help Kelsey to know that she's getting fucked by someone who's afraid of her, not someone who actually wishes her ill? She's getting fucked all the same.

"I'm not going back, end of story," Bee tells me, then storms out of the dorm.

Shit.

I at least owe her whatever support I can give. I shoot Gloria an apologetic look and hurry after Bee.

"Does it help if I say I understand where you're coming from?"

Bee rounds on me with an entire storm's worth of fury leashed behind her eyes. "Do you understand where I'm coming from?"

I wet my lips, trying to remember how to move them. Oh, and maybe some words would be nice. If I could remember any of those, which I can't when faced with Bee's anger.

"I . . . um . . ."

"That's what I thought. You're sad because Daddy's calling you back home, but for you, that just means that you don't have to worry about struggling over homework anymore. You still get to go home and be somebody. Do you know what I get? I get to go home and be nobody. Again. And for the rest of my life. I don't want any more of that kind of protection, Grey. I'm serious. You've got the day to decide whether you're siding with him so I never talk to you again or if you're standing up to him so I can actually live my life."

Her eyes bore into my soul, making it even harder than usual to sort through my thoughts and figure out the right thing to do.

"What do you mean you'll never talk to me again?" I ask. It's a little pathetic, how scared and small my voice comes out, but I guess that's how I'm feeling right now. About as scared and small as I could ever feel.

Bee's face softens with a hint of understanding, but the muscle in her jaw is still working in time with her anger.

"I mean, if you tell me you're going to go back there and side with him and try to bring me back with you, I'm going away where you'll never find me again. I know he's trying to keep me safe, but . . . maybe safe isn't really what I actually want, you know?"

I don't really know, but I'm on her side, so I nod yes. "I won't try to force you to go back," I say, and I really hope I don't have to break that promise. "And I really don't want you to disappear on me. Promise you won't?"

Bee huffs. "I'll promise to say goodbye if I do take off. How's that?"

"Is it the best I can get?"

"For now? Yes. I can't promise you anything better."

"Okay." I stick out my hand for a shake. "I promise to not send you back, and you promise to not leave without saying goodbye."

She takes my hand with a wry headshake. "I feel like we're five again."

"Yeah, but when we were five, I could have promised to run away with you."

"What happened since then," she wonders. "Why can't you promise that anymore?

I shrug, feeling like my skin is a size too tight. "I'm not

sure. I guess I stopped feeling brave enough to stand up for myself? Or maybe I realized that someone else knew better than me, so I should just follow orders instead of trying to give them?"

Bee's eyes are steady as she stares me down. "I'm not sure about that last part, you know. I'm not sure about someone else knowing better than you."

Chapter Twenty-Nine

JIMMY

Things have settled down by the time we get back in. Or maybe everyone is just waiting for Bee and me to let them in on our personal drama.

Too bad for them. I'm not telling anyone unless it's absolutely necessary, and Bee's got that jaw-clench thing going, which makes me think she's even less likely than me to start talking about this.

Gloria takes one look at us and realizes we're not talking—she's pretty damn smart like that—and changes the subject.

"Look. Theoretically, they can call me in whenever they want," she explains to the others. "Part of being a member of the pack is that you have to fall in line anytime the pack gives orders. And the Council is in charge of all the packs, so I really don't have much choice if the order is coming from them. But I can't stand the thought of leaving here before we have things settled. They'll have to come and get me if they want me to go right now. For everyone else, honestly, I wouldn't take them up on their offer of protection if there's another choice. You don't want to give up your freedom like that."

I agree with her, but I can't exactly say that.

Kelsey crosses her arms with a huff. "Well, I don't even get a choice. I honestly wouldn't have minded leaving school if it meant feeling safe again. I haven't really felt safe for a few years now, you know? It would have been nice to know someone was able to offer me some protection. Or willing to."

Selena huddles in on herself. "It's not like I really have another option. My family supports me, sure, but they're halfway across the country, and they can't afford for me to make more trouble for them by refusing an order from the Council."

Before I settle on what to say, there's a knock on the door. We all just sit, looking around the room for clues about who could be at the door. They pound on the door again, harder this time.

Accepting that I'm the person who actually lives in this dorm and that maybe makes me the best person to answer, I tiptoe to the door and open it a sliver, trying to block anyone outside from seeing the crowd gathered within.

A vampire in a suit—and I mean a nice, well-tailored, probably expensive and designer suit—stands at the door, looking intimidating.

"You knocked?" I try to channel cool and confident, maybe a little bored at the intrusion. On the inside, I'm bubbling with near panic that any vampire or shifter can probably sense from miles away.

"I already know about the friends you've got staying with you and about the trouble you're in. You're going to want to let me in so we don't have to talk in front of every random person in the hallway."

"Who are you?"

Typical for a vampire, I can't peg his age at all. He's definitely an adult, not college aged, but he doesn't look old. Because of how vampires age, I guess that could mean he's anywhere between twenty-five and one hundred and twenty-five.

I'm shit at guessing vampire ages and even worse at reading vampire emotions. I have no idea what this guy is up to or if I should trust him. Of course, there's a room full of people behind me who are far from helpless. I open the door and step back for him.

"Thank you." He looks around the room critically, then brushes at an invisible speck on his sleeve, like just coming in here has made him dirtier than he wanted. "My name is Elijah Jones, and I'm a lawyer who—among other projects—has an interest in the goings-on at Davenport Pharmaceuticals."

Great, I think. Exactly who we need right now.

"I understand that there has been an issue with Vincent Davenport?"

Bee gives a derisive snort. The rest of us stay quiet and somehow find all sorts of interesting things around the room to look at rather than looking at the vampire in front of us.

"Here." He whips a card out of somewhere in the designer jacket. "Maybe if you know I'm legitimate, it will be easier to talk openly."

I take the card but don't really look at it. I have no idea how I'm supposed to behave in this situation.

Thankfully, my mate jumps in. Apparently, she knows what the issue is.

"It's not that we don't think you're legitimate," she tells the guy. "You definitely look how I would expect a lawyer to look. What I'm curious about is what you want from us. I mean, we've all kind of been through enough."

He leans on one foot and assesses her from head to toe before answering.

"That's fair. If your stories are to be believed, you have

every reason to distrust anyone in a suit right now. You also have every reason to need protection from the Davenports right now." He holds up a defensive hand. "Yes, I know you're all protecting each other, but let's be honest, has that really been working out for you so far? The Davenports, in particular the youngest Davenport, are involved in a larger legal case I've been building. With the help of some testimony that's recently been brought to us, not to mention the stories some of you have brought to light recently, I believe we're very close to taking care of the Vincent Davenport issue."

"And by 'taking care of the issue,' do you mean we're all getting pulled out back and shot before we can embarrass the family any more?"

I want to kick Gloria for talking to him like that. What am I going to do if she gets herself thrown in vampire jail or something and leaves me to figure out what to do about all these politics and shit on my own?

I put what I hope is a calming hand on her shoulder. *Please don't piss off the vampire in the expensive suit*, I send in her direction.

The man's smile shows off his extra-sharp canine teeth, making me think that wolves and vampires might actually have more in common than I was raised to believe.

"By 'take care of the issue,' I mean that Vincent Davenport is a rotten tooth that I intend to extract, along with any other rotten teeth I can find. To my knowledge, no one in this room would be in need of that kind of . . . extraction."

We all share confused looks.

"I don't understand what you're saying," I admit. I'm already the dumb one in our group. I might as well own it.

"You were the students who found Cassie and convinced her to contact me, is this correct?"

We all share a look around the room, still completely lost.

"A few days ago, Cassie approached our organization with

evidence that someone has been stealing and using a trial drug that is still far from being approved for widespread use. Since then, we have moved her into a safe house until the repercussions of informing to us can be sorted out. My understanding is that everyone here has also faced some repercussions after coming out with their stories about Vincent Davenport? Well, I am here to conduct my own research and build a case to determine what should be done to deal with his transgressions."

I'm pretty sure my jaw just dropped so fast that my chin hit the floor.

"You're . . . planning on doing something about Vincent?" Kelsey asks.

"We are, in fact, already doing something about Vincent. In order to do more of something about Vincent, I need to take a statement from each of his victims, particularly regarding the effects of the drug he gave you."

My stomach churns with acid. Somehow, knowing that Gloria—and the others, of course—was drugged and remembering what that whole awful day was like didn't prepare me for hearing it laid out in plain language.

Gloria was drugged. Maybe it could even be argued that she was poisoned. Thinking back to the effects of the drug on her, poison seems to match the situation.

Knowing it like I did before, and really knowing it like I do now, with facts laid out in front of me, are two different things. The girl I've fallen in love with was poisoned, and I couldn't do anything about it.

I suppress a shiver and squeeze Gloria's shoulder. I need to stay calm for her. And I need to do a better job of protecting her. I can't stand the thought of how close she came to something even worse happening to her.

* * *

GLORIA

I'm back to having no idea who to trust—or not—once again.

I hate it.

"So, Cassie is okay?" I ask, latching onto the fact that seems to be spinning around my head slightly slower than the others.

Elijah, if that's actually his name, smiles reassuringly. "Maybe if I can give you some proof of life, that would make it easier to trust me?"

Honestly, I don't know. I don't even know which way is up anymore, much less whether this vampire can convince me to trust him.

I shrug. "I guess it wouldn't hurt."

He opens his oh-so-sleek, black leather tablet case and motions for everyone to come where they can see the screen. He plays a video of Cassie, and the room gasps collectively when we recognize what we're watching.

"The first time he raped me, I was at a house party for his fraternity."

She's in a small office, sitting across a desk from a man in a tweed jacket.

"Do you remember when that was?" an offscreen interviewer asks.

"The first Saturday of September, two years ago, my freshman year," she answers without hesitation.

It doesn't surprise me that she knows the exact day it happened, but hearing her say it still brings bile up my throat.

The interview continues, with Cassie describing her experience in enough detail that I feel wobbly and have to sit down. Elijah turns the video off before she's even finished, for which I'm grateful.

"Vincent has been on our radar for some time now," Elijah says as he turns off the video. Looking around the room, everyone is just as pale and shaken as I am. Elijah is the only calm and collected person here. I wonder if he's seen that video enough times to be desensitized to it. "We knew someone was stealing drugs, and we suspected it might be tied to him, but it wasn't until Cassie's testimony that we had any real proof. We'll make sure she's safe from him, just as we'll make sure all of you are safe if you come forward with official testimony."

Selena coughs politely and raises her hand. "Am I right in assuming that giving our testimony will involve more than answering some questions?"

Elijah nods. "If you were given the drug we believe Vincent stole, we need to conduct a physical examination to find out if it's still in your system and if you're experiencing any long-term effects. His most recent victims in particular may still be carrying traces of the drug, which would be useful in building our case against him. As the drug is still in trials, we also cannot offer any guarantees about its long-term effects —or lack thereof. Simply put, we need more information. Desperately."

Another look passes around the room. I'm not sure what everyone is thinking, but I imagine my fellow wolves are with me. The wolf community doesn't really do traditional medicine or doctor's offices or hospitals at all. We can heal from most things naturally and faster than a doctor could help us. The thought of letting a doctor—probably a vampiric doctor, no less—examine me makes my skin crawl.

"I don't think I can do that," I admit to the group, shooting Elijah an apologetic look. It's not his fault I've never been to a doctor and can't imagine letting myself trust one of them now.

Jimmy rubs a hand up and down my spine. He hasn't stopped touching me since this lawyer crashed into the dorm. Throughout the entire interview, he kept pulling me closer to him, like he needed to be reassured that I'm still here. Now that we aren't listening to the details of what Vincent might have done to me, Jimmy's a little more relaxed, but he's also still touching me.

"What if it was a wolf instead of a vampire?" he asks, surprising me.

"What do you mean?"

"I mean"—his cheeks are pink, and he looks more uncertain than I'm used to seeing him—"do you think it would be okay to be examined by a wolf? Would that make a difference? Just . . . since it seems important that they're able to check you out. What needs to happen so you can get the all clear?"

I'm not sure why, but Jimmy is the last person I would have expected to try to convince me to deal with doctors.

"I . . ." I look helplessly around the room, trying to find some allies. Even the other wolves seem to be nodding their heads in agreement. "I've never been to a doctor. I don't even really know what a doctor would do to me," I admit. The part I don't admit, at least not out loud, is that I'm scared. What if the doctor does something bad? Or what if the doctor finds something bad? What if there really are long-term effects from whatever drug this is? I don't want to know about it.

But Jimmy pulls me close against him again and breathes into my hair. "I need to know you're okay," he whispers into the top of my head. "Just let me make sure you're okay."

Sighing, I thread my arms around his waist and melt into the comfort he's offering. "Okay. I'll get checked out, but I don't like the thought of getting checked by a vampire. I'd prefer a wolf, if there even are any werewolf doctors?"

Elijah nods. "There aren't many, but we can find one for you. It really will help us build our case against Vincent, so thank you."

"What's going to happen to him?" Lydia asks. "I mean,

I'm guessing this isn't getting turned over to any human police organizations?"

"No," Elijah says in an ominous voice. "We intend to deal with this matter in-house. Since all of you have been affected by this, we will keep you posted, but you shouldn't expect to hear about the outcome on the news." With that, he leaves an address and phone number and tells us to go first thing tomorrow to see some corporate doctor, then leaves us, disoriented and speechless, in the living room.

* * *

The building is less intimidating than expected. I find a little comfort that it's not a true hospital, like I've seen in countless movies. It just looks like a big, corporate, soulless skyscraper. No flashing lights and sirens and mangled human bodies being wheeled out of ambulances on stretchers.

Jimmy stands right behind me, hands squeezing my shoulders reassuringly as I walk up to the sleek woman who's wearing a sleek suit and sitting at a sleek black desk near the entrance.

"I'm supposed to . . . I mean . . . Elijah . . . um . . . Jones said . . ."

"If you've got an appointment, all I need is your name," she interrupts my stammering to explain.

I give her my information, and thank all the gods, she's able to find me on her computer in an instant. Without asking for any justification or clarification, she hands matching visitor badges over to Jimmy and me before giving us directions and sending us through a security checkpoint. The guards don't seem interested in us particularly, but their eyes do have a watchfulness beyond what I would expect to see in the average airport security line. I get the creeping sensation that we've been carefully catalogued, filed away in these guys' brains and never to be forgotten again.

The doctor is nothing like I imagined. Instead of a cold-faced vampire, a jolly, grey-haired wolf shifter traipses into the office and starts talking too fast for us to get a word in.

"I'm Geordie Halifax. I'm the guy they call in when the traditional doctors won't work for whatever reason, and after reading your file, I totally get it. I'm guessing you've never so much as been in a doctor's office, much less had this type of doctor's appointment." He doesn't even give me a chance to nod yes before he starts talking again. "Well, I am here to make this whole process as comfortable as possible for you. Not that I expect your first-ever doctor appointment to be comfortable, exactly, but we can make the best of a difficult situation. Now, hold out your arm for me."

My head is whirling, but Geordie, or Dr. Halifax or whatever I'm supposed to call him, doesn't give me any time to think about it. He deftly pulls my arm toward him from across the desk.

"If you've never been to a doctor, I'm guessing you don't have much experience with needles," he goes on, and before I can explain that I've got plenty of experience with needles from working on a farm, he sticks one straight into the crook of my arm and starts pulling blood out of me.

I turn to look at Jimmy and find my own dizziness and queasiness mirrored on his face.

Halifax either doesn't notice or doesn't care about our discomfort. He keeps chatting away as he replaces a tube full of my blood with an empty tube, and then again, and again. Just when I'm wondering how much blood I have left in my body, he pulls out the needle and presses down on my arm for a second.

"Alright, you're all done," he says cheerfully.

"That's it?" I ask in disbelief. Not that it was exactly fun while it was happening, but I really expected him to do more than take a few vials of blood.

"That's all I need from you," Halifax says. "We should have preliminary results later this afternoon, but don't expect to hear back from us for a few days. This is one of those 'no news is good news' situations. If we don't get in touch in the next two days, it means there's nothing pressing for you to know about."

I let my breath out slowly. "I thought there would be more to this," I admit.

Halifax smiles at me. "I was probably about your age the first time I saw a doctor, and I remember feeling the same way. I wasn't sure what to expect, and I was sure I would never go back again. But that was the day I realized that wolves need doctors too, and I'd rather have a wolf for a doctor whenever I do need one."

"That's why you do this?" I'm not quite sure what I'm trying to ask, but I feel like my mind has kicked into a higher gear, trying to figure something out but I'm not even sure what.

"That's exactly why I do this," he confirms. "But there's still a lot of need for wolves to become doctors." He holds my gaze, not saying anything outright but communicating all the same.

Chapter Thirty

JIMMY

I think that I will never stop needing to touch her.

What started as attraction has grown to . . . I don't even know what. I don't have words to explain it.

Love. Yes. Of course.

But also, this idea that the longer I live with her in my life, the less I can live without her in my life.

Each time I touch her—and each of these touches seems like an absolute necessity to me, to reassure myself that she's actually still there—she gives me a confused look. She has no idea what I'm feeling.

I'm a fish, and she's the ocean, and it makes no difference to her if I exist or not, but I can't exist without her.

"That wasn't as bad as I expected," Gloria says in a cheerful voice. A crinkle forms between her brows for a moment as she looks at the hand I've looped around her elbow, then smooths as she turns to look at me. "I never even thought about there being wolf doctors. How about you?"

Caught off guard, I stammer for a moment. "I guess I

hadn't thought of it either. I mean, it makes sense that wolves need doctors every once in a while. And it would make sense that wolves who need doctors would want other wolves to be their doctors. And vampires become doctors all the time. Have you ever noticed that? Vampires might need doctors less often than shifters do, but there are tons of vampires who are doctors. Why is that?" Now I'm getting into the flow of my little speech, and Gloria doesn't seem to notice or care too much that I've readjusted so my arm is all the way around her back, so I keep going. "And humans seem to have no problem going to vampire doctors. Why shouldn't wolves go to doctors? Not that I'm the expert now or anything. I mean, today was my first time in a doctor's office too."

Gloria turns to face me and puts a hand on my chest to stop my rambling. "I think that's what I want to do."

"Oh?" It's hard to think of intelligent things to say when she looks at me with those wide, urgent eyes.

"Actually," Gloria goes on, "I kind of think that it's what I'm supposed to do. He said they needed more doctors who are shifters, and the thought just clicked into place. That's what I'm supposed to do with my life."

"Okay." I want to tell her how I know how brilliant she is and how she can do anything she wants to do, and—more than anything else—I want to tell her that I'll be there to support her through all of it, no matter what "it" is. I'll be there for her.

But the words all jumble together and get stuck together in my mouth and behind my tongue, so all I can manage to say is "Okay," which is obviously not what she needs to hear right now.

"So, yeah. I guess I thought you should know." She spins away and stalks toward the car without checking to see if I'm following.

* * *

The dorm has a festive atmosphere when we get back. Everyone has been to the doctor, it seems like someone is going to do something about our favorite douchebag Vincent, and now we know Cassie is alright. Beers are passed around, and everyone settles in for a small celebration. We're not ready for a full-blown party yet. Maybe after Vincent gets . . . well, whatever punishment he's going to get. I'm trying not to get my hopes up, but I can't help fantasizing about seeing some goons jump out of a van and beat him up before driving off and leaving him bleeding on the sidewalk. I don't want him dead. At least, not exactly. I just want to see him punished. And I want to know he's not going to hurt anyone else.

But the two people I want to spend time celebrating with more than anyone else seem to be avoiding me. Gloria and Bee are huddled in a corner, speaking too quietly for me to hear without actively eavesdropping on them. I maybe try to scoot close enough to hear but receive a not-at-all-subtle death glare from both of them, so I back off. Maybe Gloria will agree to share my bed again tonight. Maybe Bee will rethink going back to the pack like the pack leader demands.

Or maybe neither of them will speak to me again, and I'll have to go back to the pack alone and admit that I'm a failure in every way.

I chug my beer in an attempt to chase thoughts like that one away.

Everyone else, at least, seems content to sit back and relax. They're talking about going back to their classes tomorrow, maybe moving back to their dorms as soon as we hear news on Vincent. I hear more than one discussion about group shopping trips to replace everything that was destroyed in people's dorms while they've been hiding out here.

I love the sense of camaraderie that's sprung up with this

group since we all met just a few days ago. It sucks that we met under these particular circumstances, but I am glad I met these guys.

And pretty soon, I'm going to have to go back home and face reality with my father and probably never be allowed back on campus again. I hope some of them will keep in touch. At least Gloria will come back with me, now that things are settling down. Isn't that what she said? She wouldn't go to the pack until the Vincent stuff was sorted out. It will feel like being ripped in half, if Bee refuses to come home while Gloria goes back with me, but Bee made it pretty clear where she stands.

But what happens if the pack leader orders Gloria to drop out of school and stay with the pack? What about her becoming a doctor? What about me wanting to support her in whatever she wants to do?

Shit. This is going to be a mess. I want to go over and ask her what to do about all of these things, but she and Bee are still huddled together, having a serious talk and excluding me.

My beer tastes a lot more sour, and my hopes feel a lot dimmer as I sit and watch them and wonder what we're going to do.

Chapter Thirty-One

GLORIA

Jimmy is giving me longing looks from across the room, while Bee is whispering urgently in my ear that if I visit the pack with Jimmy, I'll never leave pack lands again. Or at least I won't leave pack lands until I've been successfully mated and produced a few cubs. Ugh. And when I ask her how she knows that or what exactly her connection to the pack is, she goes into super-spy evasion mode. What the fuck is happening?

"So what am I supposed to do?" I ask, giving up on getting any real answers about her place in all of this. "I don't want to do the pack-mate-motherhood thing. I've got other stuff to do with my life! But I can't just . . . not go. I mean, they won't let me just ignore their summons. Not for long."

Bee rocks her head side to side as she contemplates the situation. "Well, it's definitely not ideal, but my plan is to ignore them as long as I can, then run away and hide if things get worse. We've got vampire friends who could protect us now. Who would come after us—or even know where to look

—if we hid out with Taylor or Devon? Though, we would both have to deal with being shunned whenever someone did find us. You would have to decide if it's worth it to you to keep your freedom like that," she finishes with a shrug.

A shudder passes through me. I want—more than anything else in the world—to be someone and do something with my life, and I'm not convinced that my "something" and "someone" is having kids and being a mother. I'm still pretty convinced after my appointment at the doctor's that my "someone" I'm supposed to be is a doctor. I want to be someone who helps people. Maybe even saves people.

And, yes, I know that being a mother is important, but . . . why can't I wait and do that later, when I'm actually ready for it?

I ignore Jimmy's heavy-handed hints to come to bed with him and keep discussing plans with Bee late into the night. Jimmy gives up on me and goes to bed while Bee and I keep talking until we fall asleep on the couch together, all of our other temporary roommates strewn around us on the couch, chairs, and floor of the living room. Which means we're all woken up bright and early the next morning by someone pounding on the door.

Elijah bustles through the door, looking way less calm and collected than I remember seeing him before.

"Sorry if I woke you all up, but I thought you would want to see this live if possible," he explains, fiddling with something on the TV, then his phone, then the TV again until a video pops up on the big screen of a dark, formal-looking, circular room. Intricately carved chairs in shiny dark wood are placed around the perimeter of the room, while a simple wooden chair sits in the center of the room.

"What did you want us to see?" I ask.

Elijah shushes me and points at the TV screen, where I see pallid people in expensive-looking suits filing in and sitting in the ornate chairs. I don't bother asking Elijah again since it doesn't seem likely he'll answer.

We all collectively gasp when Vincent is led into the room—chin raised and looking every inch the wealthy frat boy who can get away with anything—with his hands cuffed behind his back.

I guess Elijah wasn't lying. This really is something I want to see.

"I hereby call this meeting of the board to order," the man in the most throne-like chair proclaims. "We have just one piece of business today. The matter of Vincent Davenport Jr., who stands accused of interference with other species, use of illegal substances, theft of illegal substances, and putting vampiric secrets at risk. Does anyone come forward to speak on his behalf?"

Vincent's proud and confident expression slips for a moment, revealing a sick, scared little boy. My heart flutters in glee, and I wonder if that makes me a terrible person. Up until I hear Jimmy clapping from across the room.

"Alright, we got him!" he shouts.

I wonder if it's really that easy, and I try to hold back my excitement.

The bigwig vampires pause for a long few seconds to wait for anyone to step forward, but no one does.

"As no one stands for the defense, we will continue on without," the same guy says.

A full-blown trial unfolds before our eyes, with Vincent wilting a little further as each piece of evidence is brought up and discussed by the vampires around the room. It's not like any trial I've ever seen, though my trial experience is pretty much limited to TV. For one thing, these guys don't seem interested at all in the whole "jury of your peers" thing. For another thing, they don't seem particularly interested in hearing Vincent's side of the story. They discuss each piece of evidence amongst themselves, completely ignoring Vincent as he sinks lower and lower in his chair. His eyes shift from side to side, searching for an escape.

No escape for you, asshole.

And suddenly, it's all over.

The vampire who seems to carry the most authority stands and proclaims, "Vincent Davenport Jr., we find you guilty of all charges. The punishment is one hundred years solitary confinement."

Panic fills Vincent's face. "No! You can't! I've learned my lesson!" He thrashes in the chair he's cuffed to. "Please! You can't!"

One by one, the vampires around the room stand and turn their backs to him as he continues to beg for a second chance, a more lenient punishment, or someone to listen to him. None of them responds, and two burly vampires eventually come into the room and force some kind of gag into his mouth before dragging him away, still screaming and thrashing in desperation.

Elijah shuts off the video feed, and we all inhale together. I wonder how long I've been holding my breath. It feels like it could be hours.

"Davenport Pharmaceuticals decided to move quickly once I brought the evidence to them. They seemed interested in dealing with the situation themselves instead of letting it reach the higher courts," he explains. "Good for us as far as having the problem solved quickly. Not ideal from a standpoint of trying to build a larger case, but I'm sure I'll catch another breakthrough soon."

"So, what happens to him now?" Bee asks.

"He'll be locked in a cell and gagged so he can't speak or feed until his punishment is up," Elijah answers casually, as if locking someone in a cell is an everyday occurrence for him.

"What do you mean he can't feed?" I ask, stomach twisting at the thought of what the answer probably is.

"Standard vampiric punishment. He'll survive, hopefully have a chance to reflect on his actions, and be unable to cause any more problems for the next century." Again, Elijah seems way too casual about this whole situation.

Jimmy puts his hand on my shoulder before I can object to the inhumane treatment of monsters. "Just let him be," he murmurs into my hair. "Let the vampires deal with vampire business."

I know he's not wrong about that, but I can also already feel the walls closing in around me. Or maybe it's more of a trap snapping closed.

As if my thoughts brushed against his, Jimmy says, "I guess we can go back to the pack leader now since Vincent is taken care of?" He looks relieved, but I'm internally slamming against the walls of my new cage.

"What's the deal with all of Vincent's supporters?" I ask Elijah. "Is it safe for us to go out on our own again?"

Elijah jumps in with an answer before Jimmy can insist on acting as a bodyguard.

"The fraternity has been put on tight restrictions. All of his known associates are being closely monitored. His close friends have been warned of the potential consequences should they attempt any form of retaliation. It should be safe again."

I nod and stalk out of the dorm without a backward glance. I need to think about my future without breathing in the pheromone-filled air of my mate's dorm. I need to remind myself that, as much as I want him, there are other things in life that I want so much more than him. I need to repeat Bee's words as a mantra. If I go to the pack, I won't get to leave until I've done what they want me to do. I can't do that. I can't give up my dreams and my life just so I can be the perfect mate and mother that the pack will want me to be.

Jimmy jogs to catch up with me.

"Where are you going?"

I search for an easy escape, but there is none.

"I'm not going to the pack," I tell him. "I don't know where I'm going to go, but you can't make me go there."

I walk away, feeling the burn of his hurt expression on my shoulder blades. Bee is right. I shouldn't have said I would follow the pack's orders once things were better. Being shunned, having to hide from the man I love, probably causing my family a lot of strife. They're a high price to pay, but I can't see another way of keeping my freedom or following my own dreams. Letting myself be trapped in the life the pack leader would choose for me isn't an option, no matter the cost.

I walk aimlessly until I find myself at the edge of town, then realize what I really need. I strip down and leave my clothes folded neatly by a tree before shifting, then take off with the goal of leaving all of my storming thoughts and worries behind.

Chapter Thirty-Two

JIMMY

I want to chase after Gloria again, ask her what she means, but Bee grabs my arm and yanks me back inside.

"If you don't give her some space right now," she hisses at me, "you are going to ruin whatever chance you have with her. You have to let her breathe, Grey."

I growl at her but manage to refrain from actually snapping at her in my frustration. "I don't know what to do. I can't just let her go and then get on with my life as normal. I need her. But apparently, she doesn't feel the same way about me because she can just leave anytime she feels like it."

"Yeah?" Bee gives me a significant, wide-eyed look, like there's something really obvious I should have caught on to before now. "Do you think that might be, like, the whole point for her?"

"The point of what? What are you talking about?"

She huffs and rolls her eyes. "How are you so clueless? You seriously don't deserve her, just for the record."

"Okay. Fine. I'm clueless. I'm undeserving. I'm the worst person you know. Would you please just help me out here?"

Bee throws her hands up. "She knows that giving in to you and letting you take her back to the pack will mean she never gets any freedom ever again. Of course she's running away right now. Either she runs away from you so she can live her own life, or she decides she's lived enough of her own life and then gives up and comes back to you, giving up her freedom and hopes and dreams and any chance at making an impact on the world beyond producing babies for you!" Her voice rises steadily until she's shouting loud enough for the entire building to hear.

"Why are you shouting at me?" I shout back.

"Because you don't get it, and if you keep not getting it, you're going to ruin her life by refusing to understand where she's coming from!"

"I . . . I understand . . ." I try to protest, but there's an annoying voice of doubt in my mind. I agreed to not get her pregnant, but it's not like I stood up to my father for her. It's not like I was the one who warned her away from going back to the pack leader. It's not like I actually told her that I want to support her in whatever she wants to do. "Shit." I sink down on the bed and rest my head in my hands. "What the fuck am I supposed to do?" I groan at the floor, or Bee, or the world, or whoever the hell cares to help me out right now.

Bee sits down beside me and wraps an arm around my shoulders. "You might start by doing something to prove you aren't going to drag her in front of the pack leader kicking and screaming. That might help your cause a little bit, at least."

"Shit," I groan again. "I don't want to face him again so soon." Or ever, really, but he is my father. There's no helping that.

"I know you don't." She gives my shoulder a cheerful pat,

which is anything but reassuring, then practically skips out of the room, leaving me to wallow in my own mess.

* * *

I wait an hour—okay, I wallow for an hour—trying to figure out what to say to Gloria before I can't stand to wait anymore.

Once I've made my choice, I walk out of my dorm with my head held high. And have to completely ignore my room-mates' comments in order to keep my head held high. I guess it was too much to hope that none of them would notice me making a fool of myself.

Oh well. This is what love does to people.

Unfortunately, my hopes of stepping outside and immediately catching sight or scent of Gloria are dashed pretty quickly. I can smell every other person on campus going about their business as if everything is completely normal, but I can't catch Gloria's scent in the mess. Not with my human nose, at least.

Who needs dignity anyway?

I slip out of my clothes as inconspicuously as possible and shift before too many people have a chance to see my little show.

There. With heightened wolf senses, I catch a hint of Gloria on the breeze, smelling like trees and wool and all of her delicious goodness that I want to be wrapped in for the rest of my life. Focus.

The longer I track her, the stronger her trail is. I take comfort in the fact that she apparently wasn't literally running away from me. This way, I might be able to catch her.

Finally, growling uncontrollably from my hunger for Gloria, I come across a noseful of her. But I can't find the actual her. I track the scent to a pile of clothes under a tree and bury my nose in them for a few breaths. Need surges through me just from having my face in her scent. I need to bury my face in her and be completely surrounded by her scent.

But even though I found her clothing, there's no sign of the actual person.

I howl out a call to her. Maybe it's a warning. Get back here, missy, or else. More like a cry of desperation. *Please*, I beg mentally. *Please, don't leave me like this.*

I double down on searching out her scent, running through the forest with my nose down and stopping just long enough to check my direction when the scent gets thinner or harder to read.

I need you. I need you so bad.

I don't know if she feels my need or if she's just slowing down, but her scent is getting stronger as I start to catch up with her.

Finally, she comes into view.

She's just sitting, in wolf form, staring at the sky. Not that I'm judging. I've done plenty of sky staring myself. And I'm definitely not complaining. I've finally found her, after what feels like ages of chasing after her.

I come up beside her and sit, but I can't join her in staring up at the sky because I'm captivated by staring at her. I've barely seen her as a wolf, and she's absolutely beautiful. Thick, black fur shines in the moonlight. I can still make out her perfect musculature beneath the thick pelt. And, of course, her scent is magnified because we're both wolves. If I hadn't already believed I was mated to her, this would seal it for me. She is perfection. Made for me. And I have to do whatever it takes to keep her.

It's hard to read wolves' faces for emotion, but her scent tells me a story of its own. She turns to me, resignation and sadness coming across loud and clear to me.

Right. This is my moment. What I chased after her to say.

I shift back so I can speak and quickly realize the problem

with this plan. She might not be affected by being this close to me when I'm naked, but my dick is already giving hopeful twitches that I don't have time for right now. I bring my knees to my chest and wrap my arms around them, hoping Gloria won't figure out what I'm up to.

"You don't have to say anything, but I really need you to listen for a little bit," I tell her.

Maybe I imagine her head lowering in a nod, but I decide to take it as a sign to go on.

"The first thing, which I think is more important than anything else, and which you might not agree about but I need to tell you anyway, is that I love you. I'm in love with you. I've fallen for you like . . . I don't know how to put it. Like a rock in water? I'm really, completely, head over heels in love with you."

Her wolf eyes blink at my words but give no hint as to how she's taking this news.

"Okay, so that's out of the way." I'm like a barrel rolling downhill at this point. I start babbling out my half-formed thoughts and plans to her, hoping she can make some kind of sense from it.

"I get why you don't want to go back with me to deal with the pack leader, and I'm not going to try and make you. Not until you want to. I see how that's not where you need to be right now. And I need to stand up to him first, anyway. And I should have told you before about my . . . well . . . my connection to him. And I should have stood up to him before. Bee helped me see that."

Gloria shifts and plants her hand over my mouth to stop my babbling.

"Jimmy, what the fuck are you even talking about? Do you think you could, like, organize your thoughts a little and then share them?"

Her glower almost stops me from glancing down appreciatively at her naked body, which causes her to cross her arms over her chest with an angry huff. Damn.

"The pack leader is my father," I confess, torn between watching for her reaction and looking away in shame. "And he's a complete asshole most of the time and a bigot." I heave a sigh. "And when I went to ask him for help, he only offered half of what I needed, and of course, there were a ton of strings attached because, of course, there always are. And while I was there, he . . . well, I think he smelled you on me, and now he thinks he has some kind of claim over you because he's figured out we're mated. But I will go to him and tell him he doesn't get any say in what you do. Because I don't want to be the reason you don't get to be a doctor—or whatever you want to do with your life—and he will definitely want to have a say in what you do with your life. Just . . . please give me a chance, okay? I want to be wherever you are, and I want to support you in whatever, and I can't do that if you run away from me again. So, please give me a chance to be with you."

She blinks at me, face as impossible to read as when she was in wolf form.

"That's a lot to dump on me at once," she finally says.

"I know," I say. "My father and all the shit that comes along with him is already a lot. You don't think I know that already? Why do you think I was trying to keep it secret here at school? I thought I could just be 'Jimmy' instead of 'Greyson James Carmichael III' and my life would be easier, but all of the shit with my father always catches up to me."

I realize that my voice is shaking, and I have to snap my teeth shut before even more emotion starts pouring out of me. I feel like word vomiting all my problems onto Gloria is not the best tactic to convince her to be with me.

To my relief, the tension in Gloria's shoulders visibly loosens, and she turns to sit beside me. Still not touching, though. Or giving any hints about what's going on in her mind.

"Does anyone in your real life actually call you Jimmy?" she asks. "Or was that made up too?"

"Only when I was a kid," I admit. "I guess I kind of wanted to go back to feeling like a kid again. Not some kind of heir to the empire or whatever."

"And what do people usually call you?"

"People who know me—people I like—call me Grey. Most people call me Greyson, but I really don't want you to start doing that. I always kind of feel like I'm choking when someone calls me Greyson. Like all of the pack's expectations are around my neck and tightening a little more with each responsibility and there's no way I can be what they all expect me to be. What they need me to be since I don't have any siblings who could take over—"

Gloria silences me by wrapping an arm around my shoulders. "I guess both of us have pretty good reasons for not wanting to go back there, then," she whispers, and I can't help but lean into the comfort she's offering me.

GLORIA

Jimmy says he's actually Greyson.

Fine.

Jimmy says he's the heir to the pack leader.

Oof, but also fine.

Jimmy says he needs me.

What do I do with this?

And now he's leaning into me like he really does need me.

Fuck.

"Okay," I hear myself saying in a voice way calmer than I expected. "So what will your father say if I go in front of him as pack leader?"

"Probably that we're mated and that you need to let me impregnate you with the next pack leader heir," he groans into his hands.

"But you're not going to make me do that?"

Jimmy jerks up to stare at me in disbelief. "I promised you, didn't I? I don't want you to have to do what you don't want to do. And I know that you have bigger plans than that. Didn't I say that?"

I shrug. "I had to make sure you understood. And I still have to make sure you understand. Because I plan on finishing school before having any babies. And if I'm going to be a doctor, that means a lot of school to finish. And that means you standing up to your father for a long time and probably more than you ever have before in your life."

"I get that," Jimmy insists. "Standing up to my father. Check. I totally get that. But does this mean you're willing to give me a chance?"

"Yeah. I guess it does. I mean. As long as you aren't expecting to use me as a baby-making machine. As much as I hate to admit it, you've kind of grown on me."

Jimmy grins at me. "I've grown on you?"

"At some point between you eating me out and pulling out before you came so you wouldn't get me pregnant," I tell him sardonically.

"I can keep eating you out and pulling out so I don't get you pregnant," he promises with more earnestness than any guy I've ever met before.

"Are you sure about this?" I ask. "I mean, it's one thing to make promises before I've made any commitments, but how do I know you won't throw me in front of the pack leader or lock me in your baby-making dungeon at the first opportunity?"

"What if I keep showing you that you can trust me? Time after time after time? What if I never do anything that might get you pregnant? And what if I never drag you in front of the pack leader? Do you think you might eventually trust me?"

I stretch out on the ground and sigh. "I guess you're going to have to prove it to me."

He looks at me with hope and excitement, then dives on me with kisses and tongue, tasting every bit of me before he reaches my pussy and lavishes all of his attention on it.

Of course, whether I'm ready to trust him or not, my body is fully on board. Jimmy—Grey, I remind myself, not Jimmy —didn't even have to touch me, and I can already feel myself dripping with wetness. Even if Jim—Grey—doesn't betray me and try to get me pregnant, my body definitely has its own plans.

He groans in ecstasy as his tongue slides down my cleft, and all thoughts about what name to call him or worries about pregnancy risks fly straight from my mind. The only thing is him and his mouth and the way he seems to be enjoying this as much as I am.

I grab his hair in both my fists and tug, loving the rumble of his answering groan against my clit. He alternates between slow strokes, his tongue flattened like he wants to taste every bit of me that he can, and quick licks against my clitoris that send electricity spiking through my center.

"Fuck, you taste so good for me," he moans.

At the same time, I grit out, "I'm so close," and he redoubles his efforts like his life depends on making me come. It kind of feels like my life might depend on it right now too. All of my muscles are tightening down, locking up in preparation for what's about to happen, and then my release crashes over me in waves, causing every muscle to spasm and jerk. I lose control of my form and accidentally shift halfway into a wolf before catching my human form and bringing it back.

And my mate keeps up his assault on my sensitive flesh through it all until I feel myself winding up for what seems like an impossible second orgasm, so close after such a mind-altering one.

"Fuck! Jimmy, I can't, it's too—" My attempt to protest gets swallowed in my orgasm, and only then, as I lie boneless and twitching on the forest floor, does Jimmy lay a final, achingly tender kiss on my sex, then gather me up in his arms and cuddle me close against him.

Against all reason, against anything I have ever done in my life, I fall asleep like that, naked and human and out in the open, protected only by my mate's arms.

Chapter Thirty-Three

JIMMY

This is the last place I would have ever—and I really mean ever, if there was any other option in the world—chosen to be.

"What are you doing back so soon?" My mom's eyes are worried, but she masks her worry with what seems like genuine happiness to see me.

"Oh, you know. I just love it here so much. Can't stay away."

She pauses from hugging me to draw back and give a very expressive raised eyebrow.

"Okay, fine. I need the pack leader's help again. Or . . . I need the pack leader to stop trying to help, I guess? I've . . . kind of fucked things up at school."

The fact that she doesn't call me out for my cursing means I must look like absolute shit. If I look healthy to her, she puts a stop to that shit real fast. But she just gives me an understanding look and guides me through to the living room, where she plunks me down on a couch and sits in the armchair right next to me.

"Okay. Now I'm ready to hear it. What have you gotten yourself into?"

"I didn't get myself into anything!" I protest, but she just tilts her head and waits for me to go on.

"Fine," I groan, "but if I tell you everything, please don't just pass it on to the Council, okay?"

Mom pats my knee. "You know they're going to hear about it one way or another, right? Wouldn't it be better to tell them first so you could control the narrative?"

"It's not that kind of problem," I huff back at her. Though, I suppose she has a point. My father, in all of his wisdom and . . . yada yada yada . . . believes Gloria is important, otherwise he wouldn't have asked me to bring her to him.

"So, if it's not that kind of problem, what kind is it? Are you going to tell me there isn't a girl involved?"

"She's so smart, and amazing, and she has big plans for her life, and she's afraid the Council will drag her back here and never let her leave," I admit. "Did you . . ." I'm not sure if there could be a more awkward conversation to have with my mother, but I need to hear her answer. "Are you happy to be mated to my father? I mean . . . did you ever wish you could do something else or be someone else? Or at least be with someone else?"

Mom's eyebrows climb, and her eyes look like they might pop right out. "Well, I guess I knew you would ask me something like that eventually, but I can't say I was prepared for it today."

"I'm sorry. I just—"

She cuts me off with a hand that covers my own and squeezes. "No. It's good we talk about these things. You must really care about this girl if you're asking me questions like this on her behalf, and it's probably best to sort it out before we go to the Council about it."

She squeezes my hand again, tight, before continuing. "Things have always been complicated between your father and me. You know that. You've known that forever. It's probably the first thing you learned about the world, that things can be complicated like that between people." She sighs. "I'm sorry that you've seen the complicated parts of our relationship so much. I wish we could have shielded you better from all that when you were younger, but I don't think either of us realized how affected you would be. Something you should know, that you probably can't see from your perspective, is that your father and I do love each other. It's in our own way, and it often doesn't look like the love on TV shows, but we do. Do I sometimes wish I'd run in the other direction before we could be mated to each other? Sure. It probably crosses my mind at least once a day. He's not an easy man, and this isn't an easy position in life. But the fact is, we are mated, and running away at this point would be harder than sawing off my own hands."

I cringe at that imagery, but she keeps going, ignoring my look of disgust.

"We're mated, and we've found a way to love each other, and we got you from that, and even if I daydream about leaving, the fact is I'm happy with my life and my choices. I know I'm in the place I'm supposed to be. You tell me this girl of yours has big plans. Well, how do they fit with your plans? How can you find a way to fit your lives together so you both know that you're where you're supposed to be?"

I stare at her. My jaw is probably hanging open like the village idiot, but my brain is whirring faster than it ever has before. Where am I supposed to be? With Gloria. There's no doubt in my mind. My father might think my life's purpose is to take over for him as pack leader, but he's wrong. I was made for her. The right place for me to be is wherever she is. The right thing for me to do is whatever she needs.

"I think I'll need some help convincing him," I finally say once the tornado in my brain subsides.

Mom grins. "Believe it or not, convincing your father of things is actually one of my specialties. It has a lot to do with picking my battles and a bit to do with being mated to him." She wiggles her eyebrows in a way that makes me groan and hide my face in my hands. "But I haven't fought any battles with him for a while, so I'm due to win one. Now, tell me everything so we can come up with a strategy."

* * *

"We hereby call this meeting of the Council of Wolves to order."

Fuck. Here we go again. I glance over at my mother for support, and she gives me the eyeball that I'm oh so familiar with. It says, "You can do this," and "Suck it up, buttercup," in equal measures, and I know both of these things are true, but I'm glad she's there reminding me of them anyway.

"What order of business is being brought before the Council of Wolves?"

I have to clear my throat twice before any words come out.

"I stand before you in order to formally renounce my claim as heir to the pack leader," I finally gasp out, "and, if necessary, to formally renounce my place as pack member."

"What?" My father's voice roars out before anyone else has a chance to weigh in.

"I formally ren—"

"I heard that." He strides toward me, sparing a single angry glance at Mom before coming even with me. "What the hell do you think you're playing at?"

Gulp. Remember what we talked about before. Remember what's at stake here.

"I'm not playing. I formally renounce any claim I have as your heir. It's . . ." I wet my lips and take a shaky breath. "It's not what I want. It's never been what I want."

He glares at me. Because genetics are weird, it's like looking in a magical aging mirror. My personality is a lot closer to my mother's, but I definitely got my looks from him.

"Don't you understand that it's never been about what you want?" he growls into my face. If I was any less familiar with his angry face, I probably would have already wet my pants. As it stands, I grit my teeth and take another deep, if shaky, breath.

"Okay. Fine. It's not about what I want. What is it about? Because you and I both know that if it's about what the pack needs, that's not me. If you try to force me to stay, you'll never get what you actually need from me."

My father—weird how I know him so well in a way, but he's actually a complete stranger to me in all the ways that matter—glances at Mom, then back to me. "Why now?" he asks. "What made you think to do this now?"

"I'm doing this now because I never had something I cared about more until now, but now I do. And now I've figured out that the most important thing to me isn't compatible with everything here."

"The girl?"

No use trying to keep it secret. I give a quick nod.

My father grunts and steps back. "Girls come and go. There's no reason you can't mate this one and continue your duties. And if she is going to keep you from your duties, there's no reason to believe you won't get over her. Find another girl."

It's my turn to glance at Mom before looking back at him. Her face is set in stone, just like when we entered this room together. She doesn't need to say anything to help with my argument.

"I have it on pretty good authority that some girls don't come and go," I say in a voice too low for the rest of the room to hear and jerk my head toward Mom, just in case he doesn't understand what I'm saying.

I can tell by his scowl that he's caught my message. "You're really serious about her?"

I jerk my head down in a single nod.

"And why can't you be serious about her while also fulfilling your duties here?"

I swallow. "Because my place is by her side, and my position is supporting her. And she has things to do other than become a pack mother."

He snarls and paces in front of me. "There's nothing wrong with being a pack mother." He shoots a significant look at Mom but continues his pacing.

Mom glides forward gracefully and stops his pacing with a touch.

"We can agree on that, at least," she says with an amused twist of her lips, "but can we also agree that not everyone should walk the same path? And maybe Greyson needs to start walking his own path now?"

With a not-at-all-convinced, still-angry-at-being-outplayed glower, he spins to face the Council.

"A decision will not be made yet concerning the acceptance or refusal of this pack member's status in the pack. He has a few years before we need to make any decisions on leadership. In the meantime, my second-in-command will serve as my heir."

Jacob does manage to look surprised, though it's done in the type of way that I wonder how often he's practiced that particular look in the mirror. But whatever. It's not going to be my problem.

My father turns his attention back to me. "She'd better turn out to actually be worth it," he mutters at me before turning and striding out of the meeting hall as if his feet are on fire.

* * *

"What the hell do you think you're doing?" He tears into me the moment I'm back in the house, which I find kind of ironic since he's out of this house so often I hardly think of it as his. But here he is, glowering like he's going to change my mind through the sheer force of his anger.

"Nice to see you outside of Council Chambers, Father. School has been tough but good, thanks for asking, Father. How have things been going here, Father?" I should absolutely control the sarcasm dripping from my voice, but I can't seem to get a hold on it.

His eyes narrow at me until I can only see the tiniest slit of gold flashing between his eyelids. "So, I take it you think you're really smart because you've been off at college? Being a smart college kid gives you a smart mouth too?"

Mom interrupts him with a jab to the chest. "I'm making tea, then the three of us are sitting down to have an actual conversation. Both of you sit down and don't say a word until I get back."

My father full-on rolls his eyes at her like he's the teenager in the room, but she just raises an eyebrow. Rather than get involved in that fight, I scurry to the armchair and sit before anything can escalate. He tosses his hands in the air and sits across from me with an angry huff, muttering something I can't quite hear under his breath.

"Sorry, dear, what was that you said?" Mom asks with a fake innocent quirk to her lips.

"I said, 'Tea sounds lovely, sweetheart,'" he grits out while a muscle in his jaw pulses with tension.

I choke back the snort of laughter that's threatening to bubble out of me.

"Oh, perfect. I thought that's what I heard."

We sit, stiff and silent and glaring, until Mom comes back with a tea tray.

I don't think I can manage to force anything into my mouth, much less swallow it, but I pick up one of the cookies to be polite. My father snatches three finger sandwiches—when did she have the time to make finger sandwiches, anyway?—and eats them all with a single bite each. I think about pointing out that his table manners are lacking, but that doesn't seem like it will be productive.

It would probably be satisfying, though.

"Alright," Mom starts. "I think it's time we got some things out in the open. Greyson, was there something you wanted to tell your father?"

"Yeah." I hunch my shoulders in a futile attempt to protect myself. "I don't really want to be pack leader, and I never wanted to be pack leader. And you can't force me to do it."

Mom's gaze swings toward my father. "And do you have something to say to your son?"

He gulps down an entire cup of black tea, keeping his glare trained on me the entire time. "Yes. What in god's name made you think you have a choice?" He explodes out of his chair and starts pacing, his voice rising with every word. "You don't want to take on your responsibilities? News flash, kiddo! Nobody does! You think I grew up dreaming of taking over this position? Of course I didn't! The only person who ever wanted to take over this position was Jacob, which is why he's obviously the last person who should. But you just tied my hands in front of all of them, so I had to name Jacob as heir anyway. So, let me repeat, what the hell do you think you're doing?"

"I'm not letting you dictate what I do with my life anymore! That's what I think I'm doing!" I don't think I've ever shouted at him. Not like this. And now that I've started, the dam is busted open, and there's no stopping the flow of words spilling out of me. "So you aren't happy with your life, and you wish you'd refused the responsibility when you had the chance. Well, that's exactly what I'm doing. I met someone, and I'm in love with her, and I can't be with her and also be under your thumb. I've known for a long time that I didn't want to be pack leader, but this is the first time in my life that I know what I do want!"

I stand there panting into the silence left behind by my rant. He glares at me for a minute, then takes a slow breath and sinks back onto the couch.

"If you're in love with her, doesn't that make everything easier?" He glances at Mom, then back at me. "All of this is . . . more bearable . . . if you have someone to support you. Why can't she do that for you?"

I take my own calming breath and sit back down. "Because she has better things to do with her life. She's better than me. Smarter, I mean, and she has all these dreams, and if I drag her here to support me, she'll be completely miserable, and I'll lose her."

My father nods thoughtfully. "What type of dreams are so much more important than being mated to the heir to the pack leader?"

"Dreams like . . . being a doctor." I rush through the words, praying he won't catch them or think too hard about them.

"A what?" he shouts, exploding out of his seat again. I guess he heard me.

Mom intercedes, laying a hand on his arm and pressing

him back toward his seat. "A doctor," she tells him steadily. "Apparently, there's a need for wolf doctors that isn't currently being met. I, for one, am excited to know we'll have someone with fresh ideas and ambitions coming into the family."

The two of them share a long look, and I have no idea what to make of that. All I know is that now I feel like an out-of-place third wheel. *Is it too late to sneak out the back door and let them sort this out?* a cowardly voice in the back of my head asks. *Yes*, I answer it. *It's definitely too late for that.*

Before I manage to sink into the chair and successfully become invisible, he turns his attention back to me.

"What about the family line? And what about children?"

I steal a glance at my mother to remind me of what we talked about earlier. "That's Gloria's decision," I tell him in just above a whisper. Frankly, I'm fucking relieved that any sound came out at all.

"Gloria's. Decision." Both words fall from his mouth like stones. Not quite questions. Almost accusations.

"Gloria gets to decide if we have cubs," I say, "and if that means you need to find a replacement heir, I'm prepared for that."

I can see the angry thoughts swirling behind his eyes and grinding between his teeth.

"Gloria gets to decide what you do with the rest of your life?"

I catch Mom's slanted look his way but figure it won't help anything to point it out to him.

"No. Gloria gets to decide what to do with her own life. I've decided that I'll support her in whatever that is."

"You'll support her." Again, the flat tone of voice isn't quite a question or an accusation or anything at all that I could grab onto and argue against. He's just repeating facts.

"Yes," I say through clenched teeth, ready to walk the fuck

out and never come back again. "I will support her. Whatever that looks like. Even if it means walking away from the pack."

He looks stricken at that. Come to think of it, maybe he needs a doctor. Maybe Gloria will be his doctor someday.

"You would seriously leave Jacob in charge just to . . . prove a point?"

"Yes, if that's how you want to think about it, fine! I'm doing this to prove a point! But I feel like I really need to make this part clear. I'm trying to prove myself to her. I'm not trying to prove anything to anyone else. I'm trying to prove a point to her, and if that point inconveniences you or anyone else, that's really too damn bad because I'm not changing my mind about this."

Chapter Thirty-Four

GLORIA

I'm halfway through history class when Jimmy bursts in. Though I was a little worried about any Davenport groupies coming after me again, there hasn't been any of that as far as I've seen.

But then Jimmy—or Greyson or whoever—flings open the lecture hall doors and strides toward me with a purpose.

"What the hell are you doing?" I hiss through clenched teeth. I glance around, trying to figure out how many people are watching us—too many—and whether they're dangerous—seems likely.

"I came to find you," he says, looking bewildered.

"Okay. But why are you interrupting class to do it? Everyone is looking at us."

He glances around like he just now noticed where he is. "I just got back. I missed you." His earnestness makes it hard to stay annoyed.

A pointed throat clearing from the professor convinces me to grab my books and drag Jimmy out of the lecture hall.

"Okay, what's up?" I ask once we're clear of the room.

His eyes lighting up is the only warning I get before he grabs me by the waist and spins me in a circle. "I stood up to my father, and I stood up to the Council, and my mom is on our side!"

"What? What are you talking about?" I push against his arms, trying to get him to let me down, but he just squeezes me tighter to him.

"Exactly what I said," he tells me. "I finally stood up to them and told them that I don't want to be pack leader or any of it and he had to agree, so now I can keep going to school and stay here with you, and he's not going to try and force you back there."

I shake my head in disbelief. "You really mean it? This isn't some sneaky way to get me to let my guard down?"

He marks a little X over his chest. "Cross my heart and hope to die."

I can't help it. A giggle bursts out of me at the childish saying.

I loop my arms around his neck with a grin. "I'm gonna hold you to that," I promise him.

"I hope you do." He grins back and kisses me.

* * *

Bee is alone, waiting for us when we get back to the dorm.

"I take it from the fact that you're walking together and have sickeningly lovey-dovey expressions that you've worked it out?"

"We have," I sigh, looking at Jimmy with the exact expression that I know she just described as sickening. Then, a thought snaps me back into reality. I bore into her with my eyes, trying to put the pieces of the Bethany puzzle together and failing miserably. "Okay, I give up. Would you both please give me the full story about who you are to each other?"

A look passes between her and Jimmy before she slumps and waves toward the couch. "You'd better sit down for this. It's not really a quick story to tell."

Jimmy leads me over to the couch with a hand on my back and doesn't break contact after we sit.

"It's tough to know where to start," Bee says to her fingers, which are twisting together in her lap.

I decide to jump in with the question that's bothering me the most, and fuck them if they judge me for how insecure I'm about to come across.

"How about we start with you really never ever hooked up or dated or anything?"

"What? Ew!" Bee squeals at the same time Jimmy busts up laughing.

I lift my chin. "Well? What is it, then?"

Jimmy drags me onto his lap for a bear hug and doesn't let go. He's still laughing but peppers kisses all over my hair and ears and face. "Bee is basically my sister. My father took her in as a ward when her parents . . . Anyway, we grew up together. I love her like a sister."

"And I'm really happy Grey has found someone to love him as something other than a sister because that's all I could ever imagine being to him."

I let out a relieved sigh. "Okay. I'm glad that's cleared up, and, you know . . . sorry for being neurotic and insecure."

Jimmy cuddles me closer and drops a few more kisses on my head.

"I'm fully human," Bee continues suddenly. "At least, as far as I know. Maybe I've got something else hidden in my genes, but it hasn't popped up to show itself, and both of my parents were human. But I guess they were close with Grey's father a long time ago. No one has ever been willing or able to tell me details, but they apparently went way back, so when my parents got into some trouble, they turned to the pack for help. I was just a baby at the time, but Greyson—Grey's father; he was already the pack leader by then—agreed to take us in and protect us.

"Well, even with the pack's protection, the people who were after my parents caught up with them and killed them, so I was left without parents and under pack protection. This year, I convinced the pack leader to let me leave the pack to go to school. He agreed under the condition that Jimmy would be my protector here." She shrugs. "And I guess that pretty much brings you up to speed. Grey is basically my brother, but he's been acting as my bodyguard for the past few months. The pack leader wants me to go back and let the pack protect me again, but I feel like I just started living my life, so there's no way in hell I'm going back right now." She gives us both a defiant glare.

I give a low whistle. "That is . . . a whole lot."

She shrugs again. "It is what it is. I'm figuring it out."

"I do actually have some news on that front," Jimmy mumbles. "My father has agreed to let me stay here at school for a little longer at least, so he won't be calling either of you back to him as long as I promise to continue acting as protector. So, as long as you're willing to let me keep an eye on you, it should be okay?"

I seek out Bee's eyes. We take a moment to silently communicate before giving a nod in unison.

Bee smiles at me. "Are you interested in still being my roommate, even though you know I kept a lot of secrets from you?"

I raise my shoulders noncommittally. "I mean, it's kind of on me for never directly asking you about yourself. And you've proven to be pretty reliable. I'd rather have you than a lot of other people as a roommate."

Bee's smile widens. "Not to mention, I suspect you're going to be spending less time in our dorm than before anyway."

I spare a glance at Jimmy. "You might be right about that," I admit.

* * *

It's not long after that Bee says she's going to talk to Lacey about getting a new dorm set up for us and leaves us alone with a big grin and an eyebrow wiggle.

"I feel better, now that I don't have any secrets from you," Jimmy says. "How about you?"

I give him a speculative look. "I feel like you said something about proving that you aren't going to get me pregnant, and I'm interested in testing that."

"Oh? How could we test that, exactly?"

"You're going to show me," I say with a grin.

"It's like that?" Jimmy drags me to him, already working his hands under the hem of my shirt. "So, if I can just find a few ways to make you feel good without getting you pregnant, you might start trusting me a little more?"

"I mean, it definitely won't hurt."

Jimmy strips off my shirt and walks me back toward his room. "That sounds like the kind of challenge I won't mind taking on."

He spins me as he shuts his door and presses my front flat against it.

"Do you trust me enough to not try to touch me at all?"

No. I don't know. How can I possibly answer that? I nod and let out a whimper. Needy and pathetic? Probably. Totally hot? Definitely.

Jimmy presses my hands into the door above my head and works some kind of magic with his tongue against my neck.

"Stay still for me, okay?"

I whimper and nod again, willing to do just about anything for the promise of all the ways he might make me feel good in the end.

And before I know what's happening, he's kissing down my spine and unbuttoning my pants and making me groan with desperate need all at the same time.

"That's right. Stay right there," he murmurs into my tail-bone, sending shivers shooting through me.

I flex my fingers into the door to keep myself from grabbing for him as he slips his tongue between my ass cheeks and uses his fingers to spread my labia. He's using torturously light touches, not quite reaching where I need him to at all each time he passes over me.

"Fuck, Jimmy. Please."

"Please what?" he asks in an innocent voice before gliding his tongue all too briefly over my hole.

"Need. More. Please." I have to grit my teeth and pant through each word to get past the need unwinding in me. I start to lose control over my form, wolf claws tearing out of my fingertips, my tail starting to unfurl from the base of my spine. "Please, Jimmy."

Finally, he passes his finger over my clit and focuses his tongue on my sensitive anus. Heat builds, vibrating up through me, but it's still not enough. I'm about to explode, but I can't find the thing to tip me over to the edge.

I claw into the door and thrust my hips back to try to get more traction, or friction, or something, from Jimmy. He just laughs and keeps on with his slow work to build me up to my climax.

Right when I think I might actually die from sexual frustration, he thrusts both of his thumbs inside of me roughly, and I come apart under his triple assault. He keeps rubbing and licking from every angle as I spasm around him and lose control of my legs. Jimmy supports me all the way down as I collapse in front of him.

305

Chapter Thirty-Five

JIMMY

Gloria's taste on my tongue is driving me wild. I'm desperate to come, but I promised I wouldn't put her at risk, and I'm going to prove myself to her. Besides, the way she's twitching and groaning makes me almost as desperate to see if I can make her come again.

I gather her up and carry her to the bed. She doesn't fight me when I lay her down on her back. I'm not sure she can actually move on her own.

"Is this okay?" I ask because I have to make sure. She responds with a moan and a nod, both of which shoot straight through to my cock. My erection presses insistently against my fly, but I tell it to calm the fuck down. We've got other things to take care of first.

I kneel between Gloria's legs and take a delicate taste of her. She tastes just as good as ever. I don't think it's possible for me to ever get enough of her like this.

She responds to my lick by threading her fingers through my hair to grab my head and hold it in place exactly where she needs me. Encouraged, I get back to work. With one hand, I work one finger slowly into her ass, which is still beautifully slick from my earlier work. With the other hand, I work one, then two fingers inside of her pussy, which flexes around me and makes me groan out my own need as I feast on her.

Every movement of my fingers and mouth brings out a louder, more desperate sound from her. Part of me hopes none of my roommates are back. I don't want to be the roommate everyone hates, after all. Part of me hopes we have an audience to hear how well I'm getting her off. I want a signed certificate saying I'm actually this good.

"More," she begs, and I add a third finger inside of her, flicking my tongue faster and faster against her clit, letting her rock her hips against my face for friction.

"More," she gasps again, and I manage to fit my pinky inside of her with my other fingers. Her pussy is clenching down so tight around me it hurts, but it's so hot at the same time.

Instinct takes over and forces my hips to thrust down into the mattress, searching for the friction I need to get off. Suddenly, Gloria's muscles are spasming around my fingers, clenching so tight they could almost break, and that, paired with the pressure of my fly against my cock, has me spilling out in my own pants again. I manage to ride out our orgasms with my face attached to her, licking every last drop of pleasure I can get from her before she relaxes back with a contented, exhausted sigh.

Chapter Thirty-Six

GLORIA

The next morning is the best wake-up I can imagine. The too-small dorm bed seems snug now instead of uncomfortable. Jimmy is curled tightly around me with his arms pulling me close against him. Kisses so soft they tickle are trailing down my neck and shoulder.

"Are you trying to tell me something?" I breathe.

"Just showing my appreciation," he murmurs, moving his lips back up my shoulder and neck until he can capture my mouth in his.

I let him kiss me for a moment before coming to my senses and putting my hand up to block his mouth. "I haven't brushed my teeth," I explain.

Jimmy covers his own mouth. "Is that your polite way of saying I've got morning breath?"

I giggle at the panicked look in his eyes. "No. That's my way of saying I have morning breath."

I start to get up, but he wraps his arms around my waist and tugs me back down.

"Don't leave me?"

"Not even to brush my teeth?"

"Hmmm." He starts working those magical, tickly kisses up and down my neck again as he considers it. "How about I do something that won't have you thinking about anyone's morning breath for a while?"

And that's when my stomach lets out an earth-rumbling gurgle.

He grins. "Or maybe I need to feed you before I can eat anything."

I swat his shoulder, but any serious effect I was going for is ruined by another loud stomach gurgle.

"Okay," Jimmy concedes, pulling me to my feet. "Breakfast first. Then . . ." He wiggles his eyebrows. "We'll see what happens from there?"

I snort a laugh at him and pull on my clothes from yesterday. "Breakfast, then I try to get caught up on all the math homework I've fallen behind on, then I do some research on what I have to do to get into medical school, then—if I haven't already done it—I check in with Bee about our housing sit—"

Jimmy cuts me off with a kiss. "Alright. I get the picture. How about this? Breakfast, then you take care of the things that I can't help with, and I'll work on getting your housing fixed up for tonight."

Actually, the thought of having someone to help carry the load sounds pretty damn good right now.

"You would do that for me? Face the housing demons, I mean?"

He presses his forehead to mine and rubs our noses together. "I would do anything for you, Gloria," he says. "Anything I can do to help you get where you're going, that's what I'll do. Anything, Gloria."

I manage to kiss him in spite of the giant grin on my face.

You know what? I think we're going to be just fine.

Epilogue

FIFTEEN YEARS LATER

JIMMY

"**W**ell?"

Miles is sitting up on my shoulders and can surely see better than me, but he still tugs impatiently at my hair.

"Well, what? I can't see her yet. You'll have to let me know when you see her."

Hailey gives a disgruntled sound and shifts in my arms. I cuddle her closer, the same way I have a thousand times since the day she was born. Miles is starting to be more independent, but Hailey still needs me, and I still treasure every moment I get to be close to both of them.

"There! There! There!" Miles shouts, pointing with one hand and steering my head with his other.

Okay, fatherhood can be a pain. But I've loved every fucking second of it. It helps that my own father is still in position as pack leader, so I don't have to deal with any of that bullshit. I get to just be Daddy, pretty much all the time.

Except for now, when the one person who definitely

doesn't think of me as "Daddy" is walking toward me from the arrivals gate.

"Hey," I say, still as breathless and inarticulate as ever when I see her.

"Hey." She grins back, then sweeps Miles off my shoulders. "My little man! How have you been?" she asks, swinging him in a circle, then squeezing him tight, then launching a tickle attack that he has no defenses against.

"Mom! I! Can't! Breathe!" he gasps out between squawks and giggles.

"Breathe? You care about breathing when your mom has been away for so long?"

Miles counterattacks by throwing himself around her. The full koala. And it seems pretty effective, considering she just stands there, hugging him tighter and tighter.

"I missed you, Miles. Did you know that?" she murmurs into his hair.

"I missed you too," I hear from her neck, where he's buried his face.

Hailey gives another grunt before resettling in my arms. Good thing she's there, or I might be arrested for doing all of the things I want to do to Gloria right here in the airport.

"Good trip?" I ask in lieu of laying her flat on the nearest bench and going to town.

"It was," she says, eyes bright with excitement and happy tears and also the unshed tears over missing her family. "The new pill is such a game changer. It's going to be an uphill battle to get more widespread use of it, but it's going to change so many lives in the long run."

She kisses Miles on the nose to punctuate her statement. I squeeze Hailey closer in response. Both of these kids—not to mention the miracle I wake up to every morning—came after years of waiting and planning and deciding that it was time for them. If Gloria's work has been going well, it means that other wolves will get the same option—to plan for their families instead of being forced into them—without all the trouble we had.

"You know, you are so amazing to me," I whisper in her ear.

"You're the reason I could do all of this," she whispers back.

"You know how much I love you?"

"Yes," she confirms, "and I love you too. And I'm going to show you just how much I've missed you in a few hours when we get home."

* * *

The next few hours are torture because I have to let her get in all of the time she needs with the cubs, which means I don't get to glue myself to her and get all of the touch I've been missing.

It's alright. I wouldn't take away her time with the kids for anything in the world. I wouldn't trade the kids for anything in the world or give up any part of the life we've built. It works for us. Me being the stay-at-home dad and backup pack leader when my father needs me. Gloria being the brilliant doctor whose research on shifter reproduction is changing the world for all of us. I'm so proud of her, and I would make the same choice a million times over so I could have this life with her.

"You're thinking awfully hard over there," Gloria whispers from across the cubs' bedroom.

Miles and Hailey are both already snoring softly. My heart gives a little clench every time I see the blanket lift with one of their inhales.

"I'm just feeling thankful for our little miracles here. And for you."

"Oh yeah? And what would you say if I told you I've been thinking of trying for a third little miracle?"

My eyes widen. I'm afraid to breathe in case I jinx it.

"Is that a positive silence or a negative one?" she asks, still smiling, because of course she knows what my answer is. What my answer will always be.

"Do you really mean . . . I don't want to get my hopes up if you're not serious."

Her smile broadens, and she comes over to me and grabs my hands. "I really mean it. The research is at a point where I can do most of the work from here, and every time I'm away from them"—she nods toward our sleeping cubs—"and you, it gets a little harder to be gone. I want to focus on building our lives together right now. And I keep having pangs, missing how they felt when they were growing inside me."

"If you're serious, I'm not sure why we're still in here instead of in our bed making a start on it," I whisper, gripping her fingers and praying this isn't just a dream.

"You know what? I'm not sure about that either." She tugs me to my feet, then lets out a quiet yelp when I throw her over my shoulder and carry her to our room.

* * *

I unwrap her like the gift she is, tasting every bit of her as I uncover it. She gives back just as much. When she isn't scratching fingernails down my back, she's stroking my erection through my pants. When she isn't sucking the most sensitive spot on my neck, her teeth nip at my ears.

Once I've got her bare and perfect in front of me, I drop to my knees to worship her.

"I think you taste better every time I have you," I groan into her pussy.

"I think you've just been missing me."

"Well, I have," I admit, "but that doesn't mean this isn't the best your pussy has ever tasted. I need you so bad, Gloria."

She tugs me up by my hair. "You'd better have me, then."

Gloria opens my fly with a deft flick of her fingers, then whips my cock free with a flourish.

Even after all these years, she knows exactly how to make my brain short-circuit.

"Fuuuuck" is the only word I can come up with.

"That's the idea." Gloria leads me by my cock and pushes me down on the bed.

Before I can come up with any further comment, she climbs on top of me and lines me up at her entrance.

"Are you sure we're ready for another baby?" she asks, hovering over me, tantalizing and torturing me simultaneously.

I gather my three remaining, very scattered brain cells together to answer. "I'm ready if you're ready. Wherever you want to go, whatever you want to do, you know I'll be there. That's all I've ever wanted."

She doesn't keep me waiting, just slides down on me, engulfing me in heat and pleasure.

"Babe, I'm gonna come too fast," I gasp out my warning. In our years together, whether we were trying to get pregnant or trying not to get pregnant, the constant has always been that she can make me come before either of us is ready for it to be over.

"Oh, no! Whatever will I do then?" She mock pouts as she slides up and down my length, letting me feel every perfect bit of her before burying me deep inside again. The pulse of her muscles around me almost undoes me right then.

"I mean it." I try to think unsexy thoughts so I can last a little bit longer. "I can't hold off much longer like this."

Gloria grins and reaches behind herself to play with my balls while she keeps riding me, and that's all it takes.

"God! Fuck!" I vaguely hope I don't wake the kids up with my shout as my orgasm explodes out of me. She rides me all the way through it, and I fill her up so much that my come is squeezing out from where our bodies are connected.

"I'm sorry," I tell her when I've finally got my breath back. "I really tried to hold on for you."

"But if you'd waited, I wouldn't be able to do this now."

"Do wha—" Before I finish my question, she crawls up my body and straddles my face. Taking the hint, I lick wherever I can reach with her legs bracketing my head. Maybe it should bother me, to eat her out like this after I've come inside of her, with my own semen dripping out of her and dripping down my chin, but instead, it reminds me of how much she belongs to me. I relish every taste and touch as she rides my mouth to her own orgasm.

When we eventually go to sleep, I wrap her tight in my arms, press my hand against her belly, and say a silent prayer for another miracle to grow inside of her.

Afterword

Thank you so much for reading! I don't have the words to say how much it means to me to have this story out in the world, with real, live, actual people reading it. The fact that you're here at the end with me really means the world and warms the cockles of my heart. Thank you for letting me into your life and spending this time with me!

Acknowledgments

This book could never have been written without the help of so many. I will do my best to thank everyone who helped make this book a reality, but it is possible—even likely—that I am forgetting someone important. Please forgive me, and know that I truly do appreciate everything you've done, even if I forget to write about it here.

Alex, sister, for all of the ways you've pushed me to keep going and to do it better and to be better, I can never thank you enough. If not for you, no one would know what Gloria looks like or why anyone would like Jimmy at all. Your input has made me and my book stronger and better.

To Victoria and the "Book Bitches," thank you for being my very first readers and pointing out some very important flaws in the original version of the book.

To North Texas Romance Writers and Dallas Mystery Writers, thank you for all the fun times, informative sessions, and gentle reminders of "butt in seat, fingers on keyboard." I don't think I would have made it to the starting line without the support of these awesome writing communities.

To my internet friends, the Author Pals, the Tavern at the Edge of the World, the WriMOOs, thank you for all the encouragement, brainstorming help, suggestions on how to get my shit together and build my website, etc. I am forever in your debt.

To my mom, who told me bedtime stories, and my dad, who read me Narnia, and my brother, who introduced my to the magic of Dungeons and Dragons, I love you all so much and wouldn't trade our little group of weirdos for anyone else in the world.

Oh, and Sean, who puts up with me even when I stay up all night reading and spend the next day complaining about it, and who gives me the space I need to do all this writing stuff. A girl couldn't ask for a better partner, support system, or love in this life.

About the Author

Kayla grew up in the mountains of New Mexico, where she fell in love with snow, small towns, and the idea of the redeeming power of love. Now, she lives in a big city in Texas and tries to spread the good word about romance novels wherever she goes. Kayla writes steamy romance stories about shifters, vampires, aliens, and sometimes even humans. She lives with her partner and cat, and enjoys running, playing ukulele, and watching her partner play video games.

If you want to receive a FREE bonus epilogue of Wolf Bound, if you would like monthly updates on my life and my writing, or if you want to be the first to read snippets of upcoming releases, subscribe to my newsletter here https://kaylabrook sauthor.eo.page/t9shh!

I would love to hear from you, whether you want to ask questions about the books, talk about your pets, or let me know something you wish you could see in a book. Feel free to email me with any of that and more at kayla@kaylabrook sauthor.com. I hope to hear from you!

Also by Kayla Brooks

Bound

A Berring College Short Story

Wolf Bound

Berring College 1

Blood Bound

Berring College 2 (coming 2025)

Earth Bound

Berring College 3 (coming 2025)

Keep reading for a preview of Blood Bound, coming out in 2025!

$$Blood\ Bound$$

DEVON

"I put all of your hats right on top of the dresser so they'll be easy to find without looking," mom wrings her hands while she talks, her eyes already searching for something else to do.

"Yep. I can see them." I work hard to not roll my eyes, but I can't help the annoyance that creeps into my voice.

She's too busy worrying—panicking, more like—to notice it, though. "And you're going to remember them, right? Every single time. No exceptions and no excuses."

I bring her in for a hug. I know she means well and it's coming from a place of love and all that, but I am just about out of patience and going to say something we'll all regret if she doesn't let up soon.

Dad saves me with a heavy pat on the back.

"We should probably give him some air, honey. We don't want his new roommates walking in on us getting all mushy and then teasing him all year, right?"

Trust dad to make it seem like I'm a little kid in danger of being bullied rather than an eighteen year old moving into a college dorm.

"Oh, you're probably right." My mom's voice is suspiciously watery as she pulls back from the hug. "But you promise you'll wear your hats? And call if you need anything at all? We are not too far away to come and get you if you need us."

I grind my teeth behind a smile. "I promise to wear the hats. I've got your number. I know where you live. I love you. I'm going to be okay."

The thing is, I get where they're coming from. Mom wasn't always like this, but then I made her into the mess of tears and anxiety currently standing before me. This is all my own damn fault, so I just need to suck it up and deal with the consequences of my actions. But at the same time, this is probably the worst part of becoming a vampire. Sure, the sun sensitivity and inability to taste most of the food I used to love are pretty sucky, but extra grey hairs I've noticed on my dad's head and the worry in my mom's eyes—and the way they both tend to treat me like some terribly fragile, already broken thing— are way worse than the physical changes.

"Okay, okay. We'll go away and let you get started with unpacking. Just one more hug to get me through the next few weeks."

I oblige without argument, though I do send up a silent prayer that they manage to stay away for more than my first three weeks of college.

Then dad is pulling me in for a hug that would squeeze all the air out of me if that was still and issue. "I snuck a box of condoms into your sock drawer so you can stay safe," he whispers gruffly in my ear before breaking away and leading mom away.

Good thing my blood doesn't work the same way it did

when I was human, or I would be blushing firetruck red right now.

And, just like that, I'm on my own to start putting things away and get settled in my dorm.

In the past few months, I came out, became a vampire, and moved away to college. This will be just like all of the other changes in my life, I remind myself. It will take some adjustment, but I'll survive it.

* * *

MARCUS

I clamp my fingers down on my knee to keep from fidgeting, or tapping, or giving away any of the everything that I'm feeling right now. "So, I guess this is it," I say to the empty space between my mother and me.

"It's not too late to change your mind," she tells me without shifting from her position, perched on the edge of her seat and staring straight ahead. Like a royal expecting the paparazzi to spring out at any moment and try to catch her doing something improper.

As if they could see her at all through the tinted windows of our car.

I guess that's what her non-life has done to her. It's turned her into this frozen, perfect thing. I've never known her as anything other than ice cold and hard as glass, but sometimes I try to imagine what she was like before she became the queen of ice. By definition, she was softer and warmer as a human, but I've never been able to picture her as anything other than vampiric perfection. This has been her since I was born.

I give up on waiting for some kind of loving response from her—I should know better by now that she just doesn't have that kind of emotion to throw around—and reach for the door.

"Wait," she calls me back with just one small sound. "Don't forget your hat."

I jam the cap down over my eyes and escape the car before I can let myself be hurt any more.

I hurry into the building before the sun can become an issue, not looking back to check if the movers my mom hired are following or not. They'll figure it out one way or another. And I need to worry about myself, not them.

I find the correct line to check in and settle in to wait, but a timid tap on my shoulder reveals a nervous looking vampire. Probably within a few years of my age, I decide, since he doesn't have the musty smell that vampires sometimes develop after half a century or so.

"Mr. Levine?"

His nervous blinking grates my nerves, but what good will it do to let him know that?

"Yeah, that's me."

"I've got you checked in already, if you'll just follow me. I can show you to your room."

Just what I need, someone acting like a servant and leading me to where I'm going to be living. Definitely the best way to make the right impression. Well, that's probably exactly what my father had in mind, come to think of it. He lost the battle about sending me directly to the family frat, but he can still try to control me in these other little ways.

"That won't be necessary," I tell him. "If you'll just give me the keys and the room number?"

His relief is almost embarrassing as he shoves a manila envelope in my hands and mutters a hurried, "Good luck with college," before he makes his escape.

And this is the kind of loyalty and pride that my father's brand of leadership invokes. At least I'm free to go to my dorm alone, now.

My fingers shake a little as I unlock my door, but I tell myself it's okay because there's no one here to see. It's understandable to feel some nerves in a situation like this, right? Not that my father or any of his minions would accept that kind of excuse if they were here to see me.

I work to clamp down on my self-control. That's part of what this is all about, after all. I don't think he would have let me do this at all if he thought I was actually ready to start following in his footsteps. My stomach flips at just the thought of that.

Four years, I remind myself. I've got four years to get this figured out so I can do my duty.

The shared living room of the suite is already furnished with someone's belongings in the process of being unpacked. A huge TV sits, unplugged, in front of the couch. A coffee pot, also unplugged, sits on top of the tiny counter space that supposedly serves as a kitchen.

"Hey! Roommate!" A guy shouts cheerfully as he steps out of a bedroom.

My mouth dries up like a desert when I see him.

Almost my height. Maybe an inch or two shorter. And bright red hair and a face full of freckles that make him look more alive than any vampire has a right to. But the clincher is his wide grin and sparking eyes. Topaz, I think. No, tiger's eye.

Shit.

I catch the direction my thoughts are taking and bite down hard on my tongue to bring myself back to reality.

I don't live a life that allows me to notice guys' eyes or freckles or anything else. I need to shut this down fast.

And that's when I realize I'm just standing there awkwardly and biting my tongue almost to the point of bleeding and not speaking and his smile is slipping and . . .

"Right. Um. Yes. Roommate." Come on, I beg myself. Get it together. "Marcus. That's me, I mean."

His smile returns full force and I'm able to loosen some of the tension in my shoulders.

"I'm Devon. I hope it's alright that I started unloading some stuff out here. I figured, since I got here first, I'd set up my TV and stuff out here. But if someone else wants their TV out here, that's no big deal. I can move mine into my room. Same thing with the coffee pot. And gaming consoles. I mean, if any of the roommates don't want them out here for some reason. I'm easy. Or . . . Shit, I'm kind of babbling, aren't I?"

The babbling was good, from my standpoint. It meant he wasn't expecting me to contribute anything. Now we're back to me doing the awkward, silent staring thing again.

"It's fine with me," I finally choke out from my dust dry mouth. "I like coffee."

Right then, oh joy, is when the door opens and my movers start bringing in boxes.

"Mr. Levine?" The oldest, baldest of the movers addresses me. "Which room are these headed to?"

"I . . . ummm . . . " I avoid looking Devon in the eyes but I also need to get over my embarrassment at being the guy who hires movers to move into a dorm. "Does it matter which room I take?"

Devon shrugs like this is normal—for which I am eternally grateful—and points toward his door. "I'm in there. As far as I know, none of the other rooms are claimed. I say choose whichever room you want."

Wanting this whole thing over with as soon as possible, I point to the door next to Devon's. "That one's fine. Everything can go in there."

* * *

To learn more about Devon and Marcus, sign up to my newsletter here: https://kaylabrooksauthor.eo.page/newsletter where you'll get a free, erotic M/M short story along with all of my news and updates!

www.ingramcontent.com/pod-product-compliance
Lightning Source LLC
Chambersburg PA
CBHW022309310726
48973CB00001B/285